BITTER
SWEET

Connie Shelton

Books
by Connie Shelton

THE CHARLIE PARKER SERIES

Deadly Gamble
Vacations Can Be Murder
Partnerships Can Be Murder
Small Towns Can Be Murder
Memories Can Be Murder
Honeymoons Can Be Murder
Reunions Can Be Murder
Competition Can Be Murder
Balloons Can Be Murder
Obsessions Can Be Murder
Gossip Can Be Murder
Stardom Can Be Murder
Phantoms Can Be Murder
Buried Secrets Can Be Murder

Holidays Can Be Murder - a Christmas novella

THE SAMANTHA SWEET SERIES

Sweet Masterpiece
Sweet's Sweets
Sweet Holidays
Sweet Hearts
Bitter Sweet
Sweets Galore
Sweets, Begorra

BITTER
SWEET

The Fifth Samantha Sweet Mystery

Connie Shelton

Secret Staircase Books

Bitter Sweet
Published by Secret Staircase Books, an imprint of
Columbine Publishing Group
PO Box 416, Angel Fire, NM 87710

Printed and bound in the United States of America
ISBN 1479257648
ISBN-13 978-1479257645

This book is a work of fiction. Names, characters, places and
incidents are either the product of the author's imagination or are
used fictitiously. Any resemblance to actual events or locales or
persons, living or dead, is entirely coincidental. Although the author
and publisher have made every effort to ensure the accuracy and
completeness of information contained in this book we assume
no responsibility for errors, inaccuracies, omissions, or any
inconsistency herein. Any slights of people, places or organizations
are unintentional.

Book layout and design by Secret Staircase Books
Cover illustration © Dmitry Maslov

First trade paperback edition: September, 2012
First e-book edition: September, 2012

For Dan, always.

Once again, an enormous thank-you to my editor Susan Slater, who first planted the seed of the idea for this story, at the time she read the previous book in the series, *Sweet Hearts*. As always, you have provided invaluable insights for this one and excelled at meeting my impossible deadlines.

And, as ever, my undying gratitude to my readers. I continue writing, for you, and I am so appreciative of the wonderful comments and encouragement I receive from you with each new title.

Thank you, one and all!

Chapter 1

The prospect of breaking into houses made Samantha Sweet weary as she considered the two jobs that needed her attention later in the day. Once, those break-ins had provided a living, but this past year they had increasingly become a drudgery. However, the obligation loomed and she could see no way out just yet. She sighed. Sweet's Sweets, her 'bakery of magical delights' was her life now.

She piped the final few inches of shell border on an all-ivory wedding cake and stepped back to check the finished piece, happy to see that it met with her usual exacting standards. She called over her assistant baker, Becky Harper, to help her move the five-tiered confection into the walk-in fridge.

"It's gorgeous, Sam. As always," Becky said, admiring the intricate traditional swags and piping as they wheeled the metal cart toward the back of the workroom. "No wonder every bride in town wants you to make her cake."

"Kind of a mixed blessing," Sam said. "I love creating the cakes—it's what I dreamed of for years before actually opening the shop. I just never imagined that there would be *no* down time. You know what I mean?"

She'd no sooner opened the shop last fall than the winter holidays rushed in upon her—Halloween, Thanksgiving, Christmas. Personal sorrow followed in January at the sudden death of her fiancé's mother. A huge rush of business around Valentine's Day, when her own wedding had to be postponed, and she'd suddenly found herself in the midst of the spring holidays. She couldn't begin to count how many cupcakes and cookies they'd baked and decorated with pastel bunnies, chicks and eggs. Before she could breathe she was taking orders for June weddings and the barrage of associated showers and bachelorette parties. She glanced at the wire trays on her desk, where the orders were stacking up. Now, in mid-June, she already had wedding cake orders well into September.

"You're probably beat when you get home at night," Becky said, catching Sam's expression.

"It's a good kind of tired." She didn't want to admit that she was running near her limits.

For at least the fourth time that week, she made herself a mental note to hire more help. If nothing else she should be able to get some teenage boys to mow lawns and trim hedges. She'd run ads at the end of May, the moment school let out for summer, but there were no takers—hard to imagine there was so much unemployment and nobody willing to do some actual labor. Kids wanted to work at the electronics store where playing around with the cool new devices was more enticing than fresh air and sunshine.

"Sam? Your two o'clock consultation is here." Jennifer Baca, the shop's only clerk, peeked through the curtain between the sales area and kitchen.

"Be right there." Sam quickly rinsed the perpetual sugary residue from her hands and picked up her order pad and folder of cake designs. "Becky, can you get those flowers done for the Cassidy cake? White daisies with yellow centers?"

"I'm on it. Don't worry."

An hour later, Sam realized she'd never eaten lunch and her energy was gone.

"You better give yourself a break, Sam." Jen wiped down the shop's unoccupied bistro tables. "Go get a sandwich, or at least sit here for a few and put your feet up."

"I brought an apple from home. I'll just—"

The bell on the front door interrupted.

"Zoë! Hey, what's up?"

Sam's best friend breezed in, wearing her usual cotton broomstick skirt and a crinkled top that hung just right on her slender frame. She had a foil packet and a round plastic carton in her hands.

"I made way too many tamales. One of our groups canceled. I know you like them and there's enough here for you, Beau and Kelly to have a couple of dinners."

"You sure you don't want to just stick them in my freezer here? They'll keep for your next influx of guests."

"Nah. You take them."

Zoë knew Sam rarely found time to cook these days. The 'overages' at her friend's B&B were happening fairly regularly now.

"At least let me pay you for them. These things take a lot of work."

"Nope. You're not paying for a thing. How many cakes and cookies have you made for me recently? At Easter, when Darryl's whole family showed up and you gave us all those adorable cupcakes for the kids—"

"Okay, okay. As long as you continue to let me reciprocate." Sam took the warm packet and the heavenly smell just about brought her to her knees. "Can you stay a minute? I was about to take a lunch break."

Zoë followed her into the kitchen where she unwrapped two of the tamales, placed them on a plate and poured some of her friend's famous red sauce over them. The women sat on either side of Sam's desk.

"So, is your mother still nagging about the wedding or are you and Beau about to appease her by actually going through with it?"

Sam rolled her eyes as she cut into the tamale and took her first bite. "Mother, I'm afraid, is far more stressed over our pending marriage than we are. I learned my lesson trying to plan it for Valentine's Day—there was just way too much going on. Beau and I want to wait until we see a clear spot, when we can both enjoy our wedding and get away long enough for an actual honeymoon trip."

"Makes sense to me." Zoë tactfully didn't add the fact that there was no such opening anywhere on the horizon.

"Losing Iris was still pretty fresh to us then, too," Sam said. "We had hoped she would recover from that first stroke enough to attend. It was a difficult time."

She touched the garnet ring on her left hand.

Zoë nodded, letting Sam move on to the second tamale. The telephone rang and Sam automatically noted that Jen picked up two lines in the sales room. Less than a minute later, the intercom buzzed on Sam's desk.

"Sorry about this, Sam. Line one is Delbert Crow and line two is your mother."

Sam swallowed her food. Her gaze locked with Zoë's. "I'll get Delbert," she told Jen. "Tell Mother I'll have to call her back and that it will probably be later this evening."

"Chicken," Zoë said, giving Sam's hand a squeeze as she stood. "I'll catch you later."

Sam gave her friend a lopsided grin. "Samantha Sweet here," she said to the man who was her USDA contracting officer. As much as she wanted to put the job of breaking into abandoned homes and keeping them clean and tidy out of her mind, nearly eighteen months remained on her current contract with the Department of Agriculture.

"There's another job for you. Ready for the details?" Delbert Crow's voice never changed. Perpetually grumpy sounding, he seemed to Sam like a guy who'd been in his job too long and couldn't wait to retire. She pictured him slumped at a desk stacked high with thick manila folders, a cigarette dangling from the side of his mouth. Except that there were probably no government offices that allowed anyone to smoke indoors these days.

Like it or not, she would need to spend the better part of the afternoon mowing lawns and sweeping cobwebs at the two properties already under her care and now he was assigning her a third. This past winter and spring, her caretaker duties dwindled and she'd almost become lulled into believing the influx of abandoned properties in Taos County was slowing. Suddenly, it didn't seem that way at all.

She reached for a notepad and took down the particulars for the new caretaking job. Might as well go out there now, she decided as she hung up the phone. She'd scheduled no bakery deliveries this afternoon, leaving time to mow lawns at the other two places. If she handled the preliminaries quickly on this new one she should have time to get it all done before dark. Luckily—or not—this time of year darkness didn't come until well after eight o'clock. There might be more daylight, but that didn't mean a person actually had the stamina to make full use of it.

"I'm getting too old for this," she muttered as she hung up her baker's jacket and fished in her backpack for the keys to her pickup.

Becky looked up from the rack where nearly three dozen sugar daisies hung by their stems to dry. "Sam, you okay?"

Sam forced a perky smile. Her assistant was the same age as Sam's daughter and she managed to put in a full day at the bakery, go home and cook for a husband and two little boys. Surely Sam could handle this workload. And if it got to be too much . . . well, there was another way . . .

She tamped down that thought right away and gave Jen and Becky a few last-minute instructions. They could handle two more hours and close up the shop on their own. Her red pickup truck sat in the alley behind the shop, the utility trailer with garden tractor and cans of extra gasoline hitched to it. A locking bin contained the smaller tools she needed for her jobs. Taos might be small-town in a lot of ways, but that didn't mean portable items wouldn't walk away.

She unlocked the truck and let it idle as she plotted her route. The new property was farthest away so she would save it for last. The other two places should only need mowing, and one of those was a fairly small house with just a patch of lawn. She put the truck in gear and headed out.

She polished off the postage-stamp lawn in no time and quickly swept a light coating of dirt off the porch and sidewalk of the little tan-stuccoed, flat-roofed house, then went inside and logged her appearance on the sign-in sheet that she kept at each of the properties in her care. The second place was less than a mile from the first and it, too, needed minimal work. Riding the lawn tractor around a half-acre relaxed her, and the fact that no phones were ringing and frantic brides were not nit-picking the shade of purple she'd chosen for the flowers on their cakes, well, that was an added benefit at the moment.

She made the final pass across the lawn, then rode the mower up the ramp to her trailer. When she peeked at it, the readout on her cell phone told her it was nearly six o'clock. Kelly would be leaving Puppy Chic any minute. Sam speed dialed her daughter's number.

"Hey, Mom." Kelly always sounded chipper, no matter how long the workday.

"There are fresh tamales for dinner, if you want to pop in next door and pick them up."

"Zoë's? *Yum.*"

"Her red sauce is in a little tub right beside them in the fridge. I'll be late so go ahead and eat without me."

"You're not at the bakery now?"

Sam explained about the new property assignment. "I'll probably just give it a once-over, make my list of what needs to be done. But I'm in the truck, so if the yard needs tending this might be the easiest time to do it."

They ended the call and Sam re-checked the address. She secured everything on the trailer and headed west. A series of winding lanes took her past open fields of alfalfa and fenced paddocks where horses stood swishing at flies with their tails. Street signs and address numbers were tricky to find out here so she slowed to a crawl. Turning the big truck and trailer wasn't the easiest feat and she didn't want to pass her destination and have to double back. At a straight stretch in the road an impatient driver in a yellow Audi zoomed past her. She ignored his scowl and focused on the mailboxes along the road.

Two modest houses, each on about a quarter-acre plot appeared on her right. The second one looked the way Delbert Crow had described it and she turned in at a short driveway that led to a detached garage. The front yard consisted of a parking area and turnaround, all graveled. Thank goodness, no mowing.

Beds of bright dahlias and hollyhocks fronted the mid-sized house, which was neatly sided in white with blue shutters. Two large cottonwood trees in the back cast long shadows toward the neighboring house. At a glance, the place didn't seem to be in bad shape at all. Sam maneuvered her vehicle into the parking area, leaving plenty of room to make the turn when it was time to leave.

Her job at this point would be to get inside the house, check to be sure everything was secure and post the required notices inside, on the door and in the yard to indicate that the place was now under the protection of the USDA. For shrewd property buyers this was the signal that the place would probably go up for auction soon. Once in awhile, someone would approach her and ask about buying a place but since that wasn't her department all she could do was to hand out Delbert Crow's business cards and tell them to get the details from him.

She got out of her truck and assessed the property. A few weeds grew up through the gravel in the driveway—not enough to make the place unsightly but something she should attend to before they got out of hand. When the summer rains started next month, those babies could get as large as a vehicle in a fairly short time.

She approached the house on stepping stones made of concrete shaped like bear paws and stepped onto a narrow front porch. She had the tools with her to pick the lock, but sometimes people actually made it a lot easier than that. Feeling along the top of the door frame, she discovered that this owner had done precisely that as a silver key fell into her hand. The lock and deadbolt worked seamlessly and she was inside within a minute.

The house had a dim and hollow feel to it with all the drapes closed. It was a simple floor plan, she discovered, where one entered a tiny foyer that opened directly into the living room. A dining L angled off to the right. The kitchen was probably beyond that. To her left a hallway took off into the darkness. Bedrooms and bathrooms would be found back there somewhere. She flipped the light switch nearest the front door. An overhead light came on. The second switch brought up a lamp beside a fake-leather recliner chair.

Sam walked through the living room and pulled the drapery cord at the largest window. The low sun glared in, casting the room in intense brightness. These first few minutes were always the discovery phase of the job. Sam had walked into empty houses and partially furnished ones. There had been a hoarder's den, stacked to the ceiling with papers and clothing—so much so that the owner had simply taken her kids and piled into the car, only to land in another place and start collecting all over again.

At one of Sam's earliest jobs she'd discovered she wasn't alone. The woman who lived there was dying—in fact, did die while Sam was with her. Bertha Martinez bequeathed

Sam a small relic, the wooden box that somehow conveyed special powers and complicated her life all at once. Sam pushed that thought aside and walked deeper into the house.

A quick survey showed that there were two bathrooms and three bedrooms, completely furnished. The living room furniture and knickknacks had a dated feel, stuff that would have belonged to her grandmother. Six chairs sat around a glossy cherry dining table, and a large china cabinet contained an array of serving pieces in two patterns and a silver coffee service that must be a real joy to polish. Another house, another life story. Sam always caught herself wondering about them.

In the kitchen the countertops were tidy, lined with the usual assortment of canisters and appliances, kitchen tools and block of knives. At the small two-person table were a pair of flowered yellow placemats, a holder containing a sheaf of yellow paper napkins, and a ceramic salt and pepper shaker set—a charming little white mouse and a gray one. The refrigerator hummed quietly and Sam took a deep breath before opening the door. Even in a clean home this was where the nastiest surprises usually awaited.

The wire shelves were clean and neat, with condiments precisely lined up in the door racks. A crisper held fresh lettuce and tomatoes, some carrots and a bag of apples. A loaf of bread had never been opened. A plastic half-gallon of milk was unsealed but nearly full. She turned it to read the expiration date. Something was not right here.

Chapter 2

Sam closed the refrigerator door and pulled her phone from her pocket.

"Delbert, how long did you say this house has been abandoned?"

He muttered something and she could swear she heard him chewing on corn chips. Papers rattled noisily and she held her phone away from her ear until she heard his voice once again.

"Payments are a hundred-twenty days in arrears. Our mailed notices came back and our phone calls went unanswered. We started proceedings more than thirty days ago."

"But no one verified that the house was unoccupied? There's food in the fridge that has to be only a few days old."

Indistinct words, sounds of crinkling paper. He grumbled some more and finally came up with something.

"Let's see . . . The owners are listed as Marshall and Sadie Gray. Funny—the mortgage was paid on this place a long time ago, but they took out a new loan about ten months ago. Hardly made any payments on it after that."

That didn't make a whole lot of sense. "So, what should I do? I don't feel right about clearing out the house when they might still be living here."

"Stick a notice on the door and leave my business card inside. If we don't hear from them we have to proceed with eviction and sale of the property."

Sam hung up and went out to her truck. In a folder were all the requisite forms, including the notices Crow had mentioned and a pad of USDA note paper. She scrawled a note to let the Grays know that they needed to contact Delbert Crow at his office immediately, and left the message along with Crow's business card on the kitchen counter. She could only imagine their shock at discovering someone had been in their house. Even though it was her job, invading a home felt a little creepy.

However, as long as she was here, she decided to see if there were other clues as to whether the Grays would be back anytime soon. The closets of the two smaller bedrooms were crammed with lifetime collections of boxes, shoes, extra bedding—the type of clutter that everyone accumulates but some people never part with. Most of it probably hadn't been touched in years.

The master bedroom and bath contained more recent clutter. The closet rail held clothing for both genders, the man's side a bit more sparse. Two off-the-rack business suits and a half dozen dress shirts, two pair of khakis and a few collared sport shirts. At the far end he'd shoved his out-of-season things—a heavy jacket and a couple of sweatshirts. The wife's clothing consisted mostly of pastel dusters and house-dresses, along with a number of coordinated knit pants and tops, bought for their wash-and-wear qualities far more than for their style. Sensible shoes stood perkily on a wire rack that held them with their toes pointing upward.

Sam left the closet door standing open, as she'd found it, and crossed to the triple dresser. Pulling a couple of the drawers open a few inches revealed that they were fairly full. The Grays might have packed for a quick trip, but essentially all of their things were still here. They hadn't gone very far away.

This felt too intrusive. She backed out of the room, making sure she hadn't left obvious signs of her little inspection. The living room was gloomy now, the sun having dipped below the tall trees. Sam locked the front door and reached to place the house key where she'd found it on the door frame.

"What are you doing?" The sharp voice startled Sam and she nearly dropped the key. She spun around, knowing she looked guilty as hell.

Two steps below her, on one of the bear paws, stood a wizened little man of about eighty. He wore tan walking shorts that ended just above his knobby knees and white crew socks that came halfway up his calves. A plaid button-down shirt was neatly tucked into the shorts, and thickly veined hands were planted firmly on his skinny hips. Bright blue eyes peered out from under a floppy hat.

"I, uh, excuse me? Who are you?"

"Milton Fasbinder. I live next door and I don't like the looks of a strange vehicle at Sadie's house. So I'm asking you again, what are you doing?"

Sam stood straighter and flipped open her manila folder. "I'm a property caretaker with the USDA. I have authorization to enter the premises and make the house ready for sale."

"Well, that's just a big crock of shit," he said. "You can't sell Sadie's house out from under them."

She didn't want to get into the Gray's personal finances or start arguing the fact that she truly did have the right to be here. She walked down the steps to face the neighbor at his own level.

"Mr. Fasbinder, believe me, I really don't want to take anyone's house away. It's just that they haven't answered any of the notices that were sent to them. I need to know how to get in touch with the Grays."

He'd backed down a little when Sam approached him. "Well, things got tough for them when Sadie went into the home. Poor thing. It was hard on Marshall, making that decision. Me, I can't imagine it—choosing to have your wife put somewhere. Much as I miss my wife, I'm glad I didn't have no say in the matter. My Greta, she went quick. Too quick."

His eyes grew misty and Sam pretended to look at the house, giving him a moment.

"So, Marshall Gray is still living here?" she asked casually.

Fasbinder nodded. "Ain't seen him in awhile. He still travels a lot on business. Sometimes gone a week or two at the time."

"And Sadie Gray? Is she still in a home or has she—"

"Oh yeah. She's still there. It's that place over near the hospital. That Alt-heimer care place. We used to joke around, call it old-timer's disease. Not so funny once your friends start to get it though."

Sam nodded. Sounded like the Grays were in a tough spot. "I need for Mr. Gray to contact our office. Do you have a cell phone number for him or some way to contact him?"

Milton Fasbinder shook his head slowly. "Sure don't. Him and me, we never exactly became buddies. Now Sadie's first husband, Joe. We lived next door a long time. Used to watch ball games in the summer, back when the TV was only black and white and you sometimes had to look close to figure out who the players were. None of them cameras close up in their face, you know."

"Does Sadie have any children? Anyone besides Marshall that I can contact?"

"Nope. Never had any. Like to broke her heart. But she came to accept the idea. Finally she was about forty she took up working in Joe's insurance company. Good thing, too. Joe's policy money came in real handy for her when he died. Too young, he was. Who ever heard of a heart attack at forty?"

"I guess it happens."

"Left Sadie single for a lotta years. But she did okay. Kept that agency going awhile, had a lot of hobbies—the garden club and her church work. Her and Greta both were women who liked to stay busy that way."

Sam glanced toward the west where the sun had fully set. It didn't seem that she would get much more solid information from Milton Fasbinder, so before he could launch into any more stories she excused herself, reminding him to have Marshall Gray call Delbert Crow's office if the homeowner should come around.

As she pulled out of the driveway, Sam debated whether

to stop by the care home and try to speak with Sadie Gray. But it had been a long day and weariness began to set in fast as she approached Paseo Del Pueblo Sur, the main drag through town. Instead of heading toward the hospital and nearby complex of medical facilities, she took a left and made her way home.

By the time she'd maneuvered her rig up her driveway and unhitched the trailer from the pickup truck, Kelly was standing at the back door.

"Mom, it's a good thing you're home."

"What's wrong?" Her television-addicted daughter never met her at the door, and Sam's first thoughts went to Beau. A man in a dangerous career always brought worries.

"Jen wanted you to know that the air conditioning at the bakery went out this afternoon."

A choice word or two zipped through Sam's mind. "Is the electricity out?" Visions of melted butter and drooping cakes sank her mood.

"No, just the AC. And the forecast is for it to hit ninety tomorrow."

Sam growled as she trudged into her kitchen and plunked her backpack down on the table. Dealing with her landlord, crotchety old Victor Tafoya, always put her off. Since he'd tried once to evict her last fall she usually avoided contact at all costs. But coming up with the price of fixing the AC unit on her own was out of line. It really was his duty to pay for the repairs. She looked up his number and picked up the wall phone.

His line rang seven times before she gave up. The man was too cheap to get an answering machine. She slapped her phone onto the cradle, in no mood to deal with him tonight anyway. The temperatures would cool overnight and she would call him in the morning when she was in a fresher frame of mind.

"Did you eat yet, Mom?" Kelly asked, holding up the packet of tamales Zoë had given them earlier in the day.

Sam shook her head. "I had those for lunch. I'm not that hungry anyway. Save them and there will be enough for tomorrow night."

She retrieved a deli container of macaroni salad from the fridge and a fork from the drawer, carrying the impromptu meal into the living room and staring blankly at the TV while Kelly channel surfed toward some inane thing where a bunch of gorgeous women all seemed intent on getting dates with the same man.

By nine o'clock she was dozing in the chair and since her day started early, she said goodnight to Kelly and fumbled her way to bed. She fell asleep realizing that she hadn't heard from Beau all day.

Chapter 3

Sam woke before her alarm went off, thinking of the measures they would need to take at the bakery to keep their creations from melting into puddles if the air conditioning wasn't operational by midday. June weather and chocolate didn't go together very well. She rolled over, stared at the clock and gave up on more sleep.

She couldn't very well let her business crash because of this, and she couldn't bet that Victor Tafoya would react quickly. So—first things first—how to keep it all together. Her mind churned as she showered and dressed in her quasi-uniform of black slacks, white T-shirt and the white baker's jacket with her name and the store logo embroidered on it. Somewhere out in the garage she'd stored a couple of fans. By the beam of a flashlight she found them in a far corner and loaded them into her little bakery delivery van.

The early morning air felt nice and cool—a benefit of living in a dry climate was that the temps usually dropped at least twenty degrees overnight. She drove through the quiet streets and parked in the alley behind Sweet's Sweets. Thankfully, the kitchen lit up when Sam flipped the wall switch, and her inspection of the refrigerator and freezer showed those to be working properly. But they were stuffed nearly to capacity. It took a few minutes to unload the fans and get them cleaned up enough to run in a kitchen, but once she had set them in place, drawing cool air in through the back door, she felt better. At least she was taking action.

The other obvious solution was to avoid the most fragile creations—mainly chocolate and whipped cream. They'd stopped producing a lot of the finer chocolates after the holidays. She smiled at the memory of the quirky chocolatier who'd come to work for her at Christmas and then had shared elements of his secret techniques with her just in time for the Valentine rush. Unfamiliar with exactly how to measure the special seasonings, she'd produced some chocolates with amazingly strong aphrodisiacal qualities. She blushed at the memory of how well some of them had worked.

By Easter she'd thought better of using the special powders at all—turning the town's kids into raving sex maniacs would not have been good for business. All her cute little bunnies and chickies were virginally pure. She shook off those thoughts and got busy mixing the current day's batches of breakfast breads and cookie doughs.

At six, Becky came in and began filling the display cases with each new item that came out of the oven, and Sam decided that like it or not the landlord was getting an early phone call. He groused about it and never really promised anything, so Sam was astounded when a panel truck pulled up to the front door right at nine o'clock.

"You think Tafoya took everyone's threat seriously last winter?" Jen asked, after showing the repairman how to access the roof.

Sam shrugged. When he'd threatened to evict her, the neighboring businesses—a mystery bookstore on one side, and the dog grooming shop on the other—threatened to leave at the same time. Maybe there really was safety in numbers.

She relaxed into the routine of the day, finishing two wedding cakes and reviewing the delivery schedule. Becky reminded her that there were also two birthday cakes due that day.

"I can handle those, if you want," her assistant said.

"Remember, one of them is the curly ribbon design." The fondant-covered cake with dozens of fondant ribbon curls could get tricky.

"I'll give you a shout if I run into trouble," Becky assured her.

She pulled out large balls of fondant that she'd tinted the previous day and began to roll them out. Within fifteen minutes she'd cut the ribbon shapes of red, purple and yellow and wound thin strips of the same colors around dowels to form curlicues. Sam relaxed and turned her attention to her own work.

With four dozen ivory buttercream roses Becky had made the previous day, Sam finalized the more formal of the two cakes, a tone-on-tone affair where luster powder made all the difference in giving the cake depth and glow. Into the fridge it went to set up while she applied pale pink-tinted fondant to a heart-shaped cake and added bright pink piped flowers and mossy green leaves. A simple rope border and romantic bisque bride and groom figures completed the two tiers. Sam rinsed her hands and peered through the curtain to the sales room.

"Jen, if you're not busy a second?"

The shop was empty at the moment and Jen helped load the two cakes into the van.

"I better get going immediately," Sam told her. "When the repairman is done, if you need to sign anything, that's fine. Just get the air going as soon as possible. Meanwhile, make sure Becky is running those fans in the kitchen. If you need one for the sales room, that's okay too."

Jennifer assured her everything would be fine.

Sam ran the van's air conditioning until she thought she would have to put a coat on, checking the addresses for the two deliveries. As usual, heads turned as she drove down the street in the vehicle with its vivid design—like a box of pastries on wheels. The big ivory cake went to a nearby church so she drove there first, finding the kitchen entrance and calling upon a man in custodial clothing to help her get it onto a wheeled cart and then onto the decorated table in the reception hall.

The heart-shaped cake was for an anniversary party at a private home and it took her a minute to locate the exact street address on the south end of town. The hostess was delighted with the finished piece and had Sam carry it to the center of her dining table, where the pink theme continued throughout the room.

"My sister and her husband are going to love this," the woman raved. "They eloped so this is kind of their first real wedding cake."

Sam left a couple of her business cards and turned the van's air conditioning down to a reasonable level now that she didn't have to preserve a fragile cargo. As she maneuvered out of the lane where she'd made the delivery she realized that she was probably close to the neighborhood where Sadie Gray now lived. The old man next door, Milton Fasbinder, had said the nursing home was near the hospital. Maybe she could find out something about the couple's situation.

The promised ninety degree day had indeed materialized, with a cloudless, piercing sky that bounced white-hot light wherever she looked. A haze hung over the far hills, smoke from a forest fire a hundred miles south. With no rain in the forecast until next month, the fire situation was getting scary. It hadn't been that many years since hundreds of acres had burned in the mountains right outside town.

The nursing home, Casa Serenita, sat buttoned up tight with closed blinds and no one outdoors in the fenced yard. She parked in their nearly empty lot and walked up a sidewalk bordered with chamisa and purple sage, plants that could survive the high-desert summers with little water.

Inside the double doors, a small vestibule faced a reception desk. The tan theme included brown carpeting, cream upholstered chairs, and vanilla air freshener. A tired silk plant anchored one corner and one lonely magazine brightened the laminate coffee table. Sam's gaze skimmed all this and landed on the desk, manned by a business-suited female whose name badge identified her as Martha Preston. She sent Sam a quick smile and confirmed that Sadie Gray was, indeed, a resident. Sam gave a very condensed version of the reason for her visit.

"Mrs. Gray's dementia is fairly pronounced," Preston

said. "She might be able to tell you things that happened a year ago, but anything within the past few weeks will be completely gone. She's been here four months and still has a hard time locating her bedroom. Physically, she's not in bad shape for a woman of eighty-seven. If not for the mental decline, she could quite easily fit into our assisted living program."

"Would it be all right if I asked her some questions?"

"You can try." Martha Preston led Sam through a paneled door to a communal room furnished with two flowered blue sofas and a number of high-backed chairs. A television with the volume turned loud captivated the attention of about a dozen elderly people with the latest gossip from some talk show. The air was warm, and yet nearly every one of the residents wore a sweater or light jacket. Preston paused a moment and looked around.

"I don't see Sadie. She's probably in her room." She started down a wide hallway. Sam ignored the living room's scent of despair and hurried to catch up.

Doors stood open on both sides of the hall, bedrooms furnished with single hospital style beds. Many had personal touches like family photos on a dresser, a chair that was obviously an old favorite, hand crocheted afghans in colors that were popular in previous decades. Martha stopped before a closed door and tapped twice before opening it.

"Sadie? You have a visitor." She stepped into the room and ushered Sam forward.

The room was furnished more simply than some of those others—a yellow spread on the bed, a dresser and nightstand that could have been hotel furniture, generic floral prints on the walls. Sadie Gray sat at the dresser, writing on a sheet of paper. A small stack of envelopes stood nearby. Her white hair was neatly styled and she wore pink knit slacks and a flowered blouse in a similar style to the outfits Sam had seen in her closet. Her eyes must have once been vivid blue but they seemed dim now behind the thick lenses of her glasses.

Sadie gave her a puzzled look. "Carrie? I haven't seen you in ages, dear."

Martha Preston murmured to Sam, "She tends to think everyone is Carrie. Apparently that's her neighbor's daughter whom she used to babysit, maybe fifty years ago."

"Hi, Mrs. Gray. Sorry, I'm not Carrie. My name is Samantha Sweet."

"Oh, silly me. The light is terrible in these rooms, you know." She stood up. Although her legs took a moment to get going, Sadie stood straight at a little over five feet and moved energetically.

Martha Preston had backed out of the room and Sadie urged Sam to take the seat at the dresser. She perched herself on the edge of her bed.

"I was just finishing up my paperwork for the day. So many people in this office will sit around and watch TV all day but that's just not the way I do things. I've always taken care of business first."

Sam glanced down at the sheet of paper Sadie had been writing on, lined notebook paper on which she'd listed neat columns of numbers. The envelopes stacked beside it appeared to be junk mail.

"What type of business do you do here?" Sam asked.

"Insurance," Sadie said proudly. "It's what I've done my whole career." She lowered her voice. "Of course, my previous company was a lot better. I loved working with Joe. My husband. We ran a tight ship. I don't care for the work ethic in this place."

Sam had worked for one of the local insurance offices for a few years and she tried to recall the agency that might have been Sadie and Joe's.

"Everything changed when Joe died," Sadie said with a sigh.

The conversation could go off in a dozen directions but Sam reminded herself she had work to do.

"I'm actually here on a financial matter," she said. "There seems to be a problem with the payments on your house and there's a danger of foreclosure. I was sent to take care of the property."

Sadie's pale brows pulled together. "Well, that doesn't sound right. My husband is already taking care of it. He's very good about those things. Why would you need to?"

Was she still talking about Joe?

Sam went into the explanation about the late payments but Sadie's gaze kept drifting, first to the art prints on the walls, then to the papers on her 'desk.'

"Is there a number where I can contact your husband and ask him about this?" Sam finally asked.

"Everything changed when Joe died," Sadie repeated.

Sam tried twice more to get something concrete but the conversation began to spiral into repetition and Sadie grew impatient to return to her 'paperwork.' Finally, Sam stood up.

"Well, I better let you get your work done," she said. "I'll see what I can do to straighten out this other thing."

"Yes, that would be better. I'll be home next week and we can work out all the details." Sadie followed Sam to the bedroom door and closed it gently behind her.

Home in a week? That didn't seem likely. Sam made

her way back to the reception desk where she found
Martha Preston talking with a younger woman in colorfully
patterned scrubs.

"Did you learn what you needed to?" Preston asked
Sam.

"Not really. She thinks she'll be home next week and we
can just work out the details then."

Both women shook their heads. The young nurse spoke
up. "Mrs. Gray is such a sweetheart, but there's no way she
could manage her own home. Her husband apparently is on
the road quite a lot."

"On business matters, you would have better luck
talking to Mr. Gray," Martha Preston said.

"You must have contact information for him. Can you
share that?"

Martha flipped open a blue folder, paged backward
through it and ran her finger down some kind of form.

"Sadie always talks about Joe but her husband's name is
Marshall Gray. He admitted her. She remembers him when
he visits and they seem very loving toward each other."

"Does Mr. Gray still live at the house on Tapia Lane?"
Sam thought of the conflicting evidence—payments in
arrears and food in the refrigerator.

Martha nodded. "It's listed as their residence on the
admittance forms."

Martha gave her a cell phone number and the name
of Marshall Gray's employer, a trucking company. "He's
quite a bit younger than his wife—I would guess at least
twenty years. It's not all that unusual. Some men just need a
mommy," she said with a shrug.

Sam forced a smile. Her own fiancé was younger, and

Beau certainly did not need mothering.

"He seems very devoted to her, comes by to see her at least once a week," the other woman said.

She thanked them and left, intending to call Delbert Crow with the information later in the evening. For now, she might be able to learn something on her own.

Chapter 4

Sam had just pulled into the parking area at ABZ Trucking when her cell phone rang.

"Hey, babe." Beau's voice came through as if he were a block away instead of in Phoenix. "How's everything at home?"

As sheriff of Taos County, most of Beau's work kept him within a hundred miles of home and it was rare that he was gone overnight. This required trip had now kept him away for a week and both of them were getting antsy about the situation.

"Well, it's a hot day, I've got more work than I can handle, and I miss you like crazy. How's the training course going?"

"Boring. I'd hoped we would concentrate on the gun range and tactical techniques. Instead, it's mostly a matter of studying a fat book full of rules. And I know for a fact that a hot day in Phoenix will trump any hot day Taos has to offer."

She laughed. "You're so good at putting things into perspective for me."

"I'll ditto the part about missing you like crazy, though. Boy am I glad I'm outta here in one more day."

She wanted to tell him about her new caretaking dilemma; running things past Beau often helped sort out the puzzling parts, but she heard voices in the background and he rushed through a goodbye so he could get back to his class. She stepped out of her van and approached the trucking company's offices.

An icy blast of air conditioning hit her as she walked in, a reminder that the repairman should have gotten hers fixed by now.

A girl with black, unnaturally puffy hair sat behind a grungy brown counter that ran the full length of the small office. She continued to chew her gum and didn't look up.

"Excuse me?" Sam said, after tapping a fingernail on the counter didn't elicit a response. "I'm with the USDA and I need information on one of your employees."

That statement was not exactly true—Sam was an independent contractor for the agency—but this seemed like the kind of situation where some measure of authority would be needed to get answers. The girl quickly covered the fashion magazine she'd been reading and looked up a little nervously.

"Marshall Gray. Is he in at the moment?" Sam had no idea what Gray's position was supposed to be. She'd forgotten to ask Martha Preston if that was in their file. He could be anything from a manager to a driver, she supposed.

The young woman continued to stare. Sam would have asked if she habla'd inglés but the magazine was clearly in English and the girl had been devouring that.

"Marshall Gray? He works here," Sam prompted.

A tiny wrinkle formed between her brows. "I don't think so." It wasn't a smart comeback, just genuine puzzlement.

"He doesn't work here?"

"I never heard of him. I been here three years."

"Really?" Sam wasn't sure where to turn next. "Are there other branches of the company—maybe in other towns?"

The girl shook her head.

Sam thanked her and left. Clearly, the man had lied on Sadie's admission papers. She got back into her van and let the engine idle while she dialed the cell number Martha had given her for Gray. It rang the requisite four times and went to a generic voice mail where she left a message without giving many details, just in case that, too, was a lie. With no other ideas she put the van in gear and headed toward Sweet's Sweets.

Although the repairman's truck was gone, one step inside the bakery told Sam that her problem had not been fixed. It was hotter inside than out. Her two portable fans were running full blast but Becky, with her hair clipped up off her neck, looked about ready to crack.

"This buttercream isn't acting right," she moaned. Waxed paper squares on a tray held blobs of frosting that should have been roses. There was not a sharp petal edge to be seen.

"Oh, sweetie, that's okay," said Sam. "You're right, and there's nothing to be done about it. It's the heat."

She looked around. "Just scrape the icing back into the bowl and get it into the fridge. And those tubs of frosting we made in advance for tomorrow's wedding cakes—we better keep those refrigerated too."

They picked up everything in sight that couldn't withstand a hundred degrees and carried it to the walk-in. With baked tiers for six wedding cakes and another dozen birthday cakes waiting to be assembled and decorated, things were getting crowded in there.

"What was the repairman's excuse? Why didn't he fix the AC?"

"I'm not sure. He talked to Jen."

Sam left Becky to handle the kitchen while she went up front to get the rest of the story.

"He said it needs a part that wasn't available here in town," Jen told her. Although her job kept her away from the large bake oven in the back, a sheen of perspiration gave her face a rosy glow. "He called someone and it's on order from Albuquerque. It'll be two days before the part gets here."

Sam suppressed a snarl. If old man Tafoya ever properly maintained anything this probably wouldn't have happened. She wondered if she could hold him responsible for any losses the bakery might have as a result, but what would be the point? Customers didn't care if the landlord reimbursed Sam for a damaged cake. They just wanted their cakes delivered on time and with decorations that didn't drip down the sides. Why, oh why did the wedding season have to come in June and July?

She glanced at the clock. It was nearly closing time and the evening would cool off.

"Once the outdoor air starts to cool a bit, let's open everything up and see if we can catch a breeze to blow some of this heat out of here. We're done with the oven for

the day and we've shut it off." She bit at her lip. "Tomorrow,
I'll come in way early and get the breakfast breads baked.
For the next couple of days we'll have to shut down the
oven early in the day. Otherwise, we'll never get anything
decorated."

The thought occurred to her that she'd once run the
whole business from her home. If worse came to worst,
she could take cakes home and decorate there. But what a
pain—all her equipment and tools were here now. She let
out a huge sigh and decided to take it one step at a time.

Sam arrived home, grumpy and frustrated, about the
time she really should be going to bed if she wanted any
sleep at all before starting work all over again. Marshall
Gray had never returned her call, but Delbert Crow had
called twice to step up the pace so he could put the Grays'
house on the auction schedule.

"Mom, this just isn't you," Kelly said after Sam had
stomped into the kitchen ranting about how crummy the
day had gone. "You, the original Little Mary Sunshine, the
lady who is never rattled by anything."

Sam came to a stop. Her daughter was right. Going
around in a bad mood was not her style.

"I think you're simply horny. Beau has been gone too
long." Kelly shrugged and gave her mother a half-smile then
headed toward her own bedroom.

Oh, god, Sam thought. I needed that pointed out by my
thirty-four year old daughter? But it was *so* true. She felt her
mood lift and she melted into laughter, leaning against the
refrigerator.

After a few minutes she decided that life didn't need
to consist entirely of work and that stressful times always
came and went. All she had to do was make it through

this stretch. She poured a glass of iced tea and carried it to the living room, switching on the ten o'clock news with the futile hope that the weather report would announce an impending cold front.

When her bedside alarm jolted her awake at two a.m. she had to work at reminding herself of her this-too-shall-pass mantra. It was actually a little chilly in her bedroom, where she'd slept with the window open, and that helped bolster her resolve to get the pastries done early.

By four o'clock she had a good assortment of muffins, scones and coffee cake on display for her patrons, and she'd baked layers for the next day's cake orders. She shut down the large bake oven and stood in the center of the kitchen with the back door wide open to the predawn air.

She made good progress, tackling the most difficult piping techniques in buttercream well before the sun rose. By the time Becky arrived, Sam had finished a wedding cake and four birthday pieces.

"Wow, I'm impressed," her assistant said.

"I whipped up this batch of teal, for that bride who's into vivid colors," Sam said, "so if you could just make up two dozen roses . . ."

"Absolutely."

"And I've made a couple of executive decisions. For every cake that doesn't specifically require buttercream we'll go with fondant. It's more durable. And sugar flowers instead of piped ones. It's a bit more work up front, but at least we don't have to do it over again."

No argument from Becky. Yesterday's disastrous tray of lumpy roses was still fresh in her mind, apparently. She set to work on teal roses, carrying trays of them to the fridge as soon as they were done. They could do this. As long as the repairman received the part and got himself back out here, they only had to withstand a couple more days at this pace. Or so she thought.

At nine o'clock a young woman came in and told Jen she needed a wedding cake and would be back to pick it up that afternoon. When Jen informed her that wasn't how it worked, that they were backed up nearly three weeks with orders, the lady became agitated and Sam got called away from the chocolate fondant that was giving her fits anyway.

She pasted on a smile and walked out front.

"This girl says I can't get my wedding cake today," the bride whined. "I have to. The invitations are out. The wedding is at ten in the morning."

"We'll do our best, but you have to realize that your options are limited. Most people order their wedding cakes at least a month in advance." Sam pulled out her portfolio of pictures, thinking about all the other orders that weren't getting done at the moment because she was humoring this latecomer.

Within thirty minutes, they'd struck a deal. Sam knew they had some generic layers, both round and square, which they'd baked ahead to put on display as birthday cakes. She could accommodate the bride's colors but the young woman would have to give her some leeway with design and shape, and the cake itself would have to be vanilla, chocolate or red velvet. No specialty flavors on such short notice. And someone would have to pick up the cake after eight the next morning.

"Gotta love those hangers," Jen commented as the woman left, using their code word for those customers who left important details hanging until the last moment.

Sam heaved a sigh and headed back to the kitchen, ready to throw this customer's layers together as soon as she'd finished draping the chocolate fondant for a birthday order that had to be delivered before noon.

When another hanger showed up as she was heading out the door for the delivery—a man who'd planned every detail for his wife's surprise birthday party, except for the cake—it took all Sam could muster to greet him with a smile. He'd just assumed that a cake to feed a hundred was something you could walk in and buy off the shelf. He was very apologetic and offered to pay extra. Damn right, you will, she thought. She smiled and quoted him double the normal rate.

"We have a twelve-inch square and an eight-inch square in the fridge, don't we?" she asked Becky as she hustled through the kitchen. "Cover them both in white fondant, will you? And do we have any spare sugar flowers made up, something that isn't committed to another order?"

At her assistant's nod, she breathed a little easier. "I always make extras of everything, in case of breakage."

"I'll be back in thirty minutes from delivering this birthday, and then I better have some kind of brilliant inspiration. The guy is coming back at four and wants to surprise his wife with something dazzling."

Becky rolled her eyes as Sam headed out with the chocolate birthday cake in hand. A picture of the surprise cake was already forming in her head and she started to relax as she turned up the air in her van and took the back roads to her destination.

She passed the turn where she'd gone the previous day to Sadie Gray's house, reminding her that she'd still heard nothing from the elusive husband, Marshall, who never answered his phone and couldn't even be truthful about where he worked. The agency was setting an auction date for the house despite her information that there was un-expired milk in the fridge. Delbert Crow must be feeling some pressure from above because he normally wasn't quite so prompt about his duties.

She dropped off the birthday cake to a party where kids were roaring around the backyard, already in a frenzy of red-punch-induced energy. The little birthday boy barely gave his cake a second glance but his mother gushed over the circus motif that Sam and Becky had created from peppermint sticks and candy clay animals.

On her way back to Sweet's Sweets, Sam decided to cruise past the Gray house once more, just in case. But the place seemed the same as before. No fresh tire tracks, no change in the lights or draperies, no mail or newspapers piled up. What was going on here?

Back at the pastry shop, Becky brought out the two white fondant-covered square cakes and an assortment of leftover sugar flowers. It took Sam moments to stack them and start adding yellow daisies, orange lilies, and purple asters to create a flower garden on top that trailed down to the base. Touches of tiny pink anemones and a dusting of clear edible glitter made the piece zing. A stickpin with Happy Birthday on it, and the birthday surprise was ready for the man who would be there soon to pick it up.

"He'll be very relieved," Becky said, admiring the finished cake.

"Not bad, considering how quickly it came together." Sam boxed the cake and carried it to the front so Jen would have it ready the moment the customer walked in.

She glanced at her cell phone. Still no call from Marshall Gray but there was another from Delbert Crow. She ignored it and pulled the next order form from the top of the big stack on her desk.

Chapter 5

Sam's alarm brought another two a.m. awakening. Way too soon. She rolled over to ignore it but knew that she didn't dare close her eyes. Despite the fact that her back ached and her legs felt perpetually cramped, there was too much at stake. She'd had dreams all night about trying to deliver cakes, but all the homes were abandoned and she couldn't locate the owners. With a groan she sat on the edge of her bed and switched on the lamp.

Beau would be home tonight and she couldn't greet him as an aching old bag of bones who was working herself to death.

Her gaze traveled to her dresser where her jewelry box sat, that strange-looking carved hunk of wood. Bertha Martinez, the woman who had given it to her, promised Sam it was a gift meant for her, something she could use when help was most needed. The woman had promptly died five minutes after handing the box to Sam. The very first time she'd opened the box something strange happened—an electric-like jolt, a flash of insight—and from that time on, Sam's life changed in ways she'd never dreamed.

She stared at its ugly façade—the unevenly carved quilted pattern, the nasty-looking yellowish stain, the small cabochon stones set lopsidedly at each X intersection in the carved surface. Homely and lonesome, it sat like the skinny girl at the prom with braces on her teeth and a too-large dress from the thrift store. Sam reached for it, almost as if she could comfort the poor, lonely thing.

Instead, it comforted her. The wooden box began to warm her hands and the yellowish surface glowed, rich and golden. The small stones shone red, green and blue, sparkling as Sam ran her hands over them. The tension drained from her spine, the aches from her legs.

She'd promised herself that she wouldn't become addicted to using the box's powers. She couldn't bail herself out of every tough spot by taking on its energy. Well, actually she could. But the idea frightened her. Despite trying, what she couldn't seem to do was to get rid of it. And that was the scary part.

The box became too warm and she pulled her hands away from it.

Okay, this gift was given to me so I could help others. And what's more important to a bride than her wedding cake? Well, a lot of other things should *be more important, but to those young women who come into my shop with their hearts full of dreams and their heads full of wedding plans . . . This is what I have to do . . . but only today.*

A hot shower, a quick fluff of her short, graying hair and Sam was out the door. Stars filled the black sky and she breathed deeply of the cool air. With no traffic she arrived at the bakery in under ten minutes. Determined to make the most of her mystical energy boost, she preheated the oven and pulled orders from the basket on her desk.

By the time Becky arrived at six, Sam had completed half the orders and all of the morning's breakfast pastries for the displays out front. Becky stared at the loaded worktable.

"I couldn't sleep," Sam told her assistant. "That plus a lot of coffee."

Neither claim was strictly true but it was safer than revealing the powers of the magical wooden box. Only Beau knew that part of the story.

Becky began crafting sugar flowers with a vengeance while Sam carried trays of muffins and éclairs out to the display shelves in the store. Her cell phone buzzed deep in her pocket and she pulled it out. Delbert Crow. Again. Did the man never sleep?

She let it go to voice mail, determined to speak with Marshall Gray and get some answers before trying to make more excuses to Delbert. She'd left two messages for the husband and wasn't a hundred percent sure that she even had a valid number for him. She reached below the sales counter and pulled out the telephone directory, reaching an amazingly perky receptionist at Casa Serenita, considering that the sun was barely over the horizon yet. She gave minimal explanation, asking simply that Mr. Gray be told that he needed to call her the next time he visited his wife.

With the kitchen in good shape for the moment, Sam set up the beverage bar with two pots of her signature blend coffee, plus an assortment of teas and a variety of sweeteners and creamers for the first customers who would start arriving in the next twenty minutes or so. Jen arrived to take over the front and Sam lost herself once again in her favorite part of the business, the creation of beautiful pastries.

"Sam?" Jen stepped into the kitchen, keeping her voice low. "Want a little break? There's a really cute guy here who says he's an old friend."

Sam glanced up at the kitchen clock and realized that it was well after noon. She washed her hands and stepped out to the sales room.

"Samantha! How great to see you!" Derek Sanchez greeted her with a smile and a hug.

She'd last seen him as a young man and was surprised to note strands of gray at his temples.

The son of her former boss from her days at The Sanchez Agency when Kelly was still a kid, Derek spoke with his typical salesman ebullience. The small insurance firm had been founded by Derek's father Michael, but when the elder man died, Derek couldn't resist a buyout offer from a big national firm and Sam didn't like the pace and corporate attitude the new management brought to the game. Derek, on the other hand, thrived on that hustle-bustle and the last she'd heard he had moved up to a corporate-level position in some major city—she just couldn't remember which.

"Great to see you too, Derek. Did Jen offer you some coffee?"

"She did. And it's great." He motioned toward one of the bistro tables where a steaming cup waited for him to return. "Can you sit a minute?"

She almost pleaded her way out of it but a sudden thought came to her. "Sure. I'd love to take a break."

He chatted on about how great life was in San Francisco while she made herself a cup of tea and answered questions over her shoulder about the local scene. When she sat across from him, she brought up what was really on her mind.

"I ran into a lady the other day who said she used to be in insurance here in town but I can't place her. Maybe you'd remember—her name is Sadie Gray."

His eyebrows pulled together above the strong bridge of his nose. "Gray. Doesn't ring a bell."

"Oh, wait—Gray is a new married name for her. Her first husband's name was Joe. Unfortunately, I don't know their last name."

"Joe and Sadie? Well, it's got to be the Wilsons. My gosh, they were like grandparents to me. My dad worked in Joe's agency when he first got into the business." He sipped at his coffee. "When Dad branched off to start his own agency, I suppose they must have been somewhat hurt about it, but they never said a word. Always wished him well. At least, as far as I know. I was probably in junior high when all that happened. Man, I remember Sunday pot roast dinners at their house. Sadie was a heck of a cook."

Sam gave him a minute to reminisce.

"You said you ran into her recently? And she's remarried—wow. I heard about Joe passing away, but that was years ago. At least Sadie was left financially comfortable. One thing about insurance guys—their own policies are always up to date."

"Sadie's in a nursing home, Derek. Dementia."

"Oh, man, that's rough. She was sharp as a tack when I knew her. Believe me, I got caught with my hand in the cookie jar at her house so many times, I swore she had eyes in the back of her head. A kid could pull *nothing* over on that lady." He chuckled at the memory.

"I'm trying to save her home from foreclosure. I just

don't understand how that came about. I really need to get in touch with her husband and get the payments up to date. I mean, surely from what you've said it's not a lack of money. I'm guessing she just began losing track of things."

He nodded slowly. "Probably so. It's really sad. I'd like to go by and see her if you can give me the name of the place."

Sam grabbed a business card and wrote the information on the back. "If you should happen to run into Marshall Gray there, please have him call me."

Derek assured her that he would. She watched him get into a rented Lincoln and drive away.

Jen stared out the window, a little starry-eyed.

"He's as gay as they come, girl, and last I heard his longtime partner was still around." Sam patted Jen's shoulder. "I better get back to those wedding cakes."

Her energy began to flag by mid-afternoon and Becky insisted she go home and rest. Jen told her the air conditioning repair guy had called and was on his way over, and she assured Sam that she and Becky could handle the shop the rest of the day.

"Go," Becky insisted. "Beau gets back tonight, right? Well, you might want to have a nap and some time to fancy up a little. Is he taking you out to dinner?"

"I should cook at home," Sam said. "He's been eating in restaurants all week."

Great intentions, but when she began a mental inventory of her freezer contents and couldn't think of a single thing to make, she detoured to the supermarket and picked up a deli pasta sauce that was actually better than her homemade. With some fresh garlic bread and a salad, it ought to please him. Considering that their phone conversations had increasingly taken a sexy turn, it didn't seem likely that he would be too picky about the meal anyway.

Her cell phone rang while she was standing in the checkout line.

"Hey darlin', I'm getting closer. I'm at the Albuquerque airport. Be heading your way as soon as I get my bag from that carousel over there and my car from the parking lot." His voice dropped to a near-whisper. "So, seven o'clock, my place?"

"I'll bring dinner."

"Is it something that might keep for an extra hour?"

She laughed at his urgent tone. "Yes, absolutely."

Out in the van she dialed Sweet's Sweets. "Jen, is there any way you and Becky could get there early enough to get things going in the morning?"

"Already thought of that. *You* may have been so busy that you didn't think about the morning after Beau gets home. But *we* did. There's no way you're coming in at five o'clock to start baking. We'll handle it." She paused and Sam heard Becky's voice in the background. "Oh, yeah. The AC is back on and everything's going just fine here."

Sam permitted herself a long, relaxing bath when she got home and a refreshing nap, awaking in time to pull her silk kimono from the closet, the one Beau loved to remove from her. She tossed it into a small bag, gathered the dinner ingredients and headed for his ranch, about fifteen minutes past the north edge of town.

She couldn't believe how her heart rate picked up when his blue Explorer pulled through the gate and started up the driveway. His two dogs, Ranger and Nellie, ran out to meet the vehicle and raced alongside it. Obviously, the neighbor who fed them and tended the horses was no substitute for

Beau in their estimation.

When he stepped out, she met him at the door, taking in the welcome sight of him in snug jeans and short-sleeved plaid shirt. He pulled off the Stetson and took her into his arms.

"I don't ever want to be gone a whole week again," he murmured into her ear. "Can we go upstairs right this minute?"

She smiled and took his hand.

In the master bedroom she'd turned back the thick comforter on the king-size bed and aired the room before he arrived. Now, she turned on the shower and began undoing the pearl snaps on his shirt. His kisses trailed from her mouth to her neck to her shoulder.

"You coming into that shower with me?" he asked, peeling off the jeans in record time.

Well, with an invitation like that . . .

* * *

The pasta dinner wasn't at its best when they finally emerged from the bedroom, so they settled for salads—which she'd luckily remembered to stash in the fridge—and some hot toasted garlic bread, carried to the big wooden rockers on the back deck where the mild evening air felt cool on their skin.

"You don't know how lucky you are to be in this part of the world until you spend time in the month of June in a big, hot city," he said after he'd polished off half of his salad.

"I *do* know how lucky I am," Sam answered. "And that's precisely why I'm here."

"Missed you."

"You too." She sipped from her wine glass. "Life just becomes too unbalanced without you. I felt like it was work, work, work. I'm up to three caretaking jobs now. One of them is a little weird."

She filled him on her first visit to the Gray house and the discovery that Sadie Gray was in a nursing home. "Casa Serenita . . . was that where Iris went?"

He shook his head. "No, Mama was in that other place after her stroke." He stared across the open field. "We thought she would have some physical therapy and then come home."

"Sorry I brought that up. It still hurts, doesn't it?"

"It's okay, darlin'. At least she's not in pain anymore."

Sam watched as he took a pull from his beer and rocked thoughtfully.

"The weird thing about this job is that we can't seem to reach the husband even though he visits his wife regularly. You'd think he'd want to be sure the house was all right. And the place of employment he listed on Sadie's admission forms turned out to be false."

"And you'd like for me to quietly look into it." He glanced sideways at her. "I can do a standard background check but it may not turn up much more than you already know about his employment, not if he's purposely trying to hide information."

"He'll probably respond to my messages soon."

"What's his name?" Beau's tone was firm.

"Marshall Gray. But don't go to any trouble over this."

They carried their dishes indoors and settled onto the large sofa in the living room, tucked close together in one corner. The kisses started again and about the time Beau was about to slip the silk kimono off her shoulder, Sam's cell phone jangled on the coffee table.

"I'll just ignore it," she mumbled into his neck.

He lifted his head. "What if it's Kelly? Or the girls from the bakery? Maybe there's a problem."

"Grrr . . ." Sam broke away from his embrace and picked up the phone. The readout showed an unknown number but she was already losing the mood.

"Samantha Sweet?" an unfamiliar male voice said. "This is Marshall Gray returning your call."

"Mr. Gray." She glanced at Beau and he gave her a there-you-go stare.

She turned her attention back to the telephone and explained quickly to Gray why she'd been calling.

"It's just that the auction date will be set pretty quickly. You and your wife will lose the place if you don't act soon."

"Oh, dear. Well, we certainly don't want that to happen. This downturn in my wife's health has happened so fast and it's left me rushing every which direction to handle things. I guess neither of us realized that the mortgage was falling behind."

How many notices must they have received, Sam wondered. But then she thought of the stack of mail on Sadie's dresser at the nursing home and how she thought she was taking care of business when it was really more like a little girl playing secretary.

"Sadie has always been so competent. I just didn't think . . ."

"I understand. This must be very difficult."

"But I will get right on this," he said. "Give me the name

of that USDA person and I will make the calls first thing in the morning."

Sam recited Delbert Crow's number from memory, saying that he could direct Marshall to the right people. Following procedure was definitely one of her supervisor's strong suits.

"He ignored my comment about trying to reach him at work. But he did sound very sincere and says he'll take care of the payments," she told Beau, clicking the phone shut.

"Good, because I had other plans for the rest of this night." His hand reached for the front of the kimono.

Chapter 6

Sam awoke, for the first time in days, completely relaxed. The sex must be part of it, but she had to give credit for the fact that she wasn't rising before dawn to get to the shop and the reassurance that Marshall Gray would attend to the situation at the house. She could drop by there sometime and pick up the paperwork she'd left behind, send it all to Delbert Crow and close that particular case. Hallelujah and amen, as her father would say.

She rolled over and tucked her head against Beau's chest. The next time she became conscious, the clock showed that an hour had passed.

"Much as I would love to do this all day long," Beau said, "I haven't been to my office in a week and haven't even checked in with anyone for twenty-four hours."

"I knew it was too good to be true," she muttered, "but

same for me. I better find out what's happening at my shop before some bridezilla goes nutso on Jen."

She rolled over, enjoying the view as Beau walked toward the bathroom.

"Bridezillas? And to think, you chose this business fully aware of the pitfalls," he said as he turned the taps on the shower.

"I guess I did." She left the warm bed and joined him behind the steamy glass door.

An hour later when she stepped into the sales room at Sweet's Sweets, things seemed to be under control. Kelly stood in front of the display case, holding a blueberry cream scone on a napkin. She sent a mischievous look toward her mother.

"That problem you were having yesterday?" she said. "Looks like Beau took care of it."

Sam laughed aloud. "Looks like."

In the kitchen Becky was humming softly as she stacked layers for a birthday cake that would be covered in lollipops and gumdrops for a little girl.

"I wasn't sure how to approach the dump truck for that customer with the six-year-old boy," Becky told Sam. "So I took the easy one and left that for you."

"As long as the square layers have been baked and the red and yellow fondant is already tinted, that one's no problem. I'll get to it in a minute." She wanted a cup of tea first.

Two women stood in front of the display case, poring over the goodies and trying to decide whether brownies or cheesecake would make a good mid-morning snack. Sam's gaze traveled automatically to the beverages, where everything appeared to be neat and well-stocked. Jen gave her a secretive smile, but before Sam could respond the glare of a windshield caught their attention and she saw that her friend Zoë had pulled up out front.

"You look nice this morning," Jen said, taking in Zoë's deep brown broomstick skirt and pale aqua blouse.

Zoë sent a weak smile her way. "I just came from a funeral."

"Oh. I'm so sorry," Jen said.

Sam gave Zoë an intent look. "You look like you could use a cup of tea." Without waiting for a response, she chose Zoë's favorite passionflower tea and brewed a cup for each of them. A glance told her that her friend was pretty upset so she steered her through the curtain to the kitchen.

"Sit," she ordered, pulling an extra chair up to the desk.

Zoë parked herself long enough to take a sip from her cup but Sam could tell she was restless.

"Who was it? What happened?"

Zoë's eyes welled up again. "I just can't believe it. I only saw the announcement in the paper last night. Lila was not that old, and certainly not that sick. I can't believe she's gone."

"Lila? Did I know—"

"I don't remember if you had met her. Lila Coffey."

Sam shook her head.

Zoë stood up and began pacing. "Such a talented potter—it was a lifelong dream for her, moving to Taos and working full-time at her art. She created such *beautiful* pieces—and they sold well, too. Several prizes, a big following. She'd received commissions from the governor's office and just delivered a very special piece to the White House, for a collection representing the art of each of the fifty states."

She switched directions and glanced toward Becky, who was working on the lollipop cake and not paying attention to the conversation.

"Darryl and I met her about three years ago—she stayed with us while she was looking for a house to buy. Found a beautiful place out on the ski valley road—just gorgeous, with a separate little studio. It was perfect for her. "

"So . . . what happened?"

"That's the part I just don't get. She was perfectly healthy and well. Then last Monday she stepped awkwardly off the porch or something and broke her ankle. I went to see her in the hospital and she acted like it was no big deal. They planned to keep her a couple of days, then she would spend a week or two in a rehab facility until she could navigate around a bit, then she would go home. There was truly nothing life-threatening about it at all. And now she's dead." Zoë's voice cracked. "I'm still in shock."

Sam felt a shiver go through her.

"Sixty-four years old, just at the top of her career, and now she's gone." Zoë sank back into the chair.

"My gosh, how did she die?" Sam asked.

"I don't know. No one has really said, just something about her heart."

"Maybe a hidden condition, one of those things . . ."

Zoë shook her head. "I really don't . . ." She stared out into the middle of the room. "Maybe so. I don't know." She drained her tea cup. "Sorry to bring all this to you. Life is so busy for you right now, and you didn't even know her. I really just came in for a gigantic brownie to drown my sorrows."

Sam smiled gently. "Well, that you shall have. On the house."

Sending Zoë on her way with two brownies (Darryl should have one too, she'd insisted) brightened the mood only slightly. It was hard on Sam to see her friend in such pain.

She spent the afternoon lost in the intricacies of forming a construction vehicle from cake and fondant, using a little trick she'd developed where fondant wheels actually concealed the real support for the five heavy pieces of pound cake. The cab was covered in red fondant, the bed in bright yellow, with gray for the grill and bumpers and black for the tires. The piece had a hundred tiny details but filling the bed of the truck with candy and small fondant packages made it a sure hit for the two dozen little boys who would gobble it up.

When Beau stopped in at six, offering to take her out for Mexican food she was more than ready to eat something that contained no sugar.

"I had a visit from Zoë this afternoon," Sam said as they took a corner table at their favorite little restaurant. "She was really upset. This friend went in with a broken ankle and was dead a couple days later." She filled him in about Lila Coffey while he perused the menu.

"And Zoë thinks there was something suspicious about the death, and I suppose you want me to look into it?"

"You read my mind."

"Darlin', I'm getting to where I can always read your mind." He closed his menu.

"Oh yeah? So what am I thinking now?"

"That if I don't do this favor for you, there won't be any sex for a week."

"Well, that just shows how little you know," she said, dropping her voice as their waitress approached. "It would only be three days. Things have been a little desperate recently."

He sputtered a little but recovered well enough to order the beef burrito, smothered in green chile sauce.

"I'll ask some questions," he said after the girl walked away. "But I can't promise much. If the death was attended by medical staff, the doctor's statement on the death certificate is probably going to stand."

They finished their dinners and Beau dropped her off at Sweet's Sweets, warning that he had a late night ahead, making his way through a backlog of cases at his office. She decided to go back to her own house and get a good night's sleep.

The next morning at nine, she was well into a tiered cupcake display for a bridal shower, where silver streaks of royal icing rained down over three dozen white cupcakes decorated with golden stars and about a million crystalline sparkles, all meant to look as if they were trailing from the edge of the bridal veil on the small figurine at the very top. Now that the air inside the kitchen was reasonably cool again, she was having fits getting the sparkles to adhere before the buttercream frosting dried with a light crust on it. The intercom buzzed and Jen's voice came through: "Beau is—"

"—here and on the way back to the kitchen." He finished the sentence as he strode across the room. "Hey there. How about a late breakfast out somewhere?"

"I'm kind of—"

"Covered in glittery stuff?"

"Well, yeah." She stepped back from the creation and realized it was about as good as she could make it. "Does this have enough . . . bling?"

Beau looked at the three tiers of cupcakes, back at Sam, and mouthed the word *bling?* with about three question marks after it.

Becky looked up from the cinnamon rolls she was spreading with maple glaze. "It's perfect, Sam. Stop stressing over it."

"I've got some information on that other matter," Beau said, arching his eyebrows.

No sex for three days? She almost giggled but saw that his face was serious. He meant the death of Zoë's friend Lila Coffey. It must be a lot of news if he needed an entire meal to explain it.

"I can spare a half hour," she said, picking up the stack of orders that had to be finished before day's end.

"That'll do." He waited while she rinsed a few hundred sparkles down the drain and picked up her shoulder pack.

She shed the baker's jacket and they walked out into the warm morning. His cruiser waited at the curb in front of the shop and he backed out before speaking again.

"According to the death certificate, Lila Coffey died of heart failure—no further explanation. She was staying at Life Therapy at the time. It does seem unusual for a woman in otherwise good health who only had a broken ankle. You hear stories about people who work in those places. Those angels of death or whatever they're called who think they're doing old people a favor. Putting them out of their misery or something."

Sam struggled to make the connection.

"It's the same place Mama was when she died." His voice was unusually tight. "Granted, she was older and she had other problems."

"What are you saying, Beau? You don't think—"

"I don't know. But I get an uneasy feeling about this." He waited for a clear spot in traffic. "Do you remember anything at all from January, any nurses who hung around Mama more than normal, anything like that?"

Sam searched, thinking back. "Not really. Things were so crazy for me around the holidays. I'm so sorry I wasn't able to visit her more often, to be there for her. The whole season was such a blur for me."

Beau found an opening and made a right turn.

"But Zoë's friend wasn't exactly elderly, she said. " *Twelve years older than I am—yikes!*

"I just want to check things out," he said tersely. "But I promised you breakfast . . ."

"No, this is more important." She could see him staying in this tense mood all through the meal if he didn't get some answers.

Life Therapy was located only a half mile or so from the town's other nursing facility, and from the outside didn't appear much different. He whipped into the parking lot and brought the cruiser to a quick stop within view of the office windows. If the sight of a six-foot lawman didn't bring quick answers maybe the fact that his cruiser waited outside would get someone talking.

Sam followed, trotting along after him. Inside, she noted, this place had the feel of a corporate chain—precisely matched generic furniture and staff in uniforms.

A young receptionist sat at the desk and Beau asked for the manager.

They waited while the receptionist disappeared through a doorway. A stocky white-haired man in a dark business suit appeared. He greeted them with a pleasant smile and introduced himself as Robert Woods, manager of the facility.

"Can we talk in your office?" Beau suggested.

Woods ushered them into a quiet room furnished with an oak desk and credenza, matching bookcases, and two visitor chairs upholstered in navy fabric.

"You look familiar, officer," Woods said as they sat down.

"Sheriff. Beau Cardwell."

Sam started to open her mouth. Closed it. Beau surely had a reason not to reveal all.

He unfolded the copy of Lila Coffey's death certificate and presented it to Robert Woods who glanced over it and then looked up, slightly puzzled.

"Yes? I remember Ms Coffey. The artist. It certainly came as a surprise when she died." Woods pulled a folder from a drawer behind him.

"We're mainly a physical therapy unit," he said. "Our patients are all ages and come from all walks of life. Many are elderly, for instance needing rehabilitation from a hip injury. We have specialists who work with stroke victims. There are also accident victims who need to relearn to walk or lift things. It appears that Ms Coffey came in for rehabilitation on an ankle injury."

"Do you remember the circumstances of her death? The certificate says heart failure. Was it a heart attack? Were paramedics called?"

"No, unfortunately. It happened in the middle of the night. She apparently died in her sleep." He glanced into the folder. "One of the nurses was doing a midnight bed-check and found her unresponsive, not breathing. Our on-call physician happened to be here on another case and he rushed right to her room and pronounced her."

"I understand there was no autopsy."

"Since our own doctor was here, probably within minutes after the death, we didn't order one. No one other than staff had been near her since early that morning when her husband visited. Her pastor stopped by sometime during the afternoon. According to the notation here, she refused dinner. Said she wasn't very hungry. That's not uncommon around here, and we usually don't force the issue."

"What kind of background checks do you run before hiring a new staff person?" Beau asked.

Woods sat straighter in his chair. "Why, very thorough ones, of course. We would never take on someone who had anything questionable in his or her background. I know what you're thinking, Sheriff Cardwell, and I assure you—no one in this facility has ever been accused of harming a patient."

"I'll need a list of everyone who currently works here and everyone who has left since, let's say, the first of the year."

"Absolutely. It will only take a moment to access those records." He pulled his computer keyboard closer and tapped a few keys. "If you have any other questions, please don't hesitate to ask," he said, standing up and handing Beau the pages that came off the printer.

He thanked the director and they headed back to the cruiser.

"You didn't say anything about your mother," Sam said, fastening her seat belt.

"I thought about it, but I want to see what comes of my own background checks. And I'm going to include Robert Woods in that."

"Do you think he's covering up something?"

"Not necessarily. I didn't sense anything deceptive

about him. But it's best to check out everyone. That old 'trust, but verify.' " He wheeled away from the facility and steered toward the main drag through town. "Do you still have time for breakfast?"

Sam glanced at the dashboard clock. "Only if it's a quick one."

"How about a breakfast sandwich to go, from some drive-through place?"

"Maybe a breakfast burrito from Ortega's? They come in foil wrappers and I can take it back to work with me."

He nodded.

"So, how long do you think it will take to run your background checks on those people?"

He pulled into a small parking lot in front of a tiny building with hand-lettered signs. "Not too long. I'll get someone on them the minute I get back to the office."

He got out and walked up to the window that faced the road, giving quick instructions on their food while the woman inside wrote it down and sent nervous glances toward Sam. Apparently, riding around in the sheriff's cruiser didn't especially make a person look like a model citizen.

Chapter 7

Sam wolfed down her burrito in the car on the way back to the bakery. If past experience was any indicator, something would come up to prevent her from eating once she stepped into her shop. By that evening she was glad for that foresight. Beau met her on the porch at his place where he planned to grill steaks outdoors and she intended to spend the night.

"Crazy day," she said, leaning into his chest and enjoying the warm hands that stroked her back.

"Me too. But I think the dinner I planned will boost your energy." He gave her a kiss on top of her head and turned toward the kitchen.

"So," she said a little while later as she tossed the salad, "I'm dying to know what you turned up with those background checks from the nursing home staff."

He placed a succulent filet and a baked potato on each of their plates. "Not a darn thing, unfortunately. Everything I came up with on the nurses, cooks and cleaning people turned up the same as Life Therapy's own pre-employment information. There's not a person in the place with anything more serious on their record than a speeding ticket."

He carried the plates to the dining table that faced out toward open pasture land, where his two horses grazed and the sun had already dipped below the tall cottonwood trees.

"No killer nurses in the whole bunch, then," Sam said, setting the salad bowl nearby.

"Not unless one of them is just getting started. I guess every serial killer has to begin somewhere."

"That's a gruesome thought, Beau."

"It had me worried—about Mama, I mean—but I can't really find a connection. I don't think the killer-nurse scenario is true in this case. Most of their nurses are pretty young, probably still idealistic about life. The two older ones have been at the game for a long time. One is near retirement age. If either of them had begun bumping off their patients, they probably started years ago and there would be something suspicious in their records. I'm guessing, anyway."

The steaks had turned out perfectly and Sam devoted herself to savoring both the meal and the fact that tomorrow was Sunday, her one day off. She'd bought the ingredients for her special omelets and envisioned a lazy morning with Beau—complete with all the benefits.

"I better contact Zoë and tell her what you found out—or didn't find out—about the nursing home," she told Beau as they cleared the table and loaded the dishwasher. "She was pretty upset about Lila's death. I'll need to go see her."

"Well, as someone once said . . . tomorrow is another day," he said, switching out the kitchen light and grabbing her hand. "I'm going upstairs for a shower . . . want to join me?"

He didn't need to ask twice.

* * *

It was nearing noon before Sam tore herself away from Beau's idyllic ranch house. The previous evening had worked every bit of the week's tension from her body, and their cozy Sunday breakfast provided an excellent excuse to stay in and enjoy a thoroughly domestic day at home. But by late morning he was becoming antsy about unfinished chores around the place—horses needed tending, the stalls in the barn hadn't been cleaned in a week. Sam had things to do herself, remembering her promise to check in on Zoë and give her the latest information from Beau's investigation.

Beau walked toward the barn after leaving Sam with a lingering kiss. She let her van idle for a minute while she dialed Zoë's number.

"Hey there. My guests just left and I was on my way out the door."

"Oh. Well, I can catch up with you later. Beau got some background information on the staff at Life Therapy but it didn't amount to a lot."

"Listen, why don't you meet me? I was going up to Lila Coffey's studio. One of her friends called me and said they're having a little gathering. I get the impression it's not quite a wake and not really a memorial, just a chance for friends to visit a bit."

Sam started to demur but when Zoë suggested that she

might learn something more about Lila's mysterious death she changed her mind.

"You're practically halfway there already," Zoë said, giving directions to the home-slash-studio on the ski valley road. "I should be along in no more than twenty minutes."

Sam looked down at the black slacks and baker's jacket she'd worn home from the bakery yesterday. Not exactly party duds. She shut down the van and went back inside. Beau had cleared one side of his closet for her, and when it looked like their wedding was imminent she'd brought some of her things over. But then they'd cancelled and she'd halted in mid-move.

Face it, Sam, your life is scattered over half the county.

She found a bronze-toned blouse that would look okay with the black pants, traded the baker's jacket for it, and gave the slacks a quick brush-down with a damp cloth to remove the haze of powdered sugar that tended to cling to everything she wore. Some gel to give definition to her fluffy hair and a swipe of lipstick, and she considered herself done. She wasn't going to know anyone there except Zoë anyhow.

Back in the van she negotiated Beau's long driveway and turned north.

Yellow signs with bold black print announcing an estate sale and a line of cars along the roadway began to appear about the time Sam thought she was getting close to the destination. She'd just pulled into a vacant spot when Zoë's Subaru coasted by and came to a screeching halt. The passenger side window whirred down.

"What the heck is this?" Zoë shouted.

Sam shrugged. "Am I at the right place?"

"Yeah, but a sale? I can't believe it."

Another car pulled up behind her and Zoë drove on, tucking the little car into the first open place she spotted. Sam walked over to join her.

"Lila isn't even cold yet, and someone is selling her things?" Zoë looked genuinely distressed.

"Let's go see what we can find out." Sam took her friend's elbow and steered her toward the chalet style house with its neatly planted beds of flowering plants and trimmed topiary.

The front door stood open and several women milled about, each with an armload of treasures. A small queue of people had formed at the side of the house.

"Her studio is out back," Zoë said. "That must be where they're all going."

She spotted someone she knew and hurried forward. Sam followed close behind, hoping not to lose Zoë in the crowd.

"Aggie! What is all this?" Zoë demanded.

The woman was about their age, with long hair in gray-brown wavy strands and loose cotton clothing in the same new-age style Zoë favored. Sam introduced herself when Aggie gave her a puzzled glance.

"It's Ted, he's organized this sale. It looks like he's clearing out both the studio and the house."

"Ted? Who's Ted?" Zoë's hands were on her hips now.

"Lila's husband."

Zoë started to choke. "*What?*"

"You didn't know?" Aggie reached out and patted Zoë on the back. "Lila got married a couple of months ago, although she kept her professional name. I guess they kept it very low-key, didn't even mention a honeymoon to the

Bahamas. I only found out when someone pointed him out at the funeral."

Zoë turned to Sam. "I was so upset that I left the funeral without going through the receiving line. I assumed those people in the front rows were family. I mean, Lila's siblings or cousins or something."

Aggie spoke up again. "A couple of them were—distant cousins from Alabama or someplace. But the man up front . . . I'll point him out when I see him . . . that was Ted O'Malley."

Zoë chewed at her lip, digesting all the new information. Sam slipped away and wandered toward the house, passing two women. One had a lamp in her hand and a fur coat draped over her arm. The other struggled with a large box that appeared to contain a set of china.

". . . no bargains, but boy, it's really quality stuff," the shorter woman was saying to her friend.

Sam stepped aside to let them pass, then mounted the steps to the front porch. The living room looked like sale-day at Macy's. Tables lined the walls and were stacked with everything from clothing and costume jewelry, to bottles of shampoo and perfume, to picture frames and storage boxes. A beautifully upholstered striped sofa had a red 'sold' tag pinned to it. A slender young woman in semi-official black clothing pointed people toward the kitchen or bedrooms, depending upon their wishes. Through the dining room window, Sam spotted two men struggling with a large potter's wheel.

"Oh, god," Zoë said, apparently seeing the same thing as she walked up to Sam. "I can't believe her life is just getting distributed like so much garage sale junk."

Sam put an arm around her friend's shoulders. "I know, I know. But I guess it has to go to someone, and at least people are buying things they like."

"It just seems so . . . cold, doing it this way." Zoë's lip trembled.

Sam noticed two men standing to the side, conversing quietly. "I wonder if that's the husband."

Zoë wiped at her eyes and followed Sam's gaze. "I'll bet it is. Aggie said he was wearing a dark suit with a purple tie."

Sam gave her a nudge and they approached the men.

"Excuse me, are you Ted O'Malley?" Sam asked. She put his age at about fifty. Touches of gray in his pale brown hair, worry wrinkles across the high forehead, prominent ears and a droop at the tip of his nose, as if it wanted to touch his weak upper lip.

He nodded and held out his hand. "Yes, ma'am. And you were a friend of Lila's?"

Zoë stepped forward, ignoring the hand, her eyes practically flashing. "I was a *good* friend. And I want to know why I never heard of you."

Sam gave her a gentle elbow.

"What right do you have to get rid of her things this way? I can't believe it. The funeral was only days ago."

The man he'd been conversing with cleared his throat. "I understand how upsetting this must be," he said. "I'm Joe Smith, the family attorney."

Smith's steel gray hair was brushed back in a pompadour and the color matched his suit exactly. His face, which tended toward jowly in his serious mode now brightened and he flashed a pleasant smile. Bright blue eyes grabbed and held hers. Sam was hit with a quick impression of that long-ago charmer in her life, Jake Calendar, the short affair that had resulted in her daughter Kelly. She was momentarily speechless.

"What are you saying?" Zoë demanded. "That you, the family attorney, have condoned Mr. O'Malley's getting rid of all Lila's things?"

Smith turned the charm toward Zoë and Sam shook off the feeling of familiarity. Aside from the aquamarine eyes this man really was nothing like Jake. She became distracted by two women who were reaching for a silver tea service in a nearby china cabinet.

"It's always hard to let go of loved ones," Smith was saying. "Ted has been devastated by the loss of his recent bride and I suggested that moving on, not living among her personal possessions would make this awful transition a bit easier for him."

O'Malley deepened his grief-face. "I truly hope that Lila's friends will take away personal keepsakes that will remind them of her in the most positive ways. Please—find something of hers that you loved and accept it as a gift. Except the urn." His eyes drifted toward the living room. "Her ashes will stay on my dresser, always. Wherever I go."

Zoë stared at him, her mouth tight. "Are *all* these items going out to friends, as keepsakes? Because it certainly appears that a lot of cash is changing hands."

"Zoë," Sam said. "Let's just go."

She took hold of her friend's rigid arm and steered her toward the kitchen. A dozen or more women crowded the room, handling cookware and small appliances, commenting on the quality of the items.

"Out back," Sam whispered through clenched teeth.

A door led to a wide flagstone patio, with a pathway leading to the studio where pieces of Lila's pottery were walking out the door at a rapid pace.

"Oh, Sam, I can't handle this," Zoë said, her voice cracking.

"Well, Ted did make one valid point. If you'd like something of Lila's as a keepsake, you better choose it now."

Zoë shook her head. "I can't. I just can't."

"We should go," Sam said gently.

"But . . . Can he do this? I'm sure Lila had nieces and nephews she would have wanted to leave something to. And what about her favorite causes? She supported quite a number of charities."

Sam didn't want to point out about possession being however many points . . . Ted's being on site and ready to move so quickly . . . well, the place could very well be cleared out before any court could act to stop him. She could call Beau, but had the feeling that there was nothing the sheriff's office could do without a warrant or court order or some such thing. And O'Malley had that smarmy attorney conveniently on hand to handle any objections. The whole thing stunk—big time.

"I'll speak to him again—give it one more try," Sam said. "Maybe you should just go on home and try to get this picture out of your head."

"Can you come over? Darryl went to Santa Fe for the day and I don't want to be alone."

"Sure. Put on the tea kettle and I'll be right behind you."

Sam watched Zoë walk toward her car with a dejected slump to her shoulders. She looked back at the house, squared her own shoulders and went inside. Ted O'Malley was flashing a charming smile at an older lady, wooing her into buying the dining table and chairs. He backed away when Sam approached.

"Mr. O'Malley," she said. "I've just been on the phone with the sheriff." O'Malley obviously didn't spot the lie; his face went two shades whiter. "He's got a call in for the probate judge, who wants to know by what authority you are selling these items."

His mouth worked for a moment before the gracious smile came back.

"I'm sorry, I didn't get your name," he said with a glance over her shoulder.

She simply stared him down.

The voice of the lawyer came from behind her. "Ms. Coffey rewrote her will as soon as she married. My client, Ted O'Malley, is the sole beneficiary of her trust. A trust which, by the way, keeps the entire estate out of probate. Your sheriff's judge has no jurisdiction over that."

O'Malley gave her a smug grin. They'd called her bluff. And Sam knew that he knew it.

"I can show you a copy of the documents," Smith said. "But you'll need a court order for that. Since we don't really know you from Adam."

Curses. She turned away.

Chapter 8

The conversation replayed through her head the whole time it took her to drive to Zoë's house. By the time she pulled into the long drive beside the big adobe bed and breakfast, she'd calmed down enough to know that she wasn't going to be able to force Ted O'Malley's hand. There simply was nothing she or Zoë could do to stop all of Lila's belongings from disappearing. She parked near the back door and admired the shady patio and Zoë's touch with flowering plants.

Inside her Mexican-tiled kitchen, Zoë had set out tea cups and wine glasses.

"We better go straight for the wine," Sam said.

Ever the hostess, Zoë pulled out some chips and whipped up a little bowl of guacamole.

"I didn't get anywhere at all with the husband or the

lawyer," Sam said, after admitting that she'd tried to use Beau's rank to intimidate them. "He barely flinched."

"It's not that Lila's things are most important anyway," Zoë said. "That stuff eventually has to go somewhere. It's just—I miss her. And I feel like a horrible friend for not staying in touch recently. I mean, how could I have not known that she was seeing someone and getting serious enough to marry the guy? During my quick visit to the hospital she only talked about how silly it was that she'd broken her ankle and how we would get together soon. Maybe she meant to tell me about Ted when we saw each other again."

"She surely didn't know him very long, otherwise you would have known about him."

"I have to wonder when they met. I'm going to call some mutual friends and see if *anyone* knew of Ted O'Malley. Maybe Lila got taken in by him and was embarrassed to admit it. Maybe he was after her money all along."

"Wouldn't be the first time." Sam swigged the last of her wine. "Look, I better get back to Beau's. We only have one day off this week and we haven't actually spent much of it together. If you get any juicy info from the other friends, let me know. If we could find some evidence of fraud, I'm sure Beau would help build the case."

Zoë stepped around from behind the breakfast bar and gave Sam a hug. "I'll do it. And thanks for coming over. You've been a big help."

Sam squeezed Zoë's hand and walked out to her van.

Back at the ranch, Beau stood on the porch, brushing straw off his jeans.

"You don't want to come close to me," he said. "I just finished mucking out the stalls."

She took a step back.

"But if you want to make us a sandwich or something while I take a shower, and then maybe snuggle up beside me to watch some NASCAR . . ." He wiggled his eyebrows in that way of his, the way which told her there might be some afternoon delight in the picture.

"I would love that. At some point, though, can I run something by you?"

He suppressed the sigh that meant he would either have to give up the car race or the sex and he didn't want to miss either. "Talk while I'm cleaning up? And then I'll help you with the sandwiches?"

While he showered she recounted the morning's events and conversations, admitting to the part where she'd fudged—well, lied—about him contacting the judge.

"It's just that Lila's house was literally being dismantled right in front of us," she said, watching as he suggestively pulled the towel back and forth across his back.

"Um-hm."

When she didn't stop talking long enough to take advantage of his state of undress, he began pulling on clean clothes.

"What was the lawyer's name again?" he asked.

"Joe Smith."

"Never heard of him," he said. "He's supposed to be local?"

"I assumed so, but he didn't really say."

"I'll do some checking on it, first thing tomorrow. Meanwhile, lunch?"

The rest of the afternoon went as planned, and by eight o'clock that evening Sam decided she really ought to go home for the night. She hadn't talked to Kelly all weekend, and could only assume things were all right with her sometimes scatter-brained daughter. And who knew what types of bakery messages might be awaiting on her home phone—people who knew she used to work from home often called there when they couldn't reach anyone at the store.

"See you for lunch tomorrow?" Beau asked after he'd kissed her goodnight.

"Don't forget to check on those names I gave you."

"Yes, ma'am." He grinned and kissed her again.

* * *

Sam was smoothing frosting over a pan of brownies the next morning when her cell phone rang, inside her pocket. She licked her fingers and fished it out.

"A little bit of quick news," Beau said. "I thought you might not want to wait until lunch time for this. I discovered that all of Lila Coffey's bank accounts were closed the day after she died."

"How did you—?"

"Don't ask. Ted O'Malley apparently had enough of the proper documentation that the bank let him do it. He took about two thousand from her checking account and more than a hundred thou from savings—all in cash."

"And I saw thousands in furniture and art being sold at the house yesterday. Holy cow."

"Yeah. The guy sure acted faster than the typical grieving widower."

"Huh. And that lawyer told me he was devastated. Ted

had her cremated and said he was going to keep the urn on his dresser for the rest of his life. Now I'm wondering if that didn't also get sold with the pots and pans." Sam caught herself tapping her foot. "Can you haul him in, Beau? Question him about all this?"

"If there truly was a legal will, he's probably within his rights. Bad manners aren't against the law. And before you ask the next question I know you're going to ask, yes, I did check the courthouse records and they were legally married. The groom listed his address the same as hers."

"Don't mention this to anyone yet. I need to decide how to tell Zoë about it."

She disconnected the call and carried the brownies up front for the display case.

"Everything okay, Sam?" Becky asked when she came back to the kitchen.

"I don't know. It's complicated." *But even if Beau can't act upon this officially, I can do a little snooping around.*

She sat down at her desk and pulled out the Taos directory. No listing for Ted O'Malley. No listing under attorneys for Joe Smith. Okay, maybe neither man had lived in town very long—the directory was, after all, nearly a year old. She pulled her computer keyboard toward her and searched the names online. Too many Joe Smiths in New Mexico, and no matches anywhere in the state for an O'Malley with a first name or initial that could conceivably match up to Ted. What the hell was going on here?

"Sam?" Becky's voice snapped her back to the present. "Sorry. Just wanted to remind you that one of those bridal shower cakes is supposed to be delivered early this afternoon."

"Thanks. Glad you said something—I'd forgotten."

From the walk-in fridge she pulled the traditional sheet cake with its "Congratulations, Sandy and Ron" in ordinary blue script, along with the order form for it. She remembered the woman who had ordered it—matron of honor for the happy couple—a woman so completely conventional that she'd probably never had a quirky or creative idea in her life. No matter what she tried, Sam hadn't been able to convince the woman to go with something more fun for the cake. So, anyway. She hoped the bride-to-be wouldn't be too disappointed.

The order form gave a street name Sam had never heard of, and she had to look it up on the map. It was not far from Lila Coffey's place. Suddenly, the cake delivery began to take on some interest. She checked the rest of the finished orders in the fridge but this was the only one slated for the north side of town, so she told Becky she would be back in an hour or so and carried the large box out to the van.

The affianced young woman who accepted delivery of the cake was so thrilled with it that Sam had to remind herself—never try to second-guess the customer. Obviously this girl and her matron of honor were absolutely on the same wavelength. She left the young woman to finish dressing for her shower so she could soon show off the cake to her friends. Sam was eager to get on with the second part of her errand.

The road near Lila Coffey's house looked so different today, without the dozens of cars lining the way, that Sam nearly cruised on past. She spotted the distinctive chalet roof and braked quickly, turning into the driveway at the last possible second. The front yard had lost its neat appearance—the grass looked trampled and some of the flowering shrubs were certainly the worse for wear as people had ignored the walkway altogether. She sighed and got out of the van.

The living room drapes were open and Sam stepped up to the porch to get a look. Pressing the doorbell and knocking didn't raise a response from Ted, as she'd fully expected it wouldn't, so she peered inside.

Nearly all the furnishings were gone. Built-in shelves along one living room wall held a few books and the detritus of curios that a world traveler collects for their own pleasure, but surely no one else's. A model of the Eiffel Tower lay tipped on its side, next to a set of carved wooden camels, surrounded by a few personal photos in ordinary frames that no one had wanted to buy. The tables which had displayed clothing for sale yesterday held about half the previous inventory, picked-over colorful heaps of unidentifiable fabric. She moved to the dining room window—more of the same. Papers littered one section of the floor, as if someone had bought a file drawer and simply dumped the contents where they stood.

Back in the studio, the vultures had been more thorough. Not a single item of art or pottery remained of Lila Coffey's life's work. Bare shelves showed where the pottery had once been displayed. An empty recess at the back of the room probably once held her kiln. A jar of glaze had broken and dripped from an upper shelf to the floor, marring what had once been beautiful tile. Sam was glad that Zoë had not seen this. It was too sad.

But more than learning the condition of Lila's possessions, Sam wondered if Ted O'Malley might have left behind some clues to his own whereabouts. She glanced toward the road to be sure she was alone, then used one of her lock-picking techniques to get in through the kitchen door.

The place felt cold and abandoned. After a year of breaking into houses Sam had begun to develop an instinct for whether an owner would be back. But just to be sure, she peeked into the refrigerator and saw that it was empty. No un-expired milk in this one. She would have bet money that Ted O'Malley never planned on coming back here. He'd taken all the chips he could rustle up and he'd cashed out.

She wandered through the rooms, knowing that at some point someone might decide to sell the property and a person like herself would need to come in and give it a final cleanup. Her fingers almost reached for items, old habit telling her to bag, box and otherwise get it all ready for disposal—but she couldn't. She already had enough projects on her plate for the summer. Still, she might find something of use in tracking down O'Malley, if Beau could put together any compelling evidence to put him away.

If there had been wedding or honeymoon pictures, O'Malley had done a good job of finding them. He'd apparently erased all traces of his one-time occupation of the house. In the master bedroom, the furniture was gone but someone had dumped the contents of nightstand drawers in a corner. Sam pulled the drapes open for better light. Among the usual clutter of night creams and magazines, she spotted a couple of religious tracts. Stapled to the front of one pamphlet was the business card of a Reverend Ridley Redfearn. The alliterative name caught Sam's attention and it occurred to her that maybe the church could use some of the clothing and small items, either to pass along to the poor or to generate some cash to help someone. She picked up the pamphlet and jammed it into her pack.

On the way back to Sweet's Sweets, Sam pulled off Kit Carson Road to the side street where Zoë and Darryl's bed and breakfast was located. Two guest cars were parked out front; Zoë would surely allow her to make this a quick visit. She tapped at the kitchen door and walked in.

"Hey there," Zoë said, looking up from a stack of dirty dishes in the sink.

"How are you doing today?"

A vague nod.

Sam gave the condensed version of her visit to Lila's house just now, leaving out the condition of the studio and the overall sad air about the place. "I found this," she said, pulling the preacher's card from her pocket. "If Lila attended his church, maybe she would want the extra clothing and stuff to go to them."

Zoë dried her hands, took a look and shrugged. "I don't remember her ever mentioning this name. But sure, it sounds like a good idea."

"Beau is doing a little more research on the husband. If we can find out how to contact him again, I'll suggest it."

One of the B&B guests walked into the kitchen and Sam used the moment to say a quick goodbye. Back at the bakery, Jen said that Beau had called, wanting to know if she was still on for lunch. She pulled out her cell phone and sure enough, she'd missed a call. Reception wasn't always great on those roads back in the mountains. She called him back and they agreed to meet at one of their favorite sandwich shops in thirty minutes.

When she walked in, he'd already gotten a table and she detected an air of excitement as he greeted her.

"What's up?"

"Got some background results on that Ted O'Malley. His

youth record was sealed, of course, but at eighteen he was brought in a few times for minor things in Albuquerque—graffiti, starting fires in dumpsters, drunk and disorderly. By twenty-five he'd either straightened out his act or moved out of state. Recently he's not been visible in the state of New Mexico but it turns out the Nevada police have him on their radar."

Their waiter came around and they decided to split a roast beef sandwich. When he went away Beau continued.

"O'Malley's wanted for several things ranging from traffic tickets to an intent-to-distribute charge involving some cocaine that was found in his vehicle. Las Vegas PD suspected him of leaving the state because of that, plus some unpaid gambling debts to a few unsavory types." He pulled a folded sheet of paper from his pocket, opening it to reveal a photocopy of a driver's license. "Age 45, height 69 inches, weight 162, home address in Las Vegas."

Sam looked at the picture. It was Ted O'Malley, all right. His hair was quite a bit darker, even though the issue date of the license was only a year ago. Had he added some gray, to make himself appear closer in age to Lila?

"Those are the hard facts, but the juicy stuff came from the LVPD lieutenant I spoke with." He paused to get her attention. "O'Malley is already married."

Chapter 9

"What?" Sam startled the waiter, who had brought their sandwich.

Beau waited until the young man set the plate down and left. "Ted O'Malley has a wife, Debbie, in Las Vegas. She works as a waitress, they got married right out of high school, have three kids. Looks like we can add bigamy to the misdeeds of our friend."

"Wow. I never saw that coming."

"Apparently, neither did Lila Coffey. I got names from the guest book at the funeral home and called a couple of the women who attended her service. They said she'd fallen for Ted hard and fast. He showed up in town about three months ago and met Lila at Chez Luis."

One of the most upscale restaurants in town, and a place where many of the more successful artists hung out.

Sam knew because she'd delivered pastries there a few times for special events.

"Two of the ladies I spoke with mentioned how well-traveled Ted was, how he talked about Paris and London as if he'd lived in those places. Lila loved the fact that he'd also been to more exotic spots like Bali and Peru. That, plus his slightly European accent and charming ways. One of them said he reminded her of Sean Connery when he wore his tuxedo."

Sam didn't recall Ted O'Malley speaking with an accent and she told Beau so. "How does a guy who borrows from loan sharks get into *that* lifestyle? And where are the wife and kids while he's off doing all this?"

He shrugged. "According to both of these friends, Lila was all set to book the two of them on a world cruise, just as soon as she finished her current pottery commission and got paid for it."

"I don't think I'll tell Zoë about all this. She'll feel like she should have been there for Lila. She would have probably seen through this guy."

"Well, if it's any consolation, scam artists like this are usually very good at reading their targets. They'll get the women talking about their friends and family, then they'll isolate them from anyone who seems a threat to the plan. Friends who are sharp enough to be skeptical will rarely meet the guy until it's too late."

"So you think he set Lila up, right from the moment he met her?"

"He may have even stalked her, in a way, observing from a distance. Maybe watching women collect their mail to find out who received statements from banks and brokerage houses. These guys can be pretty cunning."

Sam suddenly lost her appetite.

"There are a couple of ways we can approach the case, and I'm going to be working with the Las Vegas PD to catch this guy." Beau took another bite of sandwich. "First, they know his habits. Staying married to the same woman for more than twenty-five years, he does show up back at home now and then. Even when he has stayed away for months at a time, he always seems to go back to her. They'll be watching her house closely. Secondly, since Lila Coffey was a well-known artist, her work is recognizable. If he took pieces and tries to sell them, there will be people watching for those transactions too."

"But yesterday I saw a lot of people buying her work, right there at the studio. They have a legitimate claim to whatever they bought, don't they? I mean, some of them might try to turn their purchases for a quick profit—people who aren't remotely connected to Ted O'Malley."

"True, I suppose that could happen. The artwork is definitely the weaker link back to Ted, but one we can keep an eye on anyway."

"So, what next? Will you have to hand the case over to the Nevada authorities? Surely O'Malley is far from here by now." She picked at the French fries absently.

"I'm thinking I can budget a quick trip there, to go over the case with them and to talk personally with the wife." He gave her a quick smile. "Wanna come?"

She opened her mouth to answer, but her cell phone buzzed. She felt a guilty twinge. "It's Delbert Crow, and he's left multiple annoying messages. Hold that thought."

The restaurant noise level rose by the moment so Sam carried her phone out to the parking lot to take Delbert's call.

"Sorry I didn't get back to you. What's up?" she began.

"A glitch." In Crow-parlance, glitches were not a good thing. "That property on Tapia Lane . . . I just got word that the lady passed away. So, it's still an open file."

"What? Sadie Gray died?" Sam felt a pang for the poor, birdlike little lady she'd met only once.

He went on, but Sam only half heard him as she switched gears to remember where things had left off.

"Didn't Marshall Gray contact you?" she asked. "He told me he was going to get the payments up to date and that everything would be okay. He seemed to think there was some kind of paperwork error."

She could hear Crow flipping through pages in a file, then clicking some computer keys.

"Nope. The whole thing is still in arrears. Not a penny more has been applied to the account."

"But are you sure? Maybe there's just a delay before the record is updated."

"Ms Sweet, if you can't make time to fulfill your contract . . ."

"It's not that. It's just, I hate to see that poor lady lose everything."

"Hello? Did you not get that she *has* lost everything. She died." He paused for a moment. "I will go so far as to recheck the account and make sure no last-minute payments were made. There could be heirs to her estate and heaven forbid that they lose out because she didn't pay her bills. But don't count on any real change of plan. It looks like you'll still have to clean the place out and get it ready for auction."

Heartless creep. Sam jammed her phone into her pocket and walked back into the restaurant, where Beau had thoughtfully boxed up her half of the sandwich. He was standing over the table, dropping some cash to cover the bill.

"Darlin'? You okay?"

She turned back toward the door and he followed. "It's just that—*grr*—frustrating Delbert Crow. He thinks I'm being lazy and not wanting to do my job, but it's not that. I just can't help picturing that poor old lady, and now her husband will get kicked out of their home." She felt emotion welling up.

Beau snaked an arm around her shoulders and pulled her close. "It's not your fault, babe. You can't always make everything all better."

"I just have a hard time watching the *system* come in and take over. I mean, true, sometimes it's needed. But sometimes they just don't stop and consider the human aspect at all."

He made some more there-there noises and she realized that standing out in a parking lot and blubbering on about unfairness wasn't accomplishing anything.

"I better try to find Marshall Gray's phone number and let him know. Like he needs more to worry about at this moment, when his wife has just died."

"Do that. Staying busy with little tasks will help." Beau kissed the top of her head and steered her toward her van. "And, my offer still stands. If you want to go along to Vegas, we could stay a night. The department will pay for my ticket and I'd be happy to spring for yours."

She had absolutely no business going out of town for two days, but at the moment escaping the workload here in town really held a lot of appeal.

"I'll call you later and let you know the schedule. You can give me your answer then," he said, ushering her into her vehicle.

She watched Beau get into his cruiser and start it up. He waited, obviously not planning to leave until he saw her safely off, so she started the van, blew him a kiss and headed toward the bakery. Knowing she shouldn't do it while driving, she dialed the number she'd used before for Marshall Gray. The same generic voice mail message came on, and she felt a sense of déjà vu as she left a message, this time expressing condolences over Sadie and asking him to call her regarding the house.

"Ugh, I feel like a jerk for bringing up the house payments at a time like this," she said to the empty van as she pulled into the alley behind the pastry shop.

"Sam, did you remember that there are two wedding consultations this afternoon?" Jen said, the moment she walked in the door. Sam quickly forgot all about the Grays.

"God, no. I mean, yes, I had forgotten. Is one of them here now?"

"Actually, they're both here. You're thirty minutes late for the first one, and the second one came early."

And you didn't think to call me? But she didn't say it. Becky was feverishly working on a birthday cake, and judging from the noise level out front Jen had her hands full too. She should have remembered her own appointments.

"Give them samples of the cakes and assure them I'll be out in one minute," Sam said with a sigh. Could this week not get any more crazy? She washed her hands and slipped into her baker's jacket and picked up the portfolio of design ideas. She would have to pass on the trip to Vegas with Beau. It was insane to think she could get away. She took a deep breath and walked into chaos.

While Jen patiently waited on each of the seven customers that hovered near the display cases, Sam sized up the consultations waiting at two of the bistro tables.

Two brides, two entirely different ideas about weddings. Sam knew it the moment she looked at them. Monique Ramirez sat with her mother at one table, sampling the white cake with buttercream frosting—conservative, Catholic—this would be a traditional church wedding and Sam would bet on a traditional, and huge, cake. Since, technically, they were to be the second appointment, she left them with the photo portfolio and more cake samples.

Stacy Jones and boyfriend, decked out in black leather with metal studs sticking out of almost every surface, amazing multi-colored tattoos decorating most of the skin that the leather didn't cover, spiked hair (hers purple, his blue). Sam couldn't hazard a guess as to what their cake would be, but wasn't terribly surprised when they asked her to replicate the Harley that sat in front of the shop. She walked out with them and snapped a lot of photos, assured them they would love the finished cake, and went back inside thinking *ohmygod, what have I agreed to?* At least the wedding was a month away.

When the second bride and her mother left, Jen sent a sympathetic look toward Sam. "Busy isn't exactly a strong enough word, is it?"

"Thanks for covering with them until I got here." Sam brewed herself a cup of tea and collapsed into one of the bistro chairs. "I guess I better get more help in here. It seems we just aren't going to have a lot of lulls in business."

"And that's a good thing."

"That's a very good thing," Sam agreed. "Let's call a quick meeting while there's no one demanding our attention."

She carried her tea into the kitchen and Jen followed. Becky looked up briefly from the terra cotta colored flower pot cake that she'd topped with crushed chocolate cookie 'dirt' and started filling it with sugar flowers that waited on the drying stand.

"What would you say if we hired a baker and maybe another decorator?"

Becky's look of relief was all the answer Sam needed.

"Jen, if you're interested?"

"No decorating for me," Jen said. "It isn't that I wouldn't love to be able to do that, but you know me. I'm four left thumbs and I'd really rather interact with the customers anyway."

"Fair enough. How about if I train you to do the consultations—you probably know ninety percent of it anyway, from watching what I do. And when the front is busy either Becky or I will always be here."

Except when you're off solving some mystery or another, she reminded herself.

"I'd love that," Jen said. "I always like to hear about the ideas the customers have."

"But you have to be ready to bring them back to reality, too. Sometimes they want something that's impossible to make out of cake."

"You'll coach me on that, right? I would have never guessed about the Harley."

"Absolutely."

"Okay. Jen can handle the front most of the time

and a lot of the consultations. Becky, I'd like to teach you some more decorating techniques. If we get past the summer crunch and have a quiet spell this fall, would you be interested in taking a master decorator course? There's a great school in Chicago."

Becky's face lit up. Of course, the prospect of a couple of weeks away from husband and kids might be part of the allure.

"If we add a kitchen helper who can also pinch hit at the front counter, that would be a plus. And, if we had someone who did nothing but bake it would free up a lot of our time for decorating."

"Kind of like we did last Christmas?"

"Exactly." Almost exactly. The better of the two extra workers didn't want to stay past the holidays and the one who would have stayed had such a needy personality that on a full-time basis she would have driven Sam crazy. "We'll take our time hiring and find just the right people."

The front door chime sounded and Jen put her smile on and headed that direction. Becky inserted the final tulip blossom into the flower pot and raised her eyebrows toward Sam.

"It's gorgeous." Sam put her hands on the stainless steel work table. "You know, I am really proud of the work you're doing here."

"Thanks." Becky sent a shy smile her way and turned to box up the cake and start on the next.

Sam spent the next hour at the computer, placing a supply order, then checking the baking and delivery schedule. The next time she looked up, both Jen and Becky were saying goodnight and Sam realized she better get home too.

The next morning she woke at her usual four-thirty and

went through the rote motions of dressing, driving to the bakery, mixing up the first batches of batter—those tasks she could practically do in her sleep now. By the time the girls came in she was well into her special zone, piping strings and flounces on a wedding cake. When her phone buzzed it took her by surprise.

"Ms Sweet?" She couldn't place the male voice immediately, not until he introduced himself as Marshall Gray.

"Oh, yes, Mr. Gray. I'm so sorry I had to call you about the house again. I know it's a bad time for you."

He mumbled a reply.

"I just needed to let you know that my supervisor said they had no record of those payments you made last week and the date has been set to auction off the house. I'd hate to see you lose the place."

He seemed distracted by voices in the background.

"Mr. Gray? Can you call Mr. Crow's office again and get this straightened out? He wants me to come out there later today and make the place ready. You would have to move out."

She felt badly about pushing him and wondered if he had somewhere else to go—friends or family, or enough money to fend for himself. His work and Sadie seemed to be his life, according to her caregivers.

"I will take care of it. There are other, um, arrangements to be made right now."

The funeral, of course. Sam felt a stab of guilt as she hung up. She dialed Delbert Crow and passed along the skimpy information.

"Sorry, Ms Sweet. You'll still need to get out there today. I'm sending a photographer out tomorrow to get pictures for the auction brochure. If you don't hear otherwise from me by three o'clock this afternoon, that place better be sale-ready by tomorrow."

She dialed Gray's number back again, got the voicemail cue, left the message that three o'clock this afternoon was the absolute deadline. Jamming her phone back into her pocket, she found that her creative mood had vanished.

Becky had caught Sam's half of the conversations. "Why don't you go on, Sam? I looked through the orders yesterday afternoon and I think I can handle most of them. We'll get this wedding cake into the fridge and you can finish it tomorrow. It's not due for delivery until the next day, right?"

Sam resigned herself to switching modes—from culinary creator to charwoman. But she knew Delbert Crow wasn't going to leave her alone until she got his job done. She cruised home in the decorative bakery van, traded it for her pickup truck containing yard gear and cleaning supplies.

As she pulled up in front of the Gray house, she noted the absence of a car. Marshall Gray must be downtown taking care of those arrangements he'd mentioned. The weeds in the driveway were larger now so she got out the sprayer and covered them with something that was supposed to get rid of them in twenty-four hours. Stowing the sprayer, she decided to tackle the house next. She could at least tidy the rooms enough for photography by stashing loose items inside the closets and making sure the kitchen surfaces were clean. A kitchen usually sold a home, she figured.

But once she'd retrieved the key from the doorframe and let herself inside, Sam stared in amazement. The rooms were completely empty.

Chapter 10

She wandered through the house. Not a stick of furniture remained, not a single personal item, not a shirt or a hanger. The fresh food she'd found in the refrigerator was completely gone, as if it had never existed in the first place. Aside from some monster dust balls in the corners and dingy outlines where items had sat on the kitchen counters, there wasn't a whole lot of cleaning for Sam to do. She stood in the middle of the kitchen and looked around, getting a *Twilight Zone* feeling about the stark changes in the house.

Sadie Gray passed away only yesterday, but to completely empty this house would have taken longer than a mere twenty-four hours. And that was providing that Marshall Gray had a moving team here on a moment's notice. No, he'd been at it far longer than a day or two. Which meant that his promises to pay the mortgage and all his talk about the couple's loving times together in this house were all a complete crock. He'd been planning this all along.

Sam pulled out her phone and dialed Beau.

"I don't know what it is these days with empty houses and older women," she began, "but I've just had another weird experience."

She told him about the state of the house, even though she'd just spoken with Marshall Gray that morning and he'd acted like he was going to take care of the paperwork with the USDA.

"So, what do you want to do?" His polite way of saying *why are you calling?*

"I have a strange feeling about this. Can you do that thing you did before and check on Sadie Gray's bank accounts? I just can't let go of the feeling that he's done the same thing Ted O'Malley did and cleaned out everything."

"If you get any answers right away, you can call my cell. I'll be at the Gray house a little longer."

She made sure the phone was set to vibrate and slipped it into her pocket, then retrieved her vacuum cleaner from the truck and started to work making the carpets and window sills neat. One thing about an empty house—it took a lot less time to clean than one filled with furniture and the clutter of a lifetime. When Beau called back, nearly an hour later, she was giving the kitchen counters a final swipe with disinfectant spray.

"Same thing," he began. "Mrs. Gray's bank accounts were closed on Friday. The husband, whose name was jointly on everything, told the banker that they were moving out of state."

"Really. Four days before his wife died. As if he knew she would soon be gone."

"Exactly."

"The manager at the nursing home told me Sadie Gray was in good health, physically. Her problems were mental. I witnessed it when I visited her. She moved around well, seemed pretty energetic."

"I better go make a few official inquiries. Starting with the nursing home," he said.

"I want to go with you. I'm finished here at the house. I could meet you at Casa Serenita in fifteen minutes."

"Give me thirty. There's some other paperwork on my desk that I have to get assigned out to a deputy."

Sam made a final pass through the house, checking that it would be up to Delbert Crow's "picture perfect" standards, then stowed her cleaning supplies in the truck. She placed the house key in an official USDA lockbox and surveyed the yard. Most of the plantings looked all right. She took clippers to a couple of the junipers that bore some residual winter frost damage, decided everything else could stand as it was. She ended up arriving at Casa Serenita ahead of Beau but decided to wait in the truck until he came.

Martha Preston was her usual courteous self when they had seated themselves in her office.

"I'm sorry to say that death in a nursing home is not an unusual occurrence," she said. "I'm sure you understand that."

"But Sadie was physically healthy," Sam said.

Preston gave a sympathetic look. "There can be hidden conditions. At that age you really never know."

Beau spoke up. "Can you tell us about Mrs. Gray's death? The certificate says natural causes but can you fill us in on the circumstances?"

"It was late afternoon. She'd been napping after her husband's visit earlier in the day. A staff member went to see if she wanted to come to the dining room for dinner. It's not mandatory—residents can have a tray sent to their rooms if they'd prefer." She ran her hands over the cover of the folder sitting in front of her on the desk. "The orderly discovered Mrs. Gray had passed away in her bed, as if she were sleeping peacefully."

"You said that her husband had been to visit that day," Sam said.

"Yes, around lunch time. He often brought flowers and came to eat with her. They would chat and sometimes he brought outside food, just to give her some variety. As long as the doctor doesn't have the patient on a restricted diet, that's allowed."

"Did he bring food yesterday?"

"No, I don't think so. They ate in the dining room and I seem to remember that they went through the normal buffet line."

Sam searched Beau's face to see if this meant anything.

"Did anyone else visit Mrs. Gray yesterday?" he asked.

"I don't recall any visitors," she said, "but I could check the sign-in page. I left for about an hour to run a few errands."

"Please." Beau turned to Sam while Martha was out of the room. "I'll fill you in on Marshall Gray later."

Martha returned in less than a minute carrying a bound book. "Let's see . . . it looks like Mr. Gray signed in at eleven-thirty and signed out at one o'clock." She ran her finger down the few remaining lines, then shrugged. "I don't see anyone else who signed in to visit her. Of course there are some people who don't specify—clergy, doctors, physical therapists and such. They'll often come to visit more than one patient at a time. If the purpose of the visit is for medical care, they have to check out the patient's chart so they can make their notations, then they return the charts to the receptionist or one of the nursing staff."

She picked up Sadie's chart and opened it. "But there is no record of that sort of visit for Mrs. Gray yesterday. It was a pretty quiet and normal day for her."

Until she didn't wake up from her nap, Sam thought.

Running out of questions for Martha Preston, Beau told her he would be back in touch if he needed further information. Sam and Beau walked out toward their vehicles. A pleasant breeze came out of the north, pushing the forest fire smoke away.

"So, what were you going to tell me in there?" Sam asked the minute they were clear of the building.

"Looks like Marshall Gray loves to spend money," he said. "Along with the bank account records, there was a credit card which was initially taken out in Sadie's name but later she added a card for Marshall as well. That card was nearing the max of its twenty-thousand dollar credit line."

"Whoa. Could you find out what was charged on it?"

Beau opened the door of his cruiser and plucked a sheet of paper from a folder. "Among other things are a first-class air ticket for nearly ten thousand dollars. I've got a deputy checking to see what the destination is. A men's clothing store in Albuquerque shows three separate sales at well over a thousand dollars each. And there are regular florist charges for hundred-dollar bouquets every week or two."

"So, the gifts Marshall brought Sadie were going on her card and probably being paid for with her money."

"Looks like. Every previous payment on this card was made from her personal checking account."

Sam seethed. What a rat! "Wait—you said an airline ticket. Don't you see what this means? I heard announcements and noises over the phone when he called me this morning. He was probably at an airport and he's on a plane now, going somewhere."

Beau's eyes widened. He grabbed his phone and speed dialed. "Rico, did you get the result on that airline ticket charge yet?"

Sam watched as he nodded and um-hmmd a couple of times.

"Get on the horn to Dallas PD—now. Tell them to pull Marshall Gray off that plane when it lands. We want him held for questioning as a person of interest in the death of his wife and financial fraud. Report back to me the minute they confirm that they have him."

"What—"

"You were right. The first class ticket was to Zurich. Luckily, Albuquerque doesn't have any direct flights so his connections are in Dallas, then London. If we're lucky we can catch him while he's still on American soil."

"Good. You can arrest him for taking off with Sadie's money."

"Well, I'm not so sure about that. It's why I said to hold him for questioning. We'll only have forty-eight hours."

"But he's taken her money! He may have even killed her!"

"We don't yet have any proof of either. I'll have to get autopsy results. On the money side of it, they were married. It's a community property state. She added him as a cardholder and changed the bank accounts to jointly-held.

She may have willingly given him access to everything she had."

"Oh, god, Beau. This is awful."

"Sorry about lunch, darlin' but I think I better get right back to the office and stay on top of this. I may be on a plane to Dallas to question Marshall Gray before the day is over."

"That's okay. It's better to learn the truth and then to get this guy if he's guilty." She watched Beau back his cruiser out and hit the lights and siren. When he got in a hurry, he really could move.

She picked up a fast-food burger and took it back to Sweet's Sweets with her, feeling a tingle of anticipation along with a sense of being out of the loop. She hoped Beau would keep her up to date as the afternoon went on, but knew that mainly he just had to do his job.

Hoping to find answers about Sadie Gray's death were one thing, coming back to a bakery backed up with orders was another and, as Sam discovered when she walked in the door, the more urgent.

"Two more weddings for this weekend," Becky said, pointing toward the new order forms Jen had laid on Sam's desk.

Sam stared at the pages, feeling a little out-of-body as she forced her mind away from Sadie's death, the empty house and the whole drama unfolding as Beau and the Dallas police tried to stop Marshall Gray from leaving the country. No matter what else was going on in the world, these brides would truly believe that their weddings were the most important events on earth, and Sam knew that the cakes better be done right.

She spread out the order forms for the coming week,

calculated her supplies of sugar, butter and flour and called her wholesaler for more. After tallying the number and sizes of layers to be baked, she made up task lists: what to bake on what day, what colors of each type of icing to make, and how to fit all the custom orders into the flow of the normal work day. In twenty minutes she felt that she had a better handle on it—*if* she could figure out how to invent a forty-eight hour day.

She cranked up the big mixer and began dumping in eggs, sugar and flour, lining up cake pans and filling the large bake oven with as many as she could do at a time. Tomorrow's cakes went into the fridge, everything for the day after into the freezer. As long as she could keep track of the constant flow of what-went-where on each day, it would all come out right.

"And how soon do you plan to get more help?" Becky asked as Sam emptied four more pans and began to mix another batch of batter.

She really couldn't sustain this pace and wait until autumn for help to arrive. She knew it but wasn't sure when she could pause long enough to hire and train someone else.

"An option, if I might offer it," Becky said, not looking up from the icing rose she was forming on a flower nail. "I know a guy that worked at a commercial bakery in Albuquerque. He's a buddy of Don's from high school. Just lost the job in the city and came back here until he figures out what to do next."

"Does he want to stay in Taos permanently?"

"No idea. But he has family here and it might work in with his plans." Becky set the current flower on a tray and started another.

"Give him a call. If he can run the Hobart and follow

a recipe he would be a big help. It would free me up for decorating. If he would wash pans and do the occasional delivery he would be a lifesaver."

Becky laughed. "You'll have to negotiate all that with him." She carried her tray of roses to the fridge and picked up the phone. With a call to her husband to get his friend's number, followed by another, she'd set up an appointment for Julio to be at the bakery in an hour.

"I hope that was okay," she said to Sam. "He seemed eager to come by. Hopefully, you can interview while you decorate . . . this chocolate ganache is a little beyond my expertise."

When a noisy motorcycle rumbled up to the back door and a muscular man with tattoos up the back of his neck and a cotton 'do-rag' around his shaved head stepped into the bakery, Sam almost negated the whole idea. But he had a pleasant smile and an honest look in his deep chocolate eyes. He smelled clean and spoke softly. No one said bikers couldn't be bakers.

"Sam, this is Julio Ortiz," Becky said.

Sam asked a few questions about his past job—learned that he'd specialized in breads but in the ten years he'd worked there he'd learned all the cake recipes and had a little experience handling fondant. But the thing that won her over was when he heard the oven timer go off and without a second glance, grabbed up the potholders and began pulling out pans and expertly sliding them into the cooling racks.

"If that's your next batch of batter I could go ahead and—"

"Absolutely. It's chocolate sponge, those hexagonal pans are for the order—six- twelve- and fourteen-inch layers."

He grabbed an apron from the pegs on the wall and the pans were in the oven before Sam had time to blink twice. Julio looked around for something else to do and she hired him on the spot. A quick rundown of the hours and pay, and she set him to grating carrots for one of tomorrow's birthday cakes. She lost track of the time, realizing when she carried a finished Golden Anniversary cake to the fridge that Julio had completed all of the next day's layers, stowed them safely in the cooler and that Becky had showed him how they normally pre-mixed dry ingredients for the morning pastries. By five o'clock Sam was actually moving at a normal pace instead of feeling like she was running everywhere.

"See you in the morning," Julio said as he took off his apron. "Sam, I've really missed this. I'm glad you hired me."

With a *brum-brum* of the Harley, he was gone. Sam remembered to thank Becky for the recommendation as they turned out the lights. She indulged in a quiet moment after the girls left, savoring her business and reminding herself that when times got too crazy there was usually a simple answer. In this case, a tattooed biker had saved her day.

"Hey, Mom. Haven't seen a whole lot of you lately," Kelly said, peeking through the open back door. "Guess you and Beau are making up for lost time."

"I only wish. Between his new case and sheer craziness here at the shop . . . well, I'm not even getting regular lunches with him."

"You got plans for tonight? I was kind of thinking some chicken to take home and the latest *Desperate Housewives?*" She was picking tufts of dog hair off her T-shirt, the remains of her day at Puppy Chic, right next door.

"You know, that sounds perfect. Can you pick up the chicken? I'll check in with Beau. We kind of left it where he might be on a plane to Dallas tonight."

Of course, that required an explanation. By the time Kelly had picked up the food and they met up at home again, Sam had learned from Beau that the Gray apprehension was getting complex—something about the FBI becoming involved. He would be at the office late, wished them well with their dinner and TV show, and he would give details later.

Chapter 11

Sam was dozing on the couch in a Kentucky Fried trance, her favorite show now followed by some reality thing about a family who ran an alligator-trapping business with one disaster after another. The point, Kelly seemed to be saying, was to keep the gators from eating any of the children before the episode was over. It came as a relief when the phone rang and Sam had reason to abandon the program.

"Hey darlin'."

"Beau! Are you still here or did you head for Dallas?"

"I'm here. The FBI pulled Gray off his plane and questioned him. He got very jumpy and refused to talk without a lawyer present. Last I heard they had taken his passport and are holding him until we get autopsy results on Sadie."

"You think he killed her?"

"We don't know for sure. But his cleaning out the house before she died and then emptying the bank accounts immediately after . . . well, those don't seem like the actions of an honest man."

"But you said you could only hold him forty-eight hours. Have you heard anything on the autopsy yet?"

"The medical investigator's office is giving it priority and is supposed to get back to me any time now. And although we can't hold Gray more than two days, we can prevent him from leaving the country, at least by airplane. He can always hang around Dallas and try to get a later flight, if he can clear his name. From what the federal guy told me, Gray was squawking like a mad rooster. That Zurich ticket was non-refundable."

"Yowch."

Sam heard the intercom buzz on Beau's desk.

"Hold on a sec," he said. "Let me find out who this is."

He was gone nearly ten minutes and she was about ready to hang up when he came back on the line.

"O.M.I. in Albuquerque. They're sticking with 'natural causes' for Sadie Gray's cause of death. He says there's no evidence of violence, no drugs other than a very mild sleeping tablet that was prescribed by her doctor."

Sam pondered that for a minute. "So, does that let Gray off the hook?"

"Pretty much. Like I said, the financial stuff probably isn't illegal, as long as Sadie put him on her accounts voluntarily. I better call back the Dallas folks and discuss all this with them. Gray's actions are in bad taste, but without being able to prove that he had anything to do with his wife's death I don't know that we have much of a case."

"But this is just *so* wrong, Beau."

"It is, but you can't arrest a guy for being a jerk."

She remembered the neighbor who'd told her Sadie had no children. "Sadie doesn't have anyone else who might have been next in line for an inheritance?"

"We haven't found any relatives. It looks like we're stuck on this one."

Sam stared at the middle of her kitchen table, unable to think what to suggest next.

"Well, I better get home. It's been a long day," he said. "I'll call you tomorrow?"

She had intended to tell him about her new bakery employee but that seemed a trivial thing now. She glanced into the living room where Kelly was well into some other reality show, another one that held no appeal for Sam. She decided to wash her face and get ready for bed.

Sleep eluded her for a long time as she thought back over the day—her discovery that Sadie Gray's house was completely empty, the visit to Casa Serenita and what they'd learned about Marshall Gray's financial picture, followed by the dramatic way the feds had taken him into custody as he was trying to leave the country. She felt like she was missing something, some vital clue that she ought to have picked up.

She rolled over in bed and saw the wooden box sitting on her dresser, merely a dark block in the moonlight which filtered through her curtains. As the clock numerals clicked past 12:30 she sat on the edge of the bed and reached for the box.

"Give me some answers," she whispered as she balanced it on her palms.

The box took on a soft golden glow but no ideas popped into Sam's head. She set it back on the dresser after a couple minutes, afraid that prolonged contact would energize her to the point where she would never sleep. Pulling the sheet up over her shoulders, she closed her eyes and willed herself to relax.

Sam found herself walking the downtown Plaza in the early morning, the air cool against her face, the sidewalks uncrowded. A clear sky highlighted the shapes of the old adobe buildings and big urns of flowers gave off a heady scent. Shops were beginning to open and a few people were standing in front of the La Fonda Hotel, perhaps tourists gathering to meet their bus and leave for their next destination. She needed to pass them but the crowd grew and filled the sidewalk as she approached. 'The lawyer told me to meet him here' said one old woman. 'No, dearie, it was the priest. You're confused' another one answered. Sam excused herself and started to walk between them. 'You're both confused' said a white-haired man with a raspy voice. 'It's the same guy. I tell you, the very same.' The three of them closed in around her, arguing ever louder, and Sam couldn't find a clear path down the otherwise empty sidewalk.

When she finally used her arms to drive a wedge through, she woke to find herself tangled in the sheet. Her pillow was hot and her face felt sweaty. When she tried to make sense of the dream it vanished. She threw the sheet off and sat up, pulling at her nightshirt and trying to draw some cooler air toward her body. The bedside clock said 1:39.

"Argh—" she moaned, despairing of getting a decent night's sleep at all. Her eyelids felt heavy but her heart was racing. *The strange places my mind goes in the night.*

* * *

She arrived at the bakery at five o'clock, out of sorts and sleep-deprived. She'd barely had time to brew a pot of coffee when she heard the distinctive rumble of Julio's motorcycle outside.

Okay, Sam, don't run the new guy off by being a grump on his first full day.

She forced a smile and set him to work mixing three flavors of muffins. She stirred up glazes while he cut scones and the muffins baked. She discovered that Julio knew his way around a kitchen effortlessly and that they worked together well as a team. Once she had showed him the recipes for each of the specialty breads, he took the lead with those, leaving her to handle the complex decorating jobs.

Midweek. A slow day for wedding or shower deadlines. Those always crowded around the weekends. So, when Beau called just before six and said he was catching a ten o'clock flight to Vegas and would she come along . . . well, she didn't really have an excuse.

"It's just for the day, and don't get your hopes up about any casinos or shows," he said. "We'll be on the six o'clock coming home tonight because I've got a desk full of cases that you wouldn't believe."

She laughed. "If I were interested in casinos, I would surely stop at one of the dozen or more between here and the airport. There's no reason to go to Nevada for that."

"Good. I'll book your ticket and pick you up in fifteen minutes."

She used the time to brief the bakery staff, who all assured her they could handle things for a day, and to make sure her shirt wasn't covered in flour and that her hair looked reasonably good.

When Beau coasted to a stop in front of the bakery, she felt like a schoolgirl playing hooky.

"So, I'm guessing there are some new leads on Ted O'Malley?" she asked as they reached the highway.

"Las Vegas PD called early this morning. Their surveillance team say they've spotted O'Malley at his wife's house. Well, I guess it's probably technically his house too. They called me because all they were told was to watch for the guy. They don't know the case or what questions to ask him." He paused to concentrate on passing a slower vehicle on the curvy road.

"This has been quite the week for out of town cases," Sam said.

"Yeah, normally ninety-nine percent of my work takes place right here in the county. That's why I thought you might like the little jaunt out of town, even if it isn't exactly the romantic getaway we first talked about." He reached across the console and squeezed her hand.

"That's okay. You just happened to catch me on probably the one day this week that I could actually do this. Plus, I'm kind of eager to see how this turns out. Not every day I meet a bigamist. What will you do if you catch him?"

"Take him into custody first. Then I'm not sure which state is going to prevail—Nevada where his legal residence is, or New Mexico where he committed the act of bigamy. Prosecuting attorneys may have to argue that one out. If he has to be brought back here for a trial, it may mean another trip back for me to pick him up. I guess I'll deal with it when it happens."

Two hours later they parked at the Albuquerque

airport and by noon they were walking off the plane in Las Vegas, Sam realizing that her black slacks would be a big disadvantage in the desert heat. A police officer met them as they left the secure area and paved the way through the crowds who parted like the Red Sea at the sight of two tall, authoritative men in uniform. The officer, who introduced himself as Ruskovik, led them straight to the curb where he'd left his official vehicle with lights strobing.

"There are a few perks to this job," he said with a grin as he opened the back door for Sam.

He started the cruiser and did a quick radio call.

"Our guys watching the house haven't seen O'Malley leave, so it's assumed he's still there. Is Sam coming along on the apprehension?"

"She's the only one of us who has actually seen him face-to-face, so I'm counting on her to verify that he really is the man who was married to that woman in Taos."

So, there really was a reason for her to come along. Who knew?

They drove through what seemed to Sam an impossible tangle of streets before they actually left the airport property. It had been years since her last visit to the city and things had changed drastically. Ruskovik cruised easily through neighborhoods that became increasingly drab. He made another quick radio call, loaded with code numbers, then turned onto a street that Sam would characterize as upper lower-class—cinderblock homes with flat roofs, dirt yards that served as parking pads, thirsty-looking palm trees about every third or fourth house. This was home to the guy who talked like a Frenchman and showed up in classy restaurants in a tux?

"Here we are," Ruskovik said, pointing to the house just east of where he'd pulled to the curb. "That plain car down the street is ours and there's another on the block behind the house. Sam should probably wait here, until we know there's not going to be any trouble."

He stepped out and invited Sam to take the front seat, left the engine running and the air conditioning on. He and Beau straightened their shoulders, looking official. They strode up the cracked sidewalk. Ruskovik climbed the two steps to a tiny porch. Beau waited at the sidewalk, watching the windows. Sam couldn't see any action there. She heard the officer's firm knock on the hollow wood door.

"Theodore O'Malley," he called out. "Police. Open the door."

The door opened a few inches and Sam could see a woman's face, looking upward at the tall policeman and speaking words that Sam couldn't hear. After about thirty seconds she opened the door wide and stepped aside. Beau and the other officer went into the house, stayed about three minutes and Beau returned.

"He's not here," Beau said. "You might as well come in. Maybe you can help get Debbie O'Malley to talk."

The front door opened directly into a living room that was surprisingly neat, based on what Sam had guessed from the neighborhood. Real hardwood floors spoke to the age of the home. The walls were painted a pale cream, and the blue upholstered couch and side chair were old but clean. A bookshelf beside the small television set held stacks of paperback romances. A window unit cooled the air to a tad less than what it was outside.

"I don't know where Ted is," Debbie was saying when

Sam walked in. Her voice sounded tired and Sam got the feeling the woman said this a lot.

Debbie O'Malley wore a '50s-style waitress uniform, gray dress, white trim, white apron with a coffee stain dribbled down the front. Her brown hair was pinned away from her face with two plastic barrettes and was badly in need of a trim. Beau had said she married Ted right out of high school, which would put her age at about forty-five but it was a very worn-out forty-five. She had a lot of hard hours on her thin frame.

"I just got home ten minutes ago. I got stuck with a night shift and had to stay over this morning cause Glenda never showed. Lucky my mom wanted to take the kids. Not that a fourteen-year-old needs a sitter but I won't leave him in charge of my six-year-old overnight. Since Kyra got it in her head to move to L.A. and try acting school . . . What was I thinking, having the three of 'em so spread out?"

She muttered this last bit as she kicked off her shoes and pulled the barrettes from her hair. She blew out a breath that made her bangs flutter. "So, what's Ted done now?"

"It looks like he's married another woman," Beau said.

"Well, damn." Debbie didn't appear horrified by this news. "Can I get off my feet?" She motioned for the visitors to take seats and she flopped into the armchair and put her feet up on a small stool. Sam sat on the sofa but the men remained standing.

"Has Ted been home recently?" Beau asked. "Please be truthful. Officers have had the house staked out for a couple of days."

Debbie's eyes rolled. "Damn, I can't believe how clueless I am." She jumped up from the chair, went to the shelf and pulled out a novel titled *Unforgiving Love*. Shaking the book, she started to sob.

"That son of a bitch, he's done it again," she said, letting the tears roll as she clutched the book to her chest and sank into the chair again.

"I wish't the bastard would just stay away. I don't know why I always take him back."

"When was he here?" Sam asked, keeping her voice gentle.

"Monday night he showed up. Brought the kids presents. They got so excited. Brought me this." She held up her wrist to show an old fashioned gold bracelet. Sam guessed that it probably had belonged to Lila Coffey. She tried hard not to let her face reveal anything.

"When did he leave?" Sam asked, scooting closer to Debbie, keeping her voice soft.

Debbie's shoulders slumped. "I don't know. He was here last night when I left for work. Been watching sports on TV all day and drinkin beer, like he always does. I got the house all cleaned up and I told him he just better not make a big mess." She glanced around. "So, I suppose he left right after I did. Otherwise, there'd be beer cans all over the damn place."

Sam glanced up at Ruskovik, who looked a little chagrined. Somehow Ted had crept out in the dark and gotten past the surveillance team.

"I shoulda knowed it when he showed up with the presents," Debbie said, staring toward the middle of the room. "Usually he's flat broke and I know to guard my money. But this time he seemed so happy and relaxed-like. He flashed a little cash around, took us out for tacos. I thought he'd really been working somewheres, like he said."

She held up the paperback book. "I *knew* I shoulda hid my money better. He always gets the cookie jar and last time he found that cottage cheese container on the kitchen shelf. How could I know he'd actually open a book? There was five hundred dollars in there. I'd saved it up to put us a deposit on a bigger place, a nice apartment in one of those buildings with a pool. Me and the kids are pretty crowded in here, just the one bedroom and all. I'm not whining, I just want something nicer for them." Her face watered up.

Sam looked up at Beau in disbelief. O'Malley was clearly a first-class jerk, taking Debbie's little stash after cleaning out all of Lila's money as well.

"Do you have any idea where Ted might have gone?" Sam asked. "Maybe if the sheriff can catch up with him soon enough, they might get your money back."

Debbie shrugged and the tears kept running down her face.

"I didn't even know he'd gone off to some other woman. Did he know her very long? No, I can tell you he didn't. I'll bet he swept her up just like he did me." Her eyes narrowed. "In fact, I bet I can tell you *exactly* when he went out on the prowl. Right about Easter time. He laid off the beer for a few weeks, went to some gym and said he was gonna lose that big gut of his. I even caught him reciting movie lines, staring at himself in the mirror and talking like some foreigner."

Her mouth grew hard. "Easter weekend he took my cookie jar money and bought the kids the biggest Easter baskets they had down at the K-Mart. They was so happy that they didn't even notice he wasn't home that next day. *That's* when he went out to find himself somebody else.

And I'll bet he took her money too."

Sam kept silent. She couldn't admit to Debbie just how right she was.

"I think the law will catch up with him," she said. "We'll find a way to get your money back."

Beau knelt beside Debbie's chair. "If you can think of anywhere he might be, any of his family, some friend he could go to who would be willing to hide him for awhile?"

Debbie sighed deeply and stood up. "There's some relatives. His mama and daddy won't have nothin' to do with him. But there's a cousin or two, they might put up with him for a little while."

Beau copied some names and phone numbers from the address book Debbie pulled from a small drawer in the end table. With little else to be accomplished here, they walked to the door.

Sam wanted to speak up, to tell Debbie to divorce the bum and move somewhere that he couldn't find her, but she realized how futile that would be. The guy had charming ways, apparently, and his kids loved him. He would always have a way into this poor woman's life if he showed up with gifts for the children.

Beau simply thanked her for the information and they left.

Chapter 12

The electronic *bing-bing* of slot machines rang out incessantly in the airport lounge. After lunch at a laid-back Old West-themed steakhouse followed by a tedious crawl in traffic along The Strip —Officer Ruskovik's attempt at showing them the lights and glamour of Vegas—there had been nothing much else to do but wait for their flight.

"Does that noise never end?" Sam asked, feeling fractious among the crowds that seemed only hungover and broke.

Beau took her hand. "Think of it this way. The airplane, which you normally refer to as a 'cattle car' is going to seem really pleasant after this."

She looked into his ocean-blue eyes and smiled. "You are *so* right about that. But our little town is going to be even better. I actually can't wait for the drive—" Her cell phone vibrated, interrupting the thought.

"Samantha Jane, where are you?"

Her mother had tracked her down.

"At the moment, Las Vegas. Waiting for our flight back to Albuquerque."

"Oh my *god*, ya'll didn't *elope*, did you?"

Sam felt her eyes cross. "No, Mother, we did not."

"Because if you did, you would disappoint one *heck* of a lot of people. Your *en*tire family is planning on coming out for your wedding. You know that, don't you?"

Oh boy, did she know it. Half of west Texas would come if Nina Rae had her say.

"We *need* to know the date, Samantha. People have plans to make. You know, all the kids are only out of school for about eight more weeks. And it's going to be impossible for your sister—well, okay, not im*poss*ible exactly, but it's just so *much* easier for families to travel when the kids are out of school."

Sam pictured her mother, pacing the floor as she talked, perfectly manicured hands gesturing to emphasize her points.

"Mother, Beau and I—"

"Aunt Bessie's in a dither over what to wear. Well, you know she always has to be the fanciest—"

Sam held the phone away from her ear, but the *bing-bing* was every bit as irritating as her mother's voice.

"—family reunion?"

Oops, apparently there was a question attached to that.

"Mother, sorry. It's so noisy in here that I can barely hear you and they've just called our flight. I'll have to call you when we get back to Taos."

"You said that last week."

Stop with the guilt, Mother. It's not helping your cause. She forced a smile into her voice. "Gotta go—love you!"

Sam stood up, switched the phone's power off and jammed it into her pocket. She strode three paces away, spun around and came back—blowing out a sharp breath.

Beau looked up at her with a faint smile, looking like a guy who planned to keep his trap shut.

"Beau, she's driving me crazy about this. Are we ready to set a wedding date?" she asked.

He reached for her hand. "As in, run off to some little Vegas chapel? Play hooky from work one more day and I'd do it now."

She shook her head. "That would never work. She's talking more cousins, my sister and her brood, the works on the Sweet side of the family."

"I will do whatever you want, darlin'. You know that."

She plopped onto the plastic chair beside his. "I want—" Her eyes prickled. "I don't know what I want. I have a dress I'd like to wear and a cake design I'd love to make. Beyond that, just having some of our friends around . . .. The whole crowd scene just feels like too much."

"But your mother isn't going to let it go at that."

"Or ever speak to me again if I mess up her plan."

He squeezed her hand and slipped his other arm around her shoulders. "We'll do whatever is necessary. I get to have you all to myself for the rest of my life. I guess we can compromise with the crowd for a day."

She leaned into him, taking comfort, but not telling him that her mother was working up to a whole week of festivities. When she got home she really should sit down with the calendar and Beau and make a plan. Or never hear the end of it from Texas.

"Let's talk about something easier. Like catching this con-artist Ted O'Malley."

"First thing in the morning I'll get on the contact list Debbie gave me. If we get lucky maybe O'Malley's been in touch with someone from his past. But with all of Lila's money at his disposal he could just about do anything."

"I wish I'd gotten a better sense of his personality, that time I saw him briefly at their house. He seemed very social, chatting with people. My guess is that he might very well show up around his parents or cousins, wanting to show off his new riches. You know, the kind of guy that would be driving a new sports car and flashing some cash, just to prove what a success he's become."

Someone on a PA really did call their flight right then and they stood up and edged their way into the muddle of people standing around.

By ten o'clock as they drove north of Santa Fe, passing through the small towns of Pojoaque and Espanola, Beau pointed out the orange glow from the big fires to the west. It was eleven p.m. when they reached the outskirts of Taos; Sam dozed in the passenger seat, pretending that the brief nap would count toward the full night's rest she would need in order to be functional at the shop in the morning.

Beau pulled into her driveway and walked her into the house, offering to make her a cup of tea but she was still close enough to that dozey state that she just wanted to fall into bed.

"I'll call you tomorrow," he said, "as soon as I get anything useful to the case."

A big part of her wanted to back entirely away from the whole mess. She'd found an empty house, she'd visited a woman in a nursing home. She'd extended condolences to

Zoë over the loss of a friend and gone along to that crazy wake-turned-yard-sale. Otherwise, what business was this of hers anyway? She had a wedding to plan and a bakery to run. Beau was the sheriff. This was his job, not hers.

Debbie O'Malley's tired face appeared. *Sam, you know you won't let it go.* Her current mood was exhaustion talking. She closed the back door behind Beau and went straight to bed.

By morning she'd recovered a lot of her perk, especially when she arrived at Sweet's Sweets to find the kitchen spotlessly clean and the recipes and baking pans neatly aligned to start the day's work. Becky and Jen were good workers but she spotted the professional hand of Julio in all this.

While she was still sipping at her first cup of coffee, he arrived and with a quick greeting started right to his duties. Sam sat at her desk, the calendar in front of her. There wasn't a single weekend in June or July that wasn't crammed with other people's weddings. She would be working seven days a week to tend to her customers' needs and there was no way to wedge her family and a bunch more activities into the mix. She flipped the page to August, scanned it, looked ahead. Her schedule looked impossible until at least the middle of September, and that answer was not going to go over well with Nina Rae.

Sam picked up her cell phone, turning it over in her hand and calculating the time in Texas. Before she worked up the courage to dial it, the little instrument sent out a musical tone. Delbert Crow's number appeared on the readout.

What now?

"Hello, Delbert," she said.

"Where were you yesterday? I tried to reach you half the morning."

On an airplane. She'd never checked the log of missed calls and he must not have left messages. But she didn't say it. He wasn't one for excuses and saying that she'd dashed off to Vegas wouldn't work too well when she'd just begged him for fewer jobs because of her heavy load at the shop.

"Really? What was the problem?"

"The photographer went out to that place on Tapia Road and couldn't get inside."

"Didn't he have the standard lockbox code?"

"It didn't work. Did you reset it?"

"No. I always use the same one." She could see this little blame-game going around and round. "I'll check it out when I have a minute."

"Actually, you need to check it out now. He's on the way and will meet you there in ten minutes. He's got to upload the pictures this morning for the auction."

"I'll be there in ten minutes." *Grr . . .*

Becky and Julio were doing fine in the kitchen and Jen should be along within a few minutes to open up the front. Sam put a lid on her coffee cup and carried it with her to the van.

A blue car sat in front of the Gray's former house and a lanky guy in his twenties stretched himself out of it when Sam parked in the driveway.

"Sorry about this," he said. "I didn't want to make a fuss, but Mr. Crow insisted on interior pictures as well as exterior."

"It's okay." She tried not to grumble. If this thing was going to require a bolt-cutter she would have to go back home and get her toolbox from the truck. And that would put everyone in that much finer a mood.

She walked up to the door and looked at the little

numerical wheels on the lockbox mechanism. 2-1-3-7-9. It was one digit off. She flipped the nine to an eight and the box opened to reveal the door key.

"I guess Delbert didn't quite give you the right numbers," she said.

"So sorry," the photographer said. "I thought I'd tried other combinations. Guess I didn't try enough of them. Do you want to hang around to relock it after I'm done? It shouldn't take but a few minutes."

"I'm really swamped at my shop," she said. "Just put the key back in and make sure the little door clicks firmly. Then scramble up the numbers."

He nodded and stepped past her into the house.

She'd barely opened the door to her van when another vehicle pulled up. The white sedan looked like a rental and her first thought was that some tourist was lost. The car stopped a few feet beyond the driveway and a man in khaki slacks and a light windbreaker got out.

"May I help you?" she called out, thinking he looked vaguely familiar.

"I could ask the same thing. This is my house," he said.

She felt a jolt. "Marshall Gray?" After being released by the Dallas authorities he must have come right back to Taos. "We spoke on the phone a couple of times. Samantha Sweet. You do know that the auction date has been set?"

He stared toward the house, not meeting her eye.

"I am on my way to the funeral home," he said, turning away. "There's something I left behind here, in the garage. I'll get it and be out of your way."

He pushed past Sam and walked across the driveway to the detached garage. Sam realized that was one part of the property she'd never checked. She started after him, not at all wanting to get into a grimy cleanup project today, but a hundred questions filled her head. Would he pay up, try to save the house from the auction block? Where had all the furniture gone? And why did he never seem to answer a direct query?

Before she reached the side door to the garage, Gray came out with a small canvas toolbag in his hand. He pulled the door shut, ducked around her with his head lowered and went straight to the white car, speeding away before she could stop him. She stared after the car.

She tried to turn the knob on the garage's side door but it was locked. Well, if the possessions inside the house had been his, everything in the garage was too. She looked up to see that the photographer was closing the front door.

"Thanks," he called out.

She gave up on the garage and got into her van as the young man walked to the blue car. They both rolled out at the same time.

As she drove back to the center of town, Sam couldn't help thinking about the strange encounter with Marshall Gray. Although they'd only spoken on the phone he looked familiar, but how could that be? She was certain they'd never met. His story was even more suspect. On his way to the funeral home? The newspaper had said that there would be no service for Sadie Gray. A private memorial was planned for later, with cremation and interment of the ashes somewhere in Santa Fe. And what did he take from the garage?

She should have checked it more thoroughly on her previous visits or stopped him and asked more questions just now.

Beau was at the bakery treating himself to a cup of coffee

and chatting with Jen when Sam walked in. The display case was well stocked, with just enough items missing to show that there had already been some early business.

"Hey there," Beau said. "I hope your mother didn't call you again last night. You looked really beat."

She stretched up and kissed his cheek. "I was. But I slept fine."

"It was a long day. I was just telling Jen."

"Speaking of my mother, although I really don't want to . . . She's going to call back and the pressure to set the date is getting really intense. Can you take a look at the calendar with me?"

He followed her to the kitchen, eyed Julio's tattoos for a fraction of a second too long.

"I'll tell you more about all of it later," she said conversationally, picking up the calendar, "but for now can we see if any of these dates will work?"

Beau agreed that the summer months were impossible. It wasn't fair for Sam's family to pressure her to their schedules. She was the bride-to-be, she got to choose the date, and the rest of them could work it in. Or not.

"Thank you," she said. "Mother has a way of making me feel selfish for wanting things my way."

"Seriously?" His eyes edged sideways.

She laughed. "Okay, you're right. I outgrew a lot of that when I left Cottonville, never to return. This is more of a self-preservation thing. I don't want to start a war within the family."

"Pick a date." He stabbed his finger on the second week of September.

She scooted the finger down by a line. "Third week. The twenty-first?" She looked up and he nodded. "I shall send Mother a text so she can't talk me out of it. We'll have invitations printed before she can react."

"I love it." Beau kissed her. "I love you."

"And let's plan a spectacular honeymoon. Well, whatever we can budget. I'm thinking far away from either New Mexico or Texas. It would be so nice to have a week or so with no bakery and no emergency calls."

From across the room Becky started up with applause and some raucous cheers. Julio looked puzzled. Jen came through the doorway.

"The wedding is September twenty-first," Sam said.

Chapter 13

They decided to celebrate the decision by taking a small cake from the display case, picking up sandwiches along the way, and driving out to the spot where they'd gone for their first date.

The rocky promontory overlooking the Rio Grande Gorge might have been on another planet instead of only fifteen minutes from the center of town. Miles of land, dotted with blue sage, broken only by the jagged split in the earth. They spread a blanket on a rocky shelf and stared down into the depths of the six-hundred foot gorge, where a skinny brown ribbon of water wound its way southward, with tiny white tufts the only indication of the massive rapids where rafters loved to test their skills. In the midday heat of June it wasn't quite the same romantic ambiance as it had been on that autumn evening at sunset but Sam loved the place anyway.

They toasted each other with lemonade and shared their sandwiches. Sam gazed fondly at the antique garnet ring on her left hand.

"I'll get you something more impressive—you should get to choose your own," Beau said. "You know that Mama only insisted that I give you her ring as a token, so you would have something to wear home that night."

"I love this one. I was just thinking of Iris—the ring always reminds me what a special lady she was."

He squeezed her hand then faced the steep rock walls and let out a cowboy whoop. It echoed back and forth across the wide, empty space.

"You did that on our first date," she said. "Seeing your playful side might have been the very thing that made me fall in love with you."

"Aw, shucks, ma'am," he said. He doffed his Stetson, sweeping it low.

"Uh, you don't have to take it quite that far." She poked him in the ribs and he reached out as if to tickle her but then he slipped his arms around her waist and pulled her close for a long kiss.

"Umm . . . it would be really tempting right now to sneak away and take the afternoon off," she said. "Except we did that yesterday and I'll have desperate customers if I don't get back soon."

"I know. My phone has been going almost nonstop since we got here. I just didn't want to interrupt the mood."

"You better see who it was. One of your deputies is likely to put an APB out on you." She gathered the remains of the impromptu picnic and started to fold the blanket.

Beau pulled the phone from his pocket and scrolled through the messages. "Well, darn, I would have liked to catch this one. The others can wait."

"Something to do with the trip yesterday?"

"Yeah, I hope so. I put in some calls to the names on Debbie O'Malley's list. This looks like the right area code for Ted's cousin in Reno."

He pressed the redial button while Sam put their things in the cruiser and buckled herself in. As Beau pulled onto the winding path to the road she could hear a voice come through.

"Yeah, Mike. Thanks for returning my call. I'm driving at the moment so I'm going to put you on speaker." He pressed a button and set the phone into a little cradle mounted on the dash. "I don't know if your wife told you, but I'm trying to get hold of your cousin Ted. Wonder if you've seen him lately." He'd adopted the tone of a friend.

"Teddy?" The voice on the other end came through pretty fuzzy, a male that was probably about Ted's age and may have had a couple of beers already. "Yeah, actually. You just missed him. Didn't Marsha tell you he was just here?"

"Oh, damn," Beau said. "I need to catch up with him. I owe him some money."

"I doubt he'll miss it," the guy named Mike said. "He's doing real well now. Stayed at the MGM Grand—except it's got some other name now. Anyhow, Ted took us out for a real nice dinner. He's driving a brand new Cadillac. Man that thing was sweet. He let me drive us all around."

Sam felt her teeth grind. Hadn't she predicted this? Out on the town with the proceeds from Lila's estate and he'd still taken Debbie's small stash of cash, probably out of habit.

"Really?" Beau said. "Where'd he get that kind of dough?"

"Said some old gal left it to him in her will. Hell, I didn't care. I was just having a blast driving that car."

"So he left Reno already? Did he say where he was headed?"

There was a pause on the line. "He kept talking about how he was gonna move to London and go look up the Queen. Hey, man, I'd had a few scotches by then—the really good stuff. But then some guy called him while we was driving around. Teddy just said, 'Hey Marshall, great. I'll meet you in Albuquerque.' That's in New Mexico, right?"

Beau stayed quiet, hoping Mike would remember some more but he only seemed interested in talking about that new red Cadillac. Finally, he cut in. "Well, thanks, man. Look, if you do hear from him again find out where he is and give me a call back. I still owe him this money."

"Well, you can always send it to me," Mike joked.

Beau said goodbye and clicked off the call. "Yeah, right."

"He said Marshall—as in Marshall Gray? They know each other?" Sam asked. "I ran into him this morning and he seemed to be in a real hurry."

"The two of them are meeting up in Albuquerque. Do you suppose they plan to head for London now? Gray was trying to get out of the country a few days ago."

Sam worked to piece it all together. "So if these two are friends . . . and they both just happen to have been married to older women, and both women died within a week of each other?"

"Seems really hinky to me." He steered the cruiser onto the paved highway and coasted along, pondering the new information.

"Well, can't you get the Albuquerque police on it? Bring

the men in and question them?"

"We tried that with Marshall Gray before. There just wasn't any real evidence. We might get Ted O'Malley for stealing Debbie's little cash hoard, but he's going to deny it altogether or claim she gave him the money. I need more than this before I can really nail either of them."

"What about the real possibility that the two wives were murdered? I mean, this is looking worse by the minute. Way too many coincidences." She looked at him. "Don't you think?"

"I do, Sam. But I've already inquired about the cause of death in each case. Lila Coffey died of heart failure, Sadie Gray was nearly ninety and just went peacefully in her sleep. There's not a shred of evidence that either of them were murdered."

Sam chafed at the situation. This felt all wrong and yet there was no viable reason to arrest either of the husbands. They would simply have to dig deeper.

They passed open ranch land on the north end of town and Beau slowed the cruiser as they approached the scattering of gas stations, artisan shops and grocery markets which characterized the outskirts of town. By the time they reached the Plaza and Beau turned toward Sweet's Sweets to drop her off, her mind automatically began the shift to bakery business and the fact that all this time away wasn't helping. Within an hour she found herself immersed in her little world of sugar and chocolate.

"Sam," Jen said, interrupting her reverie. "Ivan's here for the Chocoholics order."

The weekly mystery book club met at the bookstore next door and Sam had provided them with decadent treats for as long as she could remember. The only criteria was that the creation live up to the group's name, Chocoholics Unanimous.

Sam placed the final dark chocolate rose on the white-chocolate covered cake and scrutinized it quickly before picking it up to carry to the front.

"Ah, Madame Samantha, is another of your fantastical makings," Ivan Petrenko, the bookstore owner exclaimed. He handed a check to Jen while Sam placed the cake into a box. Ivan smiled widely as he picked it up.

"I am making recommending to a friend of your shop," he said. Despite butchering the finer points of English, Ivan's heart was in the right place. "A lady, most recently married."

"Thank you, Ivan," Sam said. "Who is it? I'll be sure to personally help her."

"Renata is her name. Come original from the old country, near my home in Russia. Have been in America many years."

Ivan's own history was still a little sketchy. Rumor said he was a Russian with a ballet-dancer wife who'd defected to France, and somewhere in there he'd worked in a diamond mine, apprenticed with a Cordon Bleu chef and lived in New York. Sam had no idea how much of it to believe.

"Well, you can tell Renata to ask for me and I'll take good care of her," Sam told him. She watched as he walked out with the chocolate creation, feeling a small twinge of regret that she'd not found time to continue attending the book club since she'd opened the bakery.

"Sam, what do you think about this bridal shower cake?" Becky asked as she walked back into the kitchen. "Does it need more flowers?"

"It's gorgeous," Sam said. "I'd leave it exactly the way you have it."

She watched Becky lift the sheet cake and carry it to the walk-in.

"What else is on the schedule this afternoon?" she said, reaching for the stack of orders.

She'd no sooner verified that they had sufficient layers baked for the weddings that would come due in the next two days than Jen stepped through the curtain.

"Ivan's friend is here already," she said, sotto voce. "Renata." She grinned and gave the name a flashy accent.

Sam picked up her order pad and hurried forward.

"Madame Samantha?" A slender redhead stepped forward, extending a well-manicured hand with copper polish that matched her shoes and handbag. Her vivid turquoise sheath practically glowed in contrast. "I am Renata Fai—, um, Renata Butler. I just love saying my new name," she added with a giggle.

If she'd come from Russia, it was a long time ago. Barely a hint of accent remained. Sam guessed that she might be in her fifties, but a lot of that time must have been spent under the care of masseuses and skin care specialists. She was absolutely gorgeous.

Sam shook her hand. "Just call me Sam. Ivan tends to be a bit formal, but it's not necessary."

"Perfect. Sam, this is my husband, James." Renata turned to the man Sam had hardly noticed, a good-looking guy in khaki slacks and a navy blue knit shirt. The white skin on his neck showed that his dark hair had been recently cut, and he twirled the shiny gold ring on his finger as if he were still getting used to it. Sam got a quick vision of him in jeans and a T-shirt, very casual, longer hair. When she blinked, the image went away. Where had that come from?

"Please, have a seat at one of the tables," Sam said. "Ivan didn't mention what type of cake you wanted."

The three of them took chairs at one of the bistro tables and Renata continued. "A wedding cake. We're holding a reception for some friends—I guess you would say, after the fact. We got married at a private ceremony in Santa Fe, where James lived, then spent two weeks on Maui. My friends here in Taos are only now meeting him." Renata beamed at the groom. He crossed his legs awkwardly.

"How nice. Well. What kind of cake did you have in mind? A traditional wedding cake or something smaller?"

"Oh a traditional one, of course. Right, Jimmy?" Again with the moon eyes.

James draped an arm across the back of her chair. "Anything you want, baby." He shifted his gaze to Sam. "And money is no object. Big and showy."

"How many people will we be serving?" Sam asked.

Renata and James exchanged a glance. She spoke first. "I think we invited about twenty-five people? Maybe a few more will come. But I don't want to make the cake too small. It will look, how do you say, skimpy?" She pointed to one of the display cakes in the front window, one that could easily serve a hundred-fifty guests. "More like that one."

Not one to turn down a big order, Sam nevertheless tried to explain how much cake would be left over. But Renata loved the look of that cake and, as James had pointed out, money was no object. They ordered it anyway.

Sam wrote down the details—four tiers, covered in ivory fondant with cascades of white forget-me-not petals and framed oval cameos. "And when is your party?"

"Tomorrow afternoon," Renata announced.

"Oh, my. That's really short notice."

"But you can do it, right?" James said. "If we pay a rush fee or something."

Wedding cakes weren't often requested for Thursdays and Sam knew if she put them off they would either go elsewhere or cancel the order altogether. They certainly wouldn't change the date of their party. And Renata was Ivan's friend.

"As long as there are no changes once you sign the order, I think we can do it," she said.

Renata signed the order form with a flourish. While she wrote out a check, Sam edged to the kitchen.

"I need round tiers of almond poppyseed cake—sixteen-, twelve-, ten- and eight-inch ones. Julio?"

"Right on it, boss."

"Becky, can you take a peek and be sure we have at least an extra twenty-five pounds of fondant?"

Becky gave her the nod and Sam turned back to the customers. James was standing in front of the display case, facing the chocolate éclairs but eyeing Jennifer's v-necked shirt.

"Jen?" Sam said through her teeth, giving a head-jerk toward him.

Jen turned toward the back counter and got busy stacking paper bags.

"We're all set," Sam said to Renata, who had wandered to the window display, smiling over the design she'd chosen. "I will deliver it tomorrow between noon and three."

"Ivan told me you would be wonderful to work with," Renata said with a dimpled smile. "Thank you so much, Sam."

The glamorous client stood at the door, waiting for her new husband to open it.

"Looks to me like she's used to a little higher level of male attention than this one knows how to deliver," Jen said as they watched the couple drive away in a tan Mercedes.

"Glad I wasn't the only one who thought the guy definitely married up."

"Sam, this top isn't too low-cut, is it?" Jen asked.

"No, sweetie, it's just fine. That guy . . . Well, I better get busy on this order." Sam kept the rest of her thoughts to herself. With the new groom ogling other women already, she wondered how well this marriage would go.

In the kitchen, warm almond batter sent a heady fragrance through the room.

"The large tiers are in the oven," Julio said. "Small ones will go in as soon as those come out."

"Perfect," Sam said. "Now I need to ask everyone to kick into high gear on the fondant flowers. Julio, roll and cut. Becky, watch how I do this. We need about eight hundred small flowers and around two hundred big ones."

Becky stared at her with wide eyes.

"I know, I should have talked her into something simpler. I don't know what came over me. I've accepted the order though." She squared her shoulders and pulled a tub of white fondant from the storage shelf.

Julio fed hunks of the claylike sugar dough through the rolling machine and began to apply the larger of the flower-shaped cookie cutters, his hands moving rapidly. Sam scooped up the five-petaled shapes and demonstrated for Becky.

"Lay them on the shaping foam, take the ball tool and

give 'em a little roll, like so." The edges of each petal curled and rose under her touch and she deftly pinched the center to bunch the little piece into the shape of a flower. "Set them over here in the candy molds until they've set, then we'll let them dry on parchment overnight."

Becky messed up the first couple but soon she was turning out flowers pretty efficiently. Sam went into high gear, her hands working in a blur. By the time she paused to take the first batch to the drying rack, she ran a rough count and saw that they had only about fifty large flowers. It promised to be a late night.

By six o'clock when Jen came back to say that the sales area was clean and shut down, all the layers were baked and cooled. Julio offered to stay long enough to get the initial dirty-icing done so the layers could set up well overnight in the fridge. Becky gave Sam an apologetic look.

"I'd stay but Don has tickets to the circus and we've been promising the kids for two weeks . . ."

"You go. It's not your fault this last-minute order came in."

Becky gratefully removed her apron and left. Julio already had two of the four tiers iced and Sam marveled at how deftly he handled cake, a task that wasn't nearly as easy as he made it look. By seven she had the place to herself, with only five hundred flowers left to go. There was no way she would get them done tonight, and assembling the cake would take all her attention tomorrow. Only one answer presented itself.

Chapter 14

She slipped out the back door and into the van. At home, all was quiet. Kelly must have had other plans. Sam went to her bedroom and picked up the wooden box from her dresser. Sitting on the edge of her bed with the box on her lap she spread her fingers to touch the full width of its carved surface. Immediately the wood went from yellowish brown to rich gold. The varnish began to glow and soon the red, blue and green cabochon stones sparkled with light. In under two minutes the surface warmed, then became hot. She pressed down, the heat practically singeing her palms. Her hands flew away from the box and she waved them in the air for relief.

The energy traveled into her legs and spread throughout her body. Her heart raced. Gingerly, she picked up the box with her fingertips and set it back on the dresser. Deep breath. Another.

"Ready," she said to herself as she strode toward the back door. In the kitchen she picked up an apple and a protein bar. Not much of a dinner, but she wolfed it down on the way to the shop.

Small forget-me-nots and fluffy multi-layered roses magically slid from her fingers to the drying racks as she worked the pliable white fondant. Muscle memory took over and the flowers formed effortlessly while her mind wandered back to Beau's phone call from Ted O'Malley's cousin. They both felt frustrated over the deaths of the two elderly women and the fact that it seemed the two men knew each other. She realized just how frustrated when she twisted one of the little flowers too hard and it turned into an unusable glob. She forced herself to concentrate in the quiet kitchen with only the ticking clock for company.

It ticked around to one a.m. when Sam set the final tray of flowers aside. More than a thousand flowers, and well over five thousand individual petals. *My wrists will be speaking to me tomorrow*, she thought.

The effects of the magic box would soon wear off and Sam realized that she better sneak in at least a few hours' sleep or she would be dead on her feet before she could ever get this cake delivered. She locked up and headed home, parking beside Kelly's little red car and tiptoeing through the dark house to brush her teeth and fall into bed.

Four-thirty came way too early, but then it usually did. Sam had discovered that using the box's magic powers to put in extra time at the job usually backfired when she found herself operating on a few hours sleep. As with an addictive drug she wanted more of that energy the next day. She gave the box a tiny pat on the lid but resisted picking it up.

Julio was waiting outside the back door and he quickly started mixing and baking the standard breakfast items while Sam pulled her stack of orders, rechecked that the components for the major projects were already made, and organized the orders by delivery time. When she set the trays of fondant flowers for Renata Butler's wedding cake on the work table, she caught Julio staring.

"I worked all night," she said. "Just went home for a shower and got right back."

"Sure, boss." His tone wasn't disrespectful, but she saw a large dose of skepticism in his expression. She would have to be careful about trying to pull any tricks around him. This guy knew baking, knew what was impossible.

Becky walked in just then and noticed the trays of flowers.

"Wow," she said as she pulled on her baker's jacket and washed her hands. "I've seen you work fast, but this time you must have pulled an all-nighter."

Thanks for the validation of my story, Sam thought as she smiled and walked to the fridge. She set the sixteen-inch tier for Renata Butler's wedding cake on the table.

"The orders are stacked over there," she told Becky, with a nod toward the corner of her desk. "Remember, that sport-themed one is being picked up at ten. Maybe you could do it first?"

The round cake was to be covered in fondant cut to the shapes of footballs, baseballs and soccer balls. Sam made sure that Becky located the edible-dye pens for the details and cutters for the various shapes, then she turned her attention to the assembly of Renata's cake.

She tinted large balls of fondant a light ivory and sent them through the roller, smoothing the resulting sheets over the tiers, then stacking and checking to be sure everything was symmetrical. Lacy cameos provided focal points around the sides of each tier, then she began applying the hundreds of pre-made flowers with a little thinned fondant to stick them in place. By midmorning the cake looked like an elegant structure with froths of delicate white cascading down the top and between the tiers.

"Wow, Sam, it's amazing," Becky said. She had finished the sports cake and was well into a set of pastel "packages" wrapped with large fondant bows and adorable same-shade daisies for a bridal shower.

"Thanks. What about this for a topper?" Sam held a fistful of curved white wire strands, each covered in strands of forget-me-nots. She placed the spray of flowers on top of the cake and fussed a moment to be sure they would stay in place.

"That wedding party better be impressed," Becky said.

Julio walked around the table, admiring the cake. "She's right. It's a stunner."

Sam found a deep box that would protect the sides against an accidental bump that might crush the delicate flowers, and Julio helped her carry it to the fridge.

The rest of the morning passed in a flurry of cupcakes for a kid's birthday party, an anniversary cake for a couple who seemed surprised they'd made it ten years, and seven dozen cookies for the crowd who always seemed to fill the place for coffee and a snack around mid-afternoon.

A glance at the clock told Sam she better getting moving with Renata Butler's cake—the deadline was upon her.

The address was an upscale condominium complex where old-style Taos adobe blended with modern chic in a setting among ancient leafy trees with views of Taos

Mountain. The units were situated so that one would never guess there was a town within a stone's throw. Architect and landscape artists had worked to make this spot seem as if it existed in a world of its own. From what Sam had heard about the prices, it pretty much did. Movie stars and tech-company founders tended to be the majority owners here. She wondered how Renata and James made the cut.

She located their unit by the sounds of laughter and clinking glassware from an upper veranda. Double parking, she left the van's air conditioner running while she prowled among the walkways and shrubs to find their front door.

Musical chimes, then a woman answered assuring Sam she was in the right place and offering to help carry the cake if necessary. The two of them got it inside and Sam looked around, hoping they had a table already prepared for it.

A wide foyer with decorative tile on the floor opened to a living room that featured one of those unhindered views of the mountains. Sam noted elegant side tables and expensive wall hangings as they carried the cake toward a kitchen that the woman assured her was "just through here."

They found an empty spot on the granite countertop and she lowered the sides of the box so she could slide the cake out.

"Oh, Madame Samantha! You are here!" Renata's slightly Russian accent commanded the attention of her guests. "Everyone! The cake is here. Oh, my, Sam. It is fantastic!"

"Where would you—?"

"Oh yes, just over here."

Renata pointed to a table decorated with white flowers, situated in what was probably the breakfast nook, between the upscale kitchen and sliding doors that led to a large patio. A dozen or more people were outside, standing at the built-in adobe bar or lounging on the plump cushions of wicker furniture that formed cozy little groupings.

Sam set the cake in place and arranged some of the table's decorations attractively around it.

"Will you stay for a drink?" Renata asked. "The party is just getting started."

Sam took in the elegantly clad women and the men in slacks and sport jackets, wondering without daring a glance at how many frosting stains there must be on her baker's jacket.

"Oh, no," she said. "I can't stay. I'll just—"

"At least you must meet the marvelous woman who is responsible for my marrying Jimmy." Renata took Sam's arm and pulled her across the living room. "It took me many years to find my Jimmy, you know. After my first husband died—so very young—I traveled the world. Thirty six years old and my life was so empty."

A woman with white hair nearly to her waist turned at the sound of Renata's voice.

"Zora, this is my newest friend, Samantha," she announced.

Zora wore a flowing ankle length skirt, a handkerchief blouse in a shade of orange that didn't go with any of the colors in the patterned skirt, and about twelve bangle bracelets on each arm. She extended a veined hand thick with silver rings. Her age could have been anywhere between forty and sixty—her heart-shaped face seemed to have seen some hard wear. She had a prominent nose and space between her front teeth.

"Samantha," said Zora. "It's nice to meet you."

Renata piped up again. "I met Zora last winter, at a holiday party where she was reading palms for the guests."

"I also read tarot cards and tea leaves," Zora said. "But palms are my specialty." She grabbed Sam's hand and turned the palm upward. At the sight of ingrained yellow food coloring she put the hand back down.

Renata didn't seem to notice. "Last month I went to her place and Zora did the most amazing thing. She told me that I would soon find the man of my dreams. In fact, she said that the very next man I met would become my husband."

"Really."

"She finished my reading and I walked out the door, literally into the arms of Jimmy. Can you believe it? He was trimming the lilac bushes beside the door. I looked at him . . . he looked at me . . . We were married a week later."

Zora was nodding enthusiastically. "It's true. I saw that match, clear as day."

Uh-huh. Sam bit back a response. Out on the patio she caught sight of Jimmy leaning on the bar, coming on to a girl who should have been in an English Lit 101 class. Sam quickly looked away.

"So, what is it that you do, Samantha?" Zora was asking. *You tell me—you're the psychic.*

If the baker's jacket and sugar encrusted fingernails weren't enough clue, this woman's intuitive powers were less than that of a schnauzer puppy. Sam glanced at Renata but the new bride was oblivious.

"I better get going," Sam said. "I double parked out there . . . The bakery is really crazy today . . ."

"Thanks again for the cake," Renata said, walking her to the door.

"Look, I know you don't know me very well," Sam said, keeping her voice low. "But I'm not real sure about Zora and her powers."

Renata gave her a puzzled look.

"Just be careful about what to believe. There have been cases . . . psychics who take people for a lot of money."

"Sam, it's nothing like that. She charges very, very little for her readings." Renata's eyes drifted toward the gathering on the patio and a pair of stress lines briefly touched the edges of her mouth.

"Okay. My mistake. It's none of my business." Sam escaped.

Renata's condo was not far from Zoë and Darryl Chartrain's place, and on a whim Sam made the turn and ended up at their back door two minutes later. The last time she'd seen Zoë was right after Lila Coffey's funeral. Maybe checking in on her friend would be a good idea.

"Hey there." Zoë greeted her at the door. "I'm just making some iced tea. Can you stay a minute?"

Although she really hadn't planned on it, Sam sat at the breakfast bar and accepted a glass of Zoë's fresh raspberry tea.

"Have you ever heard of a psychic here in town called Zora? I met her just now at a reception," she said as soon as Zoë sat down.

"Madame Zora? Long white hair, thin, dressed in garish colors?"

"Sounds like the one."

Zoë laughed. "I went to the farmer's market this spring. Remember that one day it was pouring rain? Well, all the vendors and absolutely everyone in the crowd had rain gear or umbrellas. This was no quick sprinkle. And there's this woman who is getting completely drenched, standing there complaining about 'where did all this rain come from?'. The guy selling the watermelons called her Zora and teased her about if she was such a great psychic, why didn't she know it would be raining."

Sam laughed. "She asked me what I did for a living," she said, spreading her arms to show her jacket with the bakery name embroidered on it. "What's with that?"

Zoë wagged her head back and forth. "She won't be in business very long. Everyone who has mentioned her has figured out she's a big fake."

"So she does have an actual—what would you call it?—like a shop?"

"Yeah, there's a little building on the south end of town, one of those places that was once a house—right there on Paseo. Past the big lumber yard."

"Has she been around very long?"

"Oh, maybe a few months. I wouldn't be surprised to see her pack up and leave soon. Or find some other line of work."

"Apparently at least one of her predictions came true." Sam repeated what Renata had told her about Zora's prediction that led to her marriage to James Butler. "Renata is crazy about the guy—really believes that fate brought them together."

Zoë looked skyward. "Okay . . ."

Sam remembered that she'd never told Zoë the details about her visit with Beau to Las Vegas and their discovery that Ted O'Malley had another wife. When she spilled the whole story, Zoë's eyes went wide.

"A bigamist! And he's skipping the country? That's just—it's crazy! Can't Beau stop him?"

"He would if he could, but he says there's not enough evidence to hold him. He says the bigamy charges are hardly worth pursuing now that Lila has died. Did I tell you that

one of my caretaking properties had a similar situation—
the wife died and the husband cleared out everything of
value and was on his way to Switzerland? Beau had him
stopped and questioned but they couldn't hold him. The
wife had made a new will leaving it all to him."

Zoë pushed her tea glass around. "And I suppose Ted
O'Malley did the same. Remember? He had his lawyer
standing right there with him as Lila's things were being
hauled out the door."

Sam felt an electric tingle go through her. The lawyer.

"I gotta go," she said. She gulped the last of her tea and
stood up. "Sorry. Something just hit me and I need to talk
to Beau about it."

Chapter 15

Her heart raced as she put the van in gear and drove the few blocks to Beau's office. Why hadn't she picked up on it right away? Sleep deprivation? That was a lousy excuse.

She found him at his desk with stacks of files surrounding him. At her tap on the doorjamb he looked up from the form he was filling out.

"Hey, this is a nice surprise," he said, rising.

"I think . . . I've got something important," she panted. "It just—"

"Come on in, darlin'. Sit down."

"I can't sit." She paced the width of the room. "Remember I told you that I ran into Sadie Gray's husband the last time I went to their house? He came to get something from the garage. Well, I finally remembered where I'd seen him before."

Beau leaned a hip on one corner of the desk. "Yeah?"

"At Lila Coffey's. The day of the estate sale. Ted O'Malley was standing there watching the money roll in."

Beau's eyebrows raised in a so-what expression.

"Ted introduced us to his attorney, called him Joe Smith. But it was Marshall Gray."

"Sam, are you *sure* about that?"

"The way he combs his hair, his size and build, the face. And the voice. He spoke both times, and I know it was him." She had reached the far wall and turned back to him. "I can't believe I didn't pick up on it the minute I saw Marshall that day. Dang, Beau. I knew something looked familiar about him but I couldn't pinpoint it."

"But O'Malley introduced him as Joe Smith. Couldn't they just be very similar looking?"

She felt a flicker of hesitation. The eyes. "No. It was the same man."

"Well, it might go toward explaining why we didn't find either of their names in a phone book or on a credit record," he said slowly. "I wonder which name is the real one."

"I think he recognized me. Marshall, I mean. The day he came to Sadie's. He gave me kind of a funny look and then he ducked around me very quickly and walked to the garage."

Beau circled his desk and sat down, pulling the computer keyboard close. He clicked a few keys and Sam moved to look over his shoulder.

"I'm just checking to see if the state bar association lists a Joe Smith."

Sam wished her earlier search had been this specific.

A few more keystrokes and a listing of licensed attorneys and their addresses came up. There were two

Joseph Smiths, one down south in Las Cruces and the other in Albuquerque.

"Too bad those listings don't show photos. I would know in a second," she said. "I wonder . . . was one of the Joe Smiths posing as Marshall Gray, or was Gray pretending to be the lawyer?"

Beau drummed his fingers on the desk. "Could be either. Could be neither. Joe Smith could be from another state. But still, I don't like the looks of this."

"So, now at least you have something to arrest Marshall Gray for, right?"

"Darlin', it's not quite that easy." He looked up at her. "Other than practicing law without a license, we really don't have much on this Gray or Smith. If he represented himself as a lawyer and filed documents, we might get him on that. But in this state a person doesn't need a lawyer to write a will. You can do your own or use one of those kits, as long as you have it witnessed and notarized. Marshall Gray would simply say that his wife chose to write her own will."

"But then why was he standing there next to Ted Coffey, introducing himself as a lawyer?"

Beau stood up and took her hands. "Could you swear in court that's what happened if he denies it and says you're just confused about what you heard?"

Her mouth pursed. "I hate this, Beau, I know they've done something illegal. I hate that we can't catch them."

He pulled her close and wrapped his arms around her. "I know, darlin', I know. It's one of the big frustrations in law enforcement. It would be different if someone—a family member of Sadie's—had stepped forward to press charges but they haven't. And you can see by the look of this desk—I don't have time to work the official cases, much less the ones where we only suspect something. I already used department funds to check out Ted O'Malley and discovered that he committed bigamy, technically. Neither wife pressed charges on that, and he's such small potatoes that it would fall very low in a prosecutor's priorities, especially since one of the wives isn't alive anymore."

Sam's mind whirled with the implications. None of this was making much sense. When Beau released the embrace, she knew he was thinking again about the stacks of files on his desk.

"Tell you what," he said. "I'll do some more extensive backgrounds on all the names, on my own time, and see if anything interesting pops up. If it does, you'll be the first to know."

She smiled up at him. "Have I ever mentioned what a great guy you are?"

He kissed her forehead. "You might have. But you could say it again. If you want to."

Instead, she gave him a kiss that more than proved her point.

The rest of the afternoon flew by in a rush of birthday cakes and a flurry of walk-in customers who managed to clean out all the cookies, cheesecake and brownies in a little under two hours. By five p.m. Sam found herself issuing orders like a general, prepping for the upcoming weekend, and ordering adequate supplies to get them through.

Thoughts of bigamists, lawyers and shady estate deals completely left her mind until the phone rang at home. She'd changed into soft capris, shared a salad with Kelly and was just getting ready for bed when her daughter informed her that Beau was on the line.

"Turns out your feminine instincts weren't so far off," he began.

It took her a minute to figure out what he was talking about.

"Two marriages, two eerily similar scenarios. Sadie Gray had married Marshall ten months before her death. Lila Coffey married Ted O'Malley less than three months ago. Both were older women marrying younger men. Both revised their wills almost immediately after marriage. So far, nothing illegal in all that."

"Oh. But—"

"But, there's more. Both women used an attorney named Joe Smith to do their estate plans, consisting of a Living Trust, a Will and an Advanced Health Care Directive. In each, the husband had control over his wife's health care decisions."

"And both of them ended up in nursing facilities. Dead. And the husbands inherited everything."

"I believe so. Since a Trust doesn't go through probate, there is no public record of the document. A person can do their own, as I mentioned earlier, and the document stays private, known only to the person who signs it and her heirs. We can't find out who inherited."

"When I questioned whether he had the right to sell everything so quickly after she died, Ted O'Malley told me he inherited Lila's estate," Sam said. "And when you checked the banking records, both men were listed on their wives' accounts."

"Sadie Gray made Marshall her executor. He signed the nursing home admission papers as such. I was able to find out that much. Lila Coffey had named another executor, a long-time friend, but he was in a car accident and since he was unable to serve, Lila's husband Ted took over as executor to her estate."

"Oh man, what a tangle. And I'm still confused about whether Marshall Gray is who he claims to be or is he really Joe Smith, the lawyer?"

"I haven't quite gotten that far. Still checking."

It ended up being a restless night for Sam, going to bed with all that fresh information in her head. Pictures of Ted O'Malley and Marshall Gray kept zipping through her dreams, and at one point the voice of Bertha Martinez spoke. The old *bruja* told Sam to trust no one, to rely on the magic box to provide answers. She woke with a headache.

The wooden box sat benignly on her dresser, minding its own business. Sam stroked its lid for a few seconds, like petting a kitten, but decided she could best put the dreams out of her mind by taking a shower and immersing herself in bakery business.

She had just put the second batch of cranberry almond scones into the oven when the shop's phone rang. She grabbed it up before she realized they weren't officially open for business for another hour.

"Samantha Jane, I've texted you *six* times about the wedding plans and you never answered."

I sent you the date—give me a breather here. "Hello, Mother. Good morning to you too."

"Honey, I *know* you're busy. I just need to know what your *colors* are."

Sam's eyes rolled toward the work table where three wedding cakes stood in various stages of readiness, sugar cookies awaited decorations, and two large pans of brownies needed icing before they could go out to the displays.

"I haven't given it much thought, Mother. A few dozen other brides and their wishes have to come first."

"Well you don't have to get snippity with me," Nina Rae said, sounding pretty snippy herself. "Your sister and I have dresses to buy."

Sheesh. Even Zoë as matron of honor wasn't getting this worked up over what to wear.

"Anything will be fine, Mother. I know how you love shopping but you have a closet full of gorgeous clothes. Just grab anything."

"Samantha, it has to be *new*. I would *never* wear something to your wedding that's been *seen* before."

Whatever. "Mother, I'll have to get back to you on that question. This is really a crazy day. Give my love to Daddy." She made a kissy noise and hung up. The woman was going to drive her crazy before this was all over.

She turned to the pan of ganache that Julio had just finished, picked it up and began spreading it over the brownies, smoothing it repeatedly in an effort to banish her mother's obsessiveness from her mind. Becky had begun piping bright green, pink and yellow lines and whorls on the sugar cookies. Things truly were under control here, Sam reminded herself.

One of these days she would pull the folder of ideas she'd collected from the first time she and Beau made their wedding plans. They would need some revision—a Valentine theme wasn't quite going to work in September—but it should be something she could pull together quickly once she had a little break from the demands of all the other brides and *their* mothers.

"Shall I take these out front?" Becky asked, setting her pastry bag aside. The sugar cookies.

"Sure, anytime. Julio, the brownies can go too—if you'll sprinkle them with chopped walnuts first?"

He nodded and Sam turned her attention to the wedding cake orders. She tackled the hardest one first—three tiers, ivory with hand-piped ivory lace. It was enough to make her cross-eyed and she gave a deep sigh when she piped the final trim in place two hours later. It went to the fridge so the buttercream wouldn't become too soft, then she started assembling a traditional white-on-white with pale pink roses. Four small cakes formed the base for a sixteen-inch tier that would sit on all of them, topped with Grecian columns, a twelve-inch tier, more columns and an eight-inch finale with a spray of netting and ribbons at the very top. Traditional, but big. By the time she'd stacked the layers, her shoulders were screaming for a break. She left her tools in place so Julio wouldn't toss them into the dishwater, thinking she was finished, then she stepped out front for a cup of coffee.

Jen's attention focused on three women at the counter who seemed unsure about what they wanted. Sam headed for the beverage bar, automatically straightening and wiping up spilled sugar, deciding on tea instead of coffee. She unwrapped a bag called Ginger Spice and turned back to face the room while it steeped.

At the curb a tan car had just come to a stop and Renata Butler stepped out. Their last exchange had become a little testy and Sam was glad to see she hadn't lost a customer. She put on a bright smile and greeted the Russian émigré personally.

"Hi, Sam." She seemed cheery. "I need some cookies

for a little church gathering tonight."

"We can take care of that," Sam assured her.

While Renata looked over the selection in the display case, Sam inquired about her new husband.

"Jimmy is wonderful," Renata said. "I still feel very lucky that I met him."

Jen boxed the cookies and Renata handed her some cash.

"Renata, could we talk for a minute?" Sam asked, walking alongside as the customer headed toward the door.

"Certainly. But I cannot spend too much time. I have an appointment with my attorney." She opened the door and the two of them stepped outside.

Sam felt a chill, even though the air was hot and dry. "Attorney?"

"He is coming to our condo. Since I am married, a few documents must be changed. It is only standard things."

"I know this is personal," Sam said. "But was this your idea? Changing your, uh, documents?"

Renata gave her a long stare. "My husband is also changing his will. We will be together for our whole lives. We want everything to be in order."

How to ask whether the new husband was the one who suggested the changes . . .? Sam took a different tack.

"I'm getting married myself, in a few months, so I suppose I should do the same. Who is your attorney?"

"I have his card, somewhere." Renata reached for the small bag that hung from her shoulder and pulled out a card. "Here it is. Keep it. I can get another."

Sam looked at the card. Joe Smith. Name and phone number but no address. She willed her jaw not to clench.

"Mr. Smith . . . does he have gray hair?"

"I actually haven't met him yet. Jimmy went to see him yesterday. He made my appointment for me and brought me the card."

"Renata—I don't know how to say this. I know of two other women who were referred to Joe Smith. They both changed their wills. They both ended up dying very shortly afterward."

"So it was a good thing they made their papers up to date."

"That's not really what I'm saying. In each case, their husbands inherited large amounts of money."

Renata shrugged. "And if the husband died, the wife would inherit. Is that not the way it works?"

Sam took a breath. "Both of these women already had money. We think—their friends think—that the men might have planned their deaths."

Renata looked as though she didn't understand the implication.

"Just be careful." Sam pleaded.

A man's voice called out, "Renata?"

The redhead turned, one hand on her car door. "Oh, Pastor Red. How lucky you see me here. I bought the cookies for tonight. Would you like to take them now?"

The slender man walked over to the car and reached for the box of cookies. He had strawberry blond hair, thin on the top, and was dressed all in black. Sam wondered how he could handle the summer heat in those dark pants, shirt and jacket. He said hello to Renata then turned to Sam.

"Oh, is this your shop?" he said. "I've seen it here and often thought about stopping in."

"Yes, it's mine. Samantha Sweet."

"Nice to meet you. Ridley Redfearn. I'm pastor at the Fellowship of Good Works church."

For the first time, Sam became aware of a murky pink haze around him.

She froze. It had been awhile since she'd seen such an aura around someone. And Ridley Redfearn—she knew she had seen that name somewhere.

Redfearn was talking but the words blurred behind the hum in her ears. She became aware that Renata had excused herself and opened her car door. The preacher was saying goodbye. He made a comment about the cookies, how good they would be. A thousand thoughts flew through Sam's head but she couldn't think of a way to phrase a single question. She merely nodded as he walked past her shop and got into an old Toyota parked beyond Ivan's bookshop.

Renata drove away, barely giving Sam another glance.

Redfearn's Toyota was out of the lot when Sam looked that direction again.

She stepped into the shade of her own awning, wondering about the strange vision.

Chapter 16

Beau's phone rang and rang, and Sam was sure it was about to go to voicemail when he picked up.

"Sorry," he said. "Crazy here."

"I think there might be another woman who's been targeted by those guys," she blurted out.

He paused, waiting for more.

"And I met that preacher, the one whose card I found at Lila's house. He's the one who married Renata and James Butler."

"Wait, who are we talking about here?"

She had to go back and fill him in, forgetting that he didn't know Renata or James Butler or the crazy story about how they met through a psychic who undoubtedly was a fake.

"I'm getting the feeling that there's not a genuine person

left in this whole town," she said. "Everybody we've come across recently seems to be pretending to be someone else."

"And you suspect this preacher is a fake too?"

"The Fellowship of Good Works? What kind of church is that? Remember how I told you once that I could see auras around people sometimes? Well, this guy's was strong. Murky . . . well, you don't care about the colors. But I picked up a very deceptive feeling around this man."

She could hear papers shuffling in the background.

"I'm looking up that church of his. Not listed in the local directories." His voice trailed off. ". . . and I don't see that they have a business license. Even non-profits are required to have one. Did he touch anything we could get prints from? Something in your shop? If I had that I could see if he's got a record."

"No, he never came inside. I'll give it some thought," Sam said. "If I hope to stop Renata from making a big mistake, I'll need to stay in her good graces. Maybe I can figure out a way to do both."

Two things that put off nearly anybody, Sam had discovered over the years, were to criticize their spouse or express skepticism about their religion. And here she was, about to do both with Renata Butler. She stewed over it as she walked back inside, but no immediate answer came to mind and she was able to lose herself in sugar flowers and chocolate fondant for the next few hours.

As the finished orders disappeared out the front door or went into the fridge for storage, the conversation with Beau kept poking at her. He needed Ridley Redfearn's fingerprints to find out if the man was in any criminal database, and Sam happened to know where both Renata and the pastor would be that very evening. Well, not *exactly* where they would be but she could find out.

"Becky, can you and Julio handle the cleanup?" she asked. Without really waiting for an answer, she grabbed up her backpack and headed out to her van.

In Taos's version of rush hour traffic it took her ten minutes to get home, then another five to change her shirt, brush through her short hair and swish on some blusher. Leaving the brightly decorated bakery van behind, she got into her pickup truck and drove to Renata's condo complex where she parked at the north end of the lot with Renata's tan Mercedes in view. Getting to the street would take Renata the opposite direction from Sam's truck.

The key here was to find out where this barely-existent church was located and to figure out how on earth she might get Pastor Redfearn's fingerprints without his knowing it.

Ancient cottonwoods bordered the condo property, alleviating some of the summer heat but even with all her windows down Sam's face glistened with perspiration after only a few minutes. She wished Renata had dropped some hint about what time this evening function was to take place. But even if she had known, Sam didn't dare count on her quarry waiting until the last minute to leave. She was lucky to have found Renata at home and better not lose that advantage.

An hour passed at a snail's pace. At least the sun had now sunk behind the buildings and the air stirred often enough to make it bearable. Sam fanned herself with an old take-out menu that she'd found on the floor and occupied her mind with the reminder that she better decide on an accent color for her wedding, just to get her mother off her back. She found herself thinking of colors that she knew Nina Rae would wear—it seemed easier to do it that way than to get into a long discussion of why her chosen color would never work. She glanced at her dashboard clock approximately every three minutes.

"This is ridiculous," she fumed. About the time she was ready to dash away to find the nearest place to get an iced beverage, she became aware that Renata's car was in motion.

She cranked the Silverado to life and coasted toward the driveway where the tan Mercedes had just made a right hand turn. By the time Sam's truck reached that point, the Mercedes was disappearing around a bend in the road. She pressed the gas pedal to catch up. Keeping her quarry in sight on the curvy road was tricky. At last she came to the straight stretch approaching the plaza, then realized that she might get caught by the traffic light and lose Renata altogether. She had to take a chance and catch up with her.

Fortunately, the other woman didn't seem to be paying attention to the big truck behind her. They turned south on Paseo del Pueblo Sur and wound past the small plaza shops and fast food places, with Sam trying to stay a couple of vehicles back. After two or three miles Renata signaled and turned west, toward an area that Sam remembered as consisting mostly of small warehouses and car repair shops. She certainly didn't remember any churches out this way. Perhaps Renata had changed her mind and was going somewhere else entirely.

The one small SUV which had separated them turned off at a self-storage unit and Sam began to feel conspicuous in her big red truck. Surely Renata would notice she was being tailed. Sam dropped back a block and slowed way down.

Renata swung into a paved parking lot and pulled up to a metal building, the type of industrial looking thing that might normally house a workshop or warehouse. Three other cars sat outside, including Redfearn's battered old Toyota. Sam cruised past, noting the hand-lettered sign that proclaimed it to be the Fellowship of Good Works. Looked like God's riches hadn't quite bestowed themselves upon this little group as yet.

In her rearview mirror, Sam saw two other vehicles turn in. She pulled into the parking lot of a welder's shop about a block farther west, turning so she could watch the meager congregation gather. *Now what?*

She needed to get a fingerprint from Redfearn and it seemed the easiest way would be to lift one from his car. Surely the door handle would be loaded with them. A great plan until she realized she hadn't exactly come equipped. No powder, no tape—how was she going to accomplish her goal?

She chafed with indecision.

Call Beau and have him send the lab tech? The Toyota wasn't likely to move for awhile. She pulled out her cell phone and dialed his number. It went to voicemail immediately. He'd said he was super busy.

Although the crime scene team were technically on call twenty-four-seven, Sam knew that they normally worked regular office hours. Calling someone away from their dinner or family time, just to take prints from an old car, from a man they didn't have on their suspect lists, wasn't going to win her any points with Beau's staff.

She chewed at a cuticle that tasted faintly of almond extract.

C'mon, Sam, do something.

Grabbing the gearshift lever she put the truck in motion. It appeared that the little congregation was complete. Eight cars sat in the parking lot. She steered the big pickup into the lot and coasted past the Toyota, turned it around and braked, reaching for pen and paper. The sounds of guitar music floated out the open door, a tune and voices that were nothing like she'd ever heard at the First Baptist Church in Cottonville, Texas.

She eyed the door handle of the Toyota but didn't see any viable way of taking prints from it. The sky was in the last stages of twilight and deep shadows blanketed the parking lot so she got out to get a better look at the license plate on the pastor's car. She'd just finished jotting down the number when the music stopped.

A man appeared in the doorway of the building.

"I thought I saw someone pull in," he said in a jovial tone. "Come, sister, join us!"

Sam felt her facial muscles freeze.

"Oh, no," she said. "I didn't mean to interrupt."

"No child of good intention ever interrupts. We welcome you into the loving arms of our little group."

Oh boy.

"Please, child, come inside and join the fellowship." Child? He was at least ten years younger than she.

Her mind flitted in a hundred directions. Initial response: Run. Run fast and far. But her pulse slowed a little and she reminded herself that they couldn't kidnap her or brainwash her in a few minutes time. And she had a mission: Get Ridley Redfearn's fingerprints. Thoroughly uncomfortable, she worked up a smile and walked toward the man who'd spoken to her.

"We are sharing some wonderful music and a few

refreshments," he said.

She noticed that he slipped a cigarette pack into the pocket of his suit coat.

"How nice," she said, sidestepping the arm he'd intended to slip around her shoulders.

The man, who introduced himself simply as Bill, ushered Sam inside where part of the metal building had been partitioned into a plain room, about twenty by twenty feet. Some colorful lengths of cloth had been draped across the wall behind a skimpy pulpit of wood that resembled a music stand more than anything else. Folding metal chairs faced it. Overall, the room had a just-finished, hollow feel to it.

Two young male guitar players with longish hair were just picking up their instruments after the short break. When they stared toward the back of the room, the people in the chairs turned to do the same. Renata gave her a funny look but Sam only countered with the brightest smile she could muster. The rest of the little congregation were probably high-schoolers and one or two of their grandmothers. Ridley Redfearn's stare was more pointed. A hazy blue aura hung around him and Sam watched it darken to the color of a stormy sky. She edged out of his view and took a seat in the back row. She amused herself by counting the rows of chairs and calculating that there were forty, only thirteen of which had actual human bottoms in them. Three out-of-tune songs later she could tell that she was the only one dying to get out of there.

Deciding he should always leave the crowd wanting more, Redfearn stood up, thanked the guitarists, and promised refreshments in just a moment. Sam almost got to her feet but the pastor had squeezed his eyes shut and raised both hands toward the stained ceiling tiles. She watched as everyone in the tiny congregation, including that Bill who'd dragged her in here, raised their faces to the same unseen entity, closed their eyes and turned their palms upward. When the rambling prayer was over—it surely only *seemed* like twenty minutes later—the aura around Redfearn had fuzzed out to a mild gray.

As the crowd stood, Sam edged to the side of the room. Renata was the first to beeline her way to Sam's corner.

"Hello, Samantha. I did not realize you knew of our church."

Sam feigned surprise at seeing the Russian and spent a half-second coming up with a plausible response. She reached into the depths of her pack and pulled out the flyer she'd been carrying ever since the day at Lila's.

"Oh, yes, I've been very curious about this, uh, church," she said. "If I'd known there would be refreshments, I could have contributed."

That seemed to remind Renata of something and she murmured a few words as she headed for the food table, where she opened the box of cookies she'd picked up at the bakery that afternoon. One of the other ladies was starting to pour iced tea into bright plastic cups, asking folks whether they preferred it sweetened or not. Apparently the red cups meant one thing and the yellow ones another.

"I thought I recognized you." Ridley Redfearn's voice startled Sam and she bumped his arm when she jerked. She spun to find herself staring directly into his sandy eyebrows. "Renata's friend from the bakery, right?"

"Um, yes. That's right." The brochure in her hand

fluttered in explanation, but she decided what the hell. She didn't owe him anything.

A young woman who might have been barely out of high school approached the pastor with one of the red cups. "Pastor Redfearn," she said shyly, "sweet tea, just the way you like it."

"Thank you, Darla. How nice of you to remember."

The girl blushed furiously.

Sam used the few seconds that his attention wandered to sneak over to the table and pick up a cookie, one that obviously came from another bakery. It never hurt to scope out the competition. She watched the pastor as he worked the room.

He rarely got a sip of his iced tea, as someone was almost always talking to him. Eventually she saw him set the cup down on a windowsill as he offered a hug to one of the grandmotherly women. Sam edged her way between him and the cup, acting like she was eyeing a plate of brownies.

Once Redfearn had moved slightly farther into the room and she saw that he wasn't looking, she picked up the cup by the rim as if it were her own. At one point he looked around, clearly trying to figure out what he'd done with his drink but since it was impossible to tell them apart he didn't have a clue. Sam worked her way to the door as conversation flowed around her, edged out into the cool night air and fast-walked toward her truck. Dumping the sweet tea on the ground she set the cup in one of her drink holders and got the heck out of there.

Chapter 17

"I can get the answer on the vehicle right away," Beau said when Sam took him the Toyota's plate number and the pastor's drinking cup the next morning. "Fingerprints, especially if there's nothing on file in New Mexico, will take a bit longer. State crime lab is totally backed up but sometimes I can pull a favor for a simple search with a buddy in Albuquerque. APD has a lot better computers and software than we do."

He slipped the cup into an evidence bag and set it on his desk.

"Missed you last night," he said, edging near for a kiss on her neck. When he added a tiny lick to the edge of her ear, a pleasant shiver shot through her.

"I think you're changing the subject," she teased. Goosebumps raised on her arm as he ran his index finger down her arm, from shoulder to fingertips. "The DMV?"

"One vehicle search coming up," he said. It took a few keystrokes and some muttering on his part, something about how he usually talked the desk officer into doing these things, but finally the screen showed the record for the plate number she'd given him.

"Nineteen ninety-eight Toyota Camry, purchased from Bob Brown Motors in Santa Fe on April 29. It's one of those corner used car lots where the old trade-ins go to be sold real cheap. You pay cash or sign up for exorbitant interest rates. It's registered to Ridley Redfearn, 421 Pacheco Drive, Santa Fe."

He opened a new screen and entered the street address. It didn't exist. "Addresses on Pacheco Drive end in the three hundred block. It's a very short street."

"I knew there was something completely hokey about that guy," Sam said.

"It could be that. It could be someone at the DMV made a typo when they input his data." He clicked back to the DMV site and filled in a few blanks. "Doesn't have a New Mexico driver's license . . . If he moved here from another state he should have gotten that changed over as soon as he established residency. Then again, if he's using a fake address, maybe he has no intention of permanently moving here."

Sam thought about that. "I definitely got a sense of transience about the guy. That whole church thing—very new, very . . . non-permanent."

The hand lettered sign, the metal building in an industrial area, the conversations among the little congregation which had made her think a lot of them were there for the first time. Renata had said Redfearn performed their marriage ceremony but Sam didn't get the feeling that either she or James Butler had known the pastor very long. Nothing about it felt quite kosher, but she couldn't pinpoint exactly what made it feel all wrong either.

"I guess I better get back to the shop," she finally said. "Let me know when you hear anything about the fingerprints from that cup?"

He stood and pulled her close. "I will do it."

"Shall I come out to your place tonight?" She threw a little seductive edge into the question and he immediately agreed.

"Cases or no cases," he said, "I'm ready for a night alone—with you."

"We've both been working long hours. I'll be there at six-thirty, with steaks."

"I'll be there at six, pre-heating some things." He leered. "The grill first."

She raked her fingernails down the front of his shirt, wishing she had long, unchipped nails. No matter. His nipples tightened at her touch.

"You better quit that or I'm locking this office door and closing the blinds," he said.

"You're right—we do need a night at home together." She backed away and blew him a kiss from the doorway. "Later, Sheriff."

It turned to be quite a bit later before either of them thought about suspects or fingerprints. Sam arrived at the ranch with the promised sirloins from the market and two slices of decadent amaretto cheesecake from her shop, to find that Beau had not forgotten his earlier promise to lock themselves away. He pulled her into the house, stashed the food in the fridge and said he felt like a shower before dinner.

The shower turned out to be *au deux*, and in the following thirty minutes they never made it past the bedroom door.

Another quick shower, shorts and t-shirts donned, and she followed him into the kitchen.

"I drove past Sadie Gray's house when I left the shop," Sam told him while she chopped vegetables for a salad. "Figured I needed to make my weekly report to Delbert Crow, plus I guess I had some tiny hope that Marshall might have left another clue or two behind."

"And, did he?" Beau seasoned the steaks and picked up the lighter.

"No, darn it."

He held up a finger to indicate one minute, while he ducked outside and lit the gas grill. When he came back Sam could tell he was itching to tell her something.

"What?" she asked as she pulled plates from a cupboard.

"Well, I wasn't going to spoil the mood earlier . . ." Pleasure before business, for once. "But I finally found some additional info on your Marshall Gray."

She crossed her arms, letting him know that dinner wasn't proceeding until she knew what he'd found.

"Okay, remember the Dallas police had questioned him? So I finally got the chance to look at the transcript of their interviews and the background info they dug up. Gray was born in Wichita Falls, Texas, but the family moved to Albuquerque before he started school. He attended up through high school there, then left the city. College was at UTEP."

The El Paso campus was a favorite of kids from the area because of its proximity to the border town of Juarez— easy place to find booze and sex. It was a shady town, even in the '60s, but not as truly dangerous as today.

"Did he live in Texas after that or come back to New Mexico, I wonder?"

"Looks like he moved around a lot, didn't really settle. Work history is really sketchy. He describes himself as an entrepreneur, and he tried to portray a certain 'citizen of the world' sophistication. The FBI and Dallas PD didn't buy it. They came up with multiple marriages, always followed by a move to a new state."

"So, he's pulled these scams with other women in the past?" Sam gathered silverware and condiments as she talked.

Beau shrugged. "We don't know. The Feds were finding out whether they could hold him for Sadie's death and absconding with her money. It turned out they couldn't, and there were no other open charges from his past."

He took the steaks outside and Sam finished setting the table while he watched the grill.

"So, can we find out more?" she asked once they'd started eating.

"I'll try. It's not like Gray has an actual police rap sheet. Either he kept out of trouble or he managed to stay on the move well enough to stay off the radar. Remember, we're talking about the late '60s, early '70s—police departments weren't computerized back then."

Sam nodded. The whole puzzle was staying stubbornly out of their grasp. And she had to remind herself that perhaps Marshall Gray had done nothing wrong.

"What about those fingerprints for Ridley Redfearn?" she asked. "Any news on them yet?"

He shook his head. She remembered what he'd said earlier about the state crime lab being backed up, and that information on the preacher wasn't exactly a priority.

They cleared the table and carried their cheesecake and coffee out to the back deck. A billion stars made crisp points in the black sky and the air felt cool and refreshing against her skin. She decided to give herself over to the summer evening and leave everything else for another time. When Beau leaned across the settee to nuzzle her neck, forgetting became pretty easy.

* * *

As always, their alarms went off way too early, but after allowing themselves the luxury of two taps on the Snooze button, Beau dressed and went outside to tend to the horses and Sam drove to the bakery.

She was deep into the morning's routine when Jen interrupted to say that Zoë was on the phone.

"Hey there," Sam said, wiping her sugary hands on a towel. "What's up?"

"Just thought I'd throw a little business your way. I've got a big group coming in tomorrow, a family reunion of folks from Oklahoma. The ones we can't house here are staying in hotels but I'll be making breakfast for the whole crowd. It would be a big help if I could get the pastries from you. Four dozen assorted muffins and scones? Maybe some coffee cake?"

"Sure, no problem. I can deliver them later, if you like. Sounds like you've got your hands full."

"Thanks—it really would help. There'll be a glass of iced tea waiting when you get here."

Sam told Julio to double the batches on some of the pastries and he began to measure ingredients into the big

Hobart without batting an eye. When she arrived at Zoë's that afternoon, a stack of boxes in her arms, the promised refreshment did, indeed, appear, complete with fresh mint from Zoë's garden.

"Wow, I needed that," Sam said after the first couple of sips. They had taken seats at the tiled counter.

"Do I detect that someone missed her normal bedtime last night?" Zoë teased with a wiggle of her eyebrows.

"Well, yeah. Beau and I had a lot to talk about. I can't remember, did I mention that one of my properties belonged to a woman who recently died? Now Beau is investigating some weird connections to it."

"I keep thinking about Lila Coffey. Did her house ever become one of your jobs?"

"No, this is another one. But eerily similar. The husband, Marshall Gray, cleaned the place out—and the woman's bank accounts—just days after she passed away."

"Marshall Gray . . . Why does that name sound familiar to me?"

Sam shrugged. "I don't know." She gave a quick description. "Maybe you'd met Sadie? She was somewhat older than he is."

"No, that's not it. This is like a name from the really distant past." Zoë squinted her eyes nearly shut as she thought about it. "High school?"

"Seriously? You remember him?"

"My friend Nancy Gray had an older brother . . ." Zoë stood up and headed for the living room. "Hold on. Let me check something."

She came back with a stack of large, bound books and when she set them on the counter Sam saw that they were yearbooks from an Albuquerque high school. Zoë hopped back up on her stool.

"Nancy's brother was older, and I remember at twelve I thought he was *so* handsome. We were still in middle school when he left for college," she muttered, flipping pages.

"So he wouldn't be in your yearbooks." Sam didn't quite grasp the connection.

"These are Darryl's books. He's nine years older than me, and he and Marshall were probably there at the same time."

The pages turned one at a time now and she finally stopped and jabbed a finger at one of the black-and-white photos. "There."

It was the standard senior student photo of the day. Boys wore tuxedos and girls had matching V-necked drapes that made anyone look attractive despite the outlandishly large hairstyles. Sam stared at the one Zoë indicated.

His hair was dark then but Gray combed it in a similar style as now. Sam tried to mentally remove the current jowliness and facial creases. The eyes were key—they looked very similar.

"Nancy and I had sleepovers a lot back then. You know the kind where you sit up all night and giggle over boys. I guess she spotted my schoolgirl crush on her brother because she loved to dish out all the dirt on him. One time he gave his class ring to someone but Nancy knew he was seeing two other girls at the same time. Eventually, he got one of the girls pregnant. Nancy and I were shocked and a little fascinated by that fact. I don't remember how it all turned out. Marshall moved away about then, maybe to college."

"Did the family originally come from Texas?"

Zoë pursed her mouth. "Yeah, now that you mention it, I'm pretty sure they did. I lost touch with Nancy after graduation and heard that she died a few years later. Too young."

"Would there be other family members in Albuquerque?"

"Only their parents, *if* they're still living," Zoë said. "There weren't any other siblings."

Chapter 18

A light breeze carried dust whorls across the street and in the distance the haze of woodsmoke still covered the hills. Today, she could smell it. Sam carried Darryl's yearbook with her, hoping that Beau might confirm whether the picture was the same Marshall Gray. Perhaps he could use some information from the book in tracking Gray.

She thought about phoning Beau, but since his office was on the route back to the bakery she decided to drop in. Finding a parking spot for her van along the narrow street outside the civic offices was always a joy, but she managed to spot another car leaving and zipped right into its place.

Beau was on the phone, winding up a conversation when she tapped at his door. He replaced the receiver and stretched an arm to encircle her shoulders.

"Hey there, what's up?"

"The usual. But I might have found us some more information on Marshall Gray." She held out the yearbook. "Zoë was a classmate of his younger sister and remembered some stories about him."

She flipped to the marked page and pointed. "The difference between age eighteen and fifty-something makes it a little hard to know but I think it's him. Zoë said his parents might still be in Albuquerque."

"That might be a good lead," Beau said. "If only I had something to charge him with. We think he married Sadie for her money. We have no evidence that he killed her to get it."

"I know." Sam let the book slap shut, feeling the letdown of the unsolved mystery. It probably really was coincidence that she'd come across two elderly women who'd married younger men and then died rather suddenly. She wanted it to be that simple but something way inside kept telling her there was more to it. Woman's intuition, or just her stubborn streak?

"Zoë asked me about Lila Coffey again. Is there any news about the lying creep who married her?"

"Ted O'Malley seems to have vanished. Las Vegas PD doesn't have anything new. They don't have the manpower to keep watching Debbie's house, but if Ted is back in their city he's staying very low-key. I don't have enough of a case against him to put him on any national watch lists. Bigamy, especially when the second wife is now deceased, just doesn't warrant a lot of attention when there are murders, rapes and drug cases to be worked."

Sam's mood dipped again. "Yeah, I know."

Too bad they hadn't found anything to suggest that one person had killed both women. A nursing home serial killer on the loose might at least garner a little bit of law enforcement interest. Beau's phone rang and Sam told him she needed to get going anyway.

Back at the bakery things were quiet for a change. The display cases in the sales room were appropriately depleted. Kelly stood at the counter chatting with Jen, her shirt front a bit damp from the last dog-bath she'd given at Puppy Chic.

"Hey, Mom. How's things?"

Sam responded halfheartedly.

"If you're coming home tonight, I'll treat us to pizza." Kelly held up her folded paycheck. "Jen, you want to come along?"

Jen glanced toward Sam. "I better not. I've got some things . . ."

Better things to do than hanging out with your boss who was clearly in the dumps. Sam put on a smile. "Sorry, I don't mean to be such a downer. A pizza sounds great—and you girls would definitely cheer me up."

"Okay then," Kelly said. "C'mon, Jen. Our house, six-thirty?"

Sam reached into her pack and pulled out a twenty-dollar bill, which she handed to her daughter. "I'll spring for the wine."

Kelly turned to leave. "Excellent! All I have to do is finish brushing out a cocker spaniel and I'm done for the day."

She gave Sam a quick hug and wiggled her fingers at them as she flounced out the door.

Jen and Sam exchanged a smile. "She keeps me young," Sam said with a roll of the eyes.

Two hours and two glasses of wine later, Sam had to admit that her earlier funk had been useless. Sadie Gray and

Lila Coffey were gone, bless their souls, and there wasn't anything anyone could do about that. She had met Sadie once and knew Lila only through Zoë's recollections. Both of the husbands had acted suspiciously, but they'd now vanished off the radar and there was nothing she could do about that either.

"I think I'm just on overload right now," she admitted to Kelly and Jen. The three of them were sitting on her living room floor with their backs against the sofa, the open pizza box on the coffee table. They grabbed the final three slices from the box. "Too many new people have crossed my path in the last couple weeks. Between that and the crush of work at the shop . . ."

"You need a break, Mom," Kelly said. "Why don't you and Beau just run off and get married and take a honeymoon trip for about a month?"

"Yeah, and have fifty brides storming the shop? When I'm the first line of defense?" Jen said. "At least give me some warning so I can call in sick that week."

Sam popped the last bite of crust into her mouth. "Hey, you guys are good—I mean, I have a wonderful crew—but I'd never do that to you. Becky and Julio are great back there in the kitchen, but my jumping ship with no notice . . . no way."

"Oh, thank you!" Jen said, dramatically draping herself over Sam's shoulder.

Sam patted her head. "Someone's had enough wine, I think." She gently plucked Jen's arms from around her neck.

The younger woman blushed a little. "I better go potty."

She straightened her legs and made it to her feet. Sam realized she better stand up too before her limbs forgot how to do it. She ignored the crackling in her knees and picked up the empty pizza box and carried it to the kitchen.

"Mom, what's this book?" Kelly asked, nodding toward the yearbook Sam had left on the kitchen table.

Sam was in the middle of the short version of the story when Jen came back.

"My mom's got this very same book," she exclaimed. "I always got a kick out of looking at the old-school hairstyles and those crazy poses of the drama class."

"Old? I'll have you know I graduated about that same time!" Sam gave her a gentle nudge.

Jen's mouth made a little twist. "Sorry."

She picked up the book and turned to a page in the freshman section.

"Look, there's my mom. Shirley Benevides."

Kelly leaned in for a look and the two young women exchanged a knowing glance that said, *Totally old-school.*

"There's another one of her when she was in the drama club," Jen said. She flipped to another section, knowing exactly where the photo would be. "Look at that!"

Sam looked at the group shot of young thespians mugging an over-dramatized scene from a play, but the face that caught her eye wasn't of Jennifer's mother.

The caption read: "Members of the drama club during rehearsals for *The Man and the Gypsy*. Cast members include Shirley Benevides as Mrs. Chapman, Ron Daniels as Rory Chapman, and Candy Butler as Zora the Gypsy."

Zora. Even with the passage of time, Sam recognized Candy Butler. The long hair was dark then, white now, but the heart-shape of her face and space between her front teeth hadn't changed a bit. She'd obviously liked the name Zora well enough that she'd kept it.

Candy Butler.

James Butler.

Who'd recently married Renata. Sam felt her pulse quicken.

"Jen, would your mother remember these other cast members now?"

Jen shrugged. "I don't know. But she used to talk a lot about how that class was her very favorite. She loved being involved in the productions."

"Could we call her?" Sam asked. *How to explain this?*

Jen gave her a questioning look but pulled her cell phone from her pocket and speed dialed a number. After a minute's worth of odd explanations, Sam got to the questions.

"Oh, I remember Candy very well," Shirley said. "She always wanted to play the exotic one in the school plays. She would be the gypsy or the flamenco dancer. Everyone else got roles like the school teacher or the mom."

"Did you stay in touch with her after graduation?"

"No. I think I remember hearing that she moved away, probably to New York or somewhere." She said it as if New York were on another continent.

"I'm actually trying to find out if she had a brother. I'm guessing he was a few years younger."

There was a long moment as Shirley mulled that over. "You know, I think she did. I can picture this kid who might have been ten or twelve. She had to drag him along to our Saturday rehearsals sometimes. He seemed young but we were only fourteen, ourselves."

"Do you remember his name? Could it have been James?"

"Jimmy. That's it. Candy used to be in the middle of a line on stage and she would stop to yell out, 'Jimmy! Don't go outside!' I remember we all laughed because it was like he was trying to escape from the auditorium."

Sam thanked her for the information and was about to hang up when Shirley thought of something else.

"You know, I remember someone at our twentieth class reunion—we were reminiscing about those silly plays we did—and somebody mentioned Candy Butler. Now what was it they said . . .? Oh. That she'd moved to Las Vegas. I remember that because I thought there was no one less like a showgirl than Candy Butler."

That Nevada connection again. Sam pondered that as she thanked Shirley once again and handed the phone back to Jen.

"Sounds like a link to me," Kelly commented as they cleaned up the remains of their dinner and saw Jen on her way.

"She didn't stay in contact after their school days, though," Sam said. "Not surprising, I suppose. I know how many of my high school friends I've stayed in touch with—exactly zero. Of course, I didn't need to. I get all the hometown gossip through Mother."

Kelly started to ask something but their kitchen phone rang and she reached for it instead.

"Beau," she said, handing it to Sam after a minute of exchanging pleasantries.

"Hey, darlin', you guys having a quiet evening?"

She started to fill him in on the phone call about Candy Butler but realized she could hear radio static in the background. "Are you still at work?" she asked.

"Unfortunately, yes. I'm a man short this evening and ended up getting called out to a traffic accident. It's cleared now, but I thought this might be my best chance to reach you before your bedtime."

Waking at 4:30 six days a week wasn't exactly conducive to much of a social life; both of them were still getting used to the schedule.

"Anyhow," he continued, "I wanted to let you know that the lab finally got fingerprint results from that plastic cup you gave me. The guy's name really *is* Ridley Redfearn, believe it or not. He came through as a 'person of interest' in a couple of Texas cases years ago, but since there are no current wants or warrants out on him I'm guessing those were cleared without his involvement."

"What's a person of interest?"

"Well, sometimes it's an actual suspect but a lot of times it's just somebody who was near a crime scene, might have been a material witness or something. I don't know the nature of these particular cases and didn't want to get too bogged down in old details unless it turns out to be somehow related."

"Okay."

"Anyhow, the thing I thought you would find interesting is that he does actually hold a doctor of divinity degree. The catch is that it looks like it came from some online place. I'm having one of the clerks do a little further research. It might be an actual school."

Or it might be a website where you answer a dozen simple questions, get a passing grade and they mail you a certificate that looks really good on your wall.

"I searched his name in the New Mexico records too, and he's not wanted for anything here. Since we know his whereabouts, all I can really do is keep an eye on him, see if he starts doing anything suspicious."

"Like performing marriage ceremonies for elderly women who mysteriously meet their soul mates after seventy?"

"Unfortunately, that's not illegal, but something like that."

They ended the call and Sam realized that it really was getting close to her bedtime. Her stay at Beau's last night hadn't exactly given her a full eight hours rest. She pondered all the new information she'd gained in the past forty-eight hours. There seemed to be connections all over the place but she still couldn't figure out where it was all heading.

Sleep came quickly but she woke with a start. A voice filled her head. Bertha Martinez, the old *bruja* who had practically died in her arms.

Use the box to find your answers, the voice said. *Use the box. Use the box.* Over and over.

Sam rolled to her back, stared at the ceiling, rolled to her other side. The clock's red numerals showed 1:27.

Chapter 19

At some point she must have fallen back to sleep because the alarm's insistent buzz startled her. Within the hour she'd showered and dressed, driven through the quiet streets, the sky only beginning to lighten in the east, and now she stood in the open doorway of the walk-in refrigerator. More than four dozen cake tiers stared back at her, awaiting assembly, decoration and delivery. She pushed the door shut and walked to the front for coffee.

At her desk, steaming mug at hand, she sorted through her stack of orders knowing there must be some way to computerize the mass of information and sketches, also knowing there was no way she had time to change her system now. With the weekend fast approaching and more than a dozen weddings in town, she had no choice but to get busy.

She made quick work of the sorting: Simple birthday
and shower cakes would go to Becky, assembly of multi-
tiered wedding cakes for herself, and Julio could bake the
layers that hadn't been made yet. On the storage racks sat
batches of sugar flowers and trim. Sam saw that Becky
had neatly labeled each section with a customer's name
that matched Sam's order forms. Inside the fridge, the
buttercream flowers were similarly organized. She really
better give that girl a bonus.

Checking the delivery times, she pulled the elements
together for the two cakes that would have to go out this
morning. By the time she heard Julio's Harley rumble to a
stop by the back door, the first cake was finished and she'd
stacked tiers for the second.

He'd barely said good morning before she asked him
to make up more white buttercream. Bless him, he didn't
take offense but got right to it. When Becky walked in a
few minutes later, she immediately sensed the urgency in
the air and started on the orders Sam had left at her end of
the worktable.

"Is it getting hot out there?" Sam asked, without taking
her eyes off the shell border she was piping.

"Unfortunately, yes," Becky said.

Sam sighed, making a mental note to pre-cool the van
before taking the cakes outside. As if balancing the schedule
weren't hard enough, dealing with a product that wilted so
easily wasn't making the summer wedding season any easier.

Jen came through right before seven, picking up a heavy
tray of stock pastries on her way to open the shop and greet
the day's first customers. Soon, the tinkle of the front door
bells sounded every few minutes. The reassuring sound of

money coming into the till. At least Sam couldn't complain that she wasn't making a decent living from the business. And when she thought of that, plus the fact that her wares contributed to people's happiness, her mood brightened.

It stayed bright until the intercom buzzed and Jen announced that Nina Rae was on the line. Sam balanced the receiver on her shoulder and continued piping trim on the four-tier cake in front of her.

"Mother, hi, how are you?"

"I tried callin' your cell phone all evening and *again* this morning, Samantha. Don't you *ever* check your messages?"

Sam pictured her mother pacing the length of her bedroom.

"Things have been pretty busy, Mother. I just haven't had a moment—"

"Well, if you *didn't* hear the messages, then you probably don't *know* that I'm still *won*derin' about your colors for the *wedding*."

For a full thirty seconds Sam couldn't think what wedding she was talking about. There were so many.

"Samantha, please don't tell me you've changed the date again. Please don't. It's still on for September twenty-first, isn't it?"

"Sure. I guess so."

"You *guess* so?"

Sam almost bit her tongue. That had been the totally wrong thing to say. "Yes, Mother, it's still on for the twenty-first, as long as I can confirm it with Zoë. She's still planning on hosting us for the ceremony and reception at the B and B, but I just haven't had a minute to make sure that date works for her."

She thought of the several times she'd seen Zoë recently, but the subject of the wedding had never come up. Of all the wedding plans that must be handled soon, that was foremost. She piped a frosting note on the stainless steel worktable: Ask Zoë—Sept 21?

". . . colors would be so nice," Nina Rae was saying.

"Sorry, I stopped for a second to write myself a note. What was that last part?"

"*Autumn colors,* I said. Wouldn't autumn colors be *so* beautiful in September?"

Sam had a comforting flash of cool air, yellow cottonwood trees, vivid orange chrysanthemums. Compared to the hot dusty days of June . . . "That does sound nice," she said.

"Oh, yes! I can see it now. You'll carry yellow roses and the chairs can be decorated in reds and yellows and oranges. Rayleen looks so good in yellow, with her dark hair and I'll look for something dramatic for myself. Bronze, I think." A high giggle came over the line. "Oh, Samantha, you'll make such a beautiful bride. Have you lost any weight, dear?"

White buttercream squirted out of the pastry bag. Luckily, Sam jerked it away from the cake, averting disaster.

She gritted her teeth. "Mother—" *Oh, never mind.* "You and Rayleen have fun shopping for your outfits. I really need to get back to—"

"Oh, heavens yes. You've got a million plans to make. I'll let you go." The line went dead.

Like I have time to plan anything. Her breath hissed out through her teeth. She slapped the portable phone down on her desk and returned to the worktable to clean up the shot of white frosting that had nearly ruined a whole tray of burgundy roses. Becky and Julio were diligently minding their own projects.

Sam blew out a breath. "It's okay. I'm not going to bite anyone's head off."

Julio sent her a timid glance. Becky caught it. "It's okay, Julio. She really won't."

Sam paused with a paper towel coated in buttercream in her hand. For a split second she thought of how de-stressing it would be to relieve the tension with a good old fashioned food fight. But she didn't have the time it would take to clean up afterward. She settled for pretending to aim the towel at Becky before turning to throw it in the trash.

"You're right. I really won't." She sent them a smile. "The completely weird thing is that I just stood there and let my mother choose my wedding colors for me. Would someone slap me and remind me that I'm over fifty? That I can make my own decisions?"

"Call her back and tell her what *your* decision is," Becky suggested.

Sam rolled her eyes. "You know, the thing is that it really doesn't matter to me. How important can it be if I didn't have a ready picture in my mind when she asked the question? And she really is kind of right about the fall colors. September is such a beautiful month here and Zoë's garden will be lovely."

She caught sight of the frosting note she'd made. "Speaking of which, I better make sure this whole idea is going to work."

She put the finishing touches on the cake with the burgundy flowers and went outside to start the van and get the air conditioning up to speed. Julio gave her a hand with the cakes and she headed out to make her deliveries.

The first was simple—a hacienda-style restaurant where

Sam knew the chef. Although the wedding reception wasn't to take place until the following afternoon, he'd agreed to make a spot to store the cake in their refrigerator after the bride had practically gone ballistic in her fear that it wouldn't arrive on time. No matter how early she called to check on it, he could show that it was there, on site.

Her second delivery took her out to the north end of town, past the ranch land where Beau's place was, through the little town of Arroyo Seco. Nestled among the tall trees that flanked a narrow creek, a spacious adobe on what had once been a large estate now hosted private events from art retreats to dances and weddings. It took her a few minutes of backtracking before she located their driveway, an unassuming trail between the trees. She hoped they would have some way to better mark the spot when the wedding guests began to arrive in six hours' time.

With the second cake safely at its destination she turned back toward town and wound her way to Zoë's, where the last of the day's bed and breakfast guests were just throwing their bags into the trunk of a small sedan. Sam pulled down the driveway to the back of the house, plucked the yearbook from the passenger seat of her van and met Zoë at the kitchen door.

"Before I do one other thing," Sam said, "I have to see if you have a date open on your calendar. For Beau's and my wedding."

Zoë led the way through the kitchen to her small office. "For you, dear, anything. Well, nearly anything. If someone has already paid a deposit . . ."

She picked up her reservation book in its leather cover. Sam knew from past experience that Zoë kept two years' calendars in there, since many of her guests booked next year's vacation before they left.

"September twenty-first," she said as Zoë began turning pages.

A hiss as Zoë inhaled sharply. "Ooh."

"Oh, no, don't tell me." Sam felt her mood dip. "If you don't have that date, you'll have to call my mother. I can't do it."

"Well, we do have one group." She chewed at her lip. "How many rooms would you need? I know we'd talked about putting your whole family up here."

"What do you have?"

"I have one room for the twentieth and twenty-first. Nothing before that. Wide open after that."

"It'll work. Put Mother and Daddy in that room for those two nights. I'll just tell them that Rayleen's bunch and anyone else will have to get hotel rooms."

Zoë drew a line through the boxes on the calendar, making sure no one could inadvertently take those away.

"Now, the ceremony and reception? Back in February we'd talked about using the parlor but in September . . ."

"I think you've read my mind. Out in the garden would be beautiful. If Darryl doesn't mind getting it ready?"

"He won't have a choice." Zoë grinned at Sam. "No, hon, he won't mind at all. There might be extra leaves to rake but otherwise, that's the best spot on the property in the fall."

Sam blew out a deep breath. "Looks like we're set then."

"All set." Zoë set down the appointment book. "Want to take a look? Decide how you want it arranged?"

She led the way out back where her bright freeform beds of wildflowers framed a perfectly trimmed lawn. Huge elms and cottonwoods bordered the property and a pair of blue spruce flanked a small pergola with a stone fountain at the rear.

"The pergola would be a nice place for you and Beau to stand while you say your vows," she said. "We can put folding chairs on the lawn for the guests."

Sam gazed around. Zoë was walking toward the large flagstone patio where groupings of furniture formed a cozy spot for her guests to lounge.

"We'll rearrange these," she was saying, "and we can add round tables for the meal. Depending on the number of guests, I can either do a Mexican buffet or if you had something else in mind and want to work with a caterer . . ."

Vows. Caterer. This was really going to happen. The beautiful garden dimmed in her vision for a second.

She shook off the momentary freeze. Of course it was going to happen. She'd been ready for it back in February and she was ready now. Except that her cell phone rang down in her pocket. Flipping it open, she saw the bakery's number.

"Sam, how soon will you be back?" Jen asked. "There's some kind of mixup with Mrs. Sanchez's order."

Back to reality.

"I gotta go," she told Zoë after assuring Jen that she could be there in five minutes.

She parked her van behind the bakery and walked through the kitchen. At Sam's inquiry about Mrs. Sanchez's problem, Becky shook her head and Julio shrugged. Sam took a deep breath and walked out front.

"My fifteen year old daughter is *not* getting married," the customer said.

Sitting on the counter was a tiered white cake with purple flowers, ten bridesmaid figurines dressed in long purple gowns, and a traditional bride-and-groom topper.

"This was to be her quinceañera cake. Vanessa can be at the top of the cake in white, but there is *no* groom!"

Oh boy. How did this happen?

Sam looked at the order sheet Jen had pulled out. Becky had decorated the cake but there was no point in trying to lay blame. At this moment all she could do was fix the customer's problem.

"Can you give me twenty minutes? I can fix it." *In the spare time I have between the other three cakes I have to deliver later this afternoon.*

Mrs. Sanchez didn't look especially thrilled at the delay, grumbling about how the party was starting in an hour, but Jen handed her a cup of their special blend coffee and a complimentary slice of cheesecake and settled her at one of the bistro tables.

Sam carried the cake to the kitchen, her mind racing with ideas to make it look less bridal. Off came the topper with the happy plastic couple.

Becky set down her pastry bag. "Oh no, I did this one. What's the matter with it?"

"It needs a few changes. Can you set up the airbrush for me? Quick!"

Sam tested shades until she came up with a lavender that set off the darker purple trim that was already on the cake. Holding a sheet of parchment to mask off the figurines she gave quick airbrushed spritzes of the lavender to the tiers and trim, effecting an elegant shading of white, lavender and purple. She found a spare bridesmaid figurine and quickly piped a white frosting dress over the standard purple one and set the little lady on top of the cake.

"What do you think? Does this look more appropriate

for a fifteen year old?"

"She'll love it."

"And hopefully her mother won't make a big deal of the fact that we changed it at the last minute."

"Sam, I am so sorry. I just saw that it was two tiers, bridesmaids . . ."

"It's okay. It's fixed now. We'll all be sure we double check our instructions from now on."

She gave the cake a final check-over and picked it up.

Becky was right, the cake was beautiful, although Mrs. Sanchez gave it a critical inspection before she accepted it. At last she said that her daughter would love the colors and she let Sam box it and carry it out to her car, where she placed it safely on the floor.

"Whew, that was a close one," Jen said when Sam walked back inside.

In the kitchen, Becky went into apologies all over again and Sam had to spend a couple minutes reassuring her that those things sometimes happened. She'd finally turned back to her work, carrying a sixteen inch tier for another cake from the fridge when her hip bumped the edge of her desk.

The fondant-covered tier veered precariously and before Sam could recover, the twenty pounds of cake and fondant crashed to the floor, smashing into a hundred pieces.

Chapter 20

The rest of the afternoon didn't go any better. By the time Julio baked replacement layers for the smashed ones, Sam knew she would miss her delivery time. The cake was to have been delivered to the bride's mother's home by six o'clock, for a ten a.m. wedding the following day. But that wasn't happening. Sam phoned the customer and assured her she could have the cake there in the morning.

"Sam—are you sure?" Becky asked. "Should I plan to stay late? I can call Don. He can handle the boys for one night."

"No, that's all right." Sam felt her energy lagging but to accomplish what she needed, she really didn't want her employees around.

Despite several more fumble-fingered delays she finished the other two wedding cakes and, leaving Becky and Julio with specific instructions to finish out their workday, she once again climbed into the van and set out. It was after six when she made the final delivery—she could hear the wedding music coming from the adjoining room at the hotel.

At home she found a note from Kelly saying that she would be out with friends for the evening. Sam wondered what that would be like—to meet up with your pals and have dinner and see a movie or something. It had been ages.

But she had promises to keep. She stretched out on her bed for fifteen minutes, hoping the headache that had plagued her for the past two hours would go away. She'd pacified her mother and organized the venue plans for her own wedding. Appeased a frantic customer and dealt with a few disasters. Surely she could take a moment or two for herself. Her eyes drifted shut.

She awoke with a snap and discovered that an hour had passed. Even with magical help she was going to need every spare minute. She pulled the wooden box from her dresser top and held it between her palms. As always, the wood began to warm, then to take on a golden glow. Sam sat on the edge of the bed and placed the box on her lap, running her hands over the uneven lumps of its quilted top, watching as the small stones began to shine.

I know I promised myself I'd quit relying on this to get my work done, she thought.

The glow dimmed slightly.

Use the box to find your answers, Bertha's gentle voice said.

"My everyday work shouldn't require these kinds of answers," Sam muttered. She took a deep breath. "But there are times . . ."

Heat suffused her hands. When it became too hot she

pulled them away. The box's colors began to dim as soon as she set it back on the dresser. Her muscles no longer ached. The nagging headache had vanished entirely. She traded her soiled baker's jacket for a fresh one and washed her face at the bathroom sink. In the mirror her face seemed younger, less tired. Her hair looked fresh and fluffy, not matted as she'd half expected.

Thank you, Bertha.

Whatever power that box conveyed, Sam knew she should be grateful for it. In the past she'd fought the scary feeling of having powers that she didn't understand. She'd tried to get rid of the object; she'd avoided telling Beau about it for a very long time. But maybe it was time to simply accept that this thing had come into her life and that as long as she used these new abilities for good purposes, maybe it was all right.

For the first time in days she felt very much at peace. She gathered her pack and picked up an apple from the fruit bowl on the table.

The pastry shop always had a different feel at night. Sam parked in the back and switched on the kitchen light as she entered. A peek into the sales room told her that Jen had left everything clean and neat, with the small night lights illuminating the window displays. All was quiet.

With a certain Zen that had eluded her all week, she moved between worktable and fridge, picking up her pastry bags and tools. Her hands moved in rhythm, placing, smoothing, piping, finishing. In the cool night hours and into the morning she set a completed order aside, picked up another, let her artistic eye tell her what to do. Her hands obeyed. Beautiful pastries emerged under her touch.

When the low sound of Julio's motorcycle rumbled into

her consciousness, she was surprised to see that it was five o'clock. She stared at her surroundings. The stack of order forms was nearly gone. The worktable held a scattering of her tools. A glance into the fridge revealed that all the unassembled bits and layers of cake were now beautifully arranged and ready for their places at parties and weddings and gatherings over the weekend.

"Sam? Everything all right?" Julio's voice startled her. He'd walked in and was peering over her shoulder at the miraculous number of finished cakes in the fridge. "What—?"

She backed out, forcing him away from the evidence.

"How did you do that?" he asked, staring at her. Julio, an experienced baker, knew she'd accomplished the impossible.

The back door opened just then and Becky stepped in. "Morning, everyone." She caught the tension in the air. "What's up?"

"I just pulled an all-nighter," Sam said, keeping her tone light.

"It looks like she finished three days' worth of work," Julio said, his eyes still on Sam.

Becky paused. She'd seen this before, although she didn't know the secret. A long two seconds of silence passed. "Oh, she does that sometimes," she said lightly. "Either she brings in little elves to help out, or what I think—she just works better without interruption."

I owe you one, Becky. Sam smiled brightly. "Well, you know. I just go to town when the phone's not ringing and all that."

As if to reinforce her point, her cell phone went off just then. She raised one shoulder—see?—and flipped it open.

"Hey, darlin'. Tried to reach you at home last night."

Sam turned away from her employees and headed to the sales room. She noticed that they started their normal work, Julio pulling out ingredients for muffin batter and Becky grabbing a tray of cookies she'd baked the day before so she could decorate them.

"I decided to work late, hon. Stuff here has just piled up on me." She didn't elaborate and he didn't ask.

"Figured as much. Look, I've got some new information. Could I take you to breakfast?" His voice sounded unusually tight, reserved.

"Sure. I'd like that." She suddenly realized she was starving. "Will it involve eggs and green chile?"

They agreed to meet at the Taoseño in fifteen minutes.

Back in the kitchen, Becky was humming the theme from a kid's cartoon show as she spread glaze on sugar cookies. Julio's non-committal expression only revealed that he was paying attention as he cut scones and placed them on baking sheets. Sam told them she would return in an hour or so.

She knew something was bothering him the minute she saw Beau. His normally open expression was tight, the smile gone. His skin looked slept-in, to borrow one of her father's sayings.

He'd already gotten a table and she joined him, dying to ask what was wrong, but the waitress appeared with her coffee pot at the ready and it took forever for her to finish reciting the specials and filling their mugs.

"Hon, what's the matter?" Sam said, the minute the woman walked away.

"Looks like I'll have to promote you to detective," he said, a tiny smile tugging at his mouth. "You don't miss a clue."

"So, what's happened?"

He gave her hand a squeeze. "I went by Life Therapy yesterday. Just a couple of unanswered questions about Lila Coffey's death."

"Hers did seem pretty suspicious. She goes in for rehab on a broken ankle and soon she's dead."

"It's the same place they took Mama for her rehab after the stroke."

She nodded. She knew this. So what was the news?

"The director there told me something I'd never known before. He said that Mama's pastor visited her several times."

"I never knew your mother had any religious affiliation."

"She didn't. And she wouldn't have welcomed a visit by any preacher." He paused when the waitress approached to take their orders. Once they were alone again he continued. "It's a little complicated. Mama was a churchgoer once, back when I was a kid. But something happened when Daddy died. I don't know all the details because she refused to talk about it much. I got the feeling it had to do with money. Whatever it was she came away with a bitter, bitter feeling about the church. She never went back."

"She might have become interested in another denomination?"

"No. This went real deep. I seriously doubt she would have let anyone through the door once he said he was a preacher." He sipped from his coffee. "I plan on asking some more questions."

The waitress approached with their steaming breakfast burritos and Sam unwrapped her knife and fork from the paper napkin encasing them.

"Speaking of phonies," Beau said after they'd eaten in silence for a few minutes, "I've learned a few more interesting things about our friends Ted O'Malley and James Butler. The two of them knew each other in high school. Apparently they got into some trouble in Nevada, mostly juvenile stuff that gets locked away off-record. When Butler's family moved to Albuquerque he lost touch with O'Malley for a few years. But those types of bad pennies always seem to find each other again. They both did time for getting caught in a junk-bond scam a few years later."

Sam chewed slowly, mulling over the new information. "I just wish we could put together the whole 'big picture' of these guys. There seem to be so many connections, but it gets confusing as to who knew whom at what point."

"And, are they just a bunch of sleazy types who gravitate toward each other, or are they actually working together in some way?" He scraped up the last of his green chile sauce as he spoke.

"I know. I feel like the answer has to be close. Look, I hate to eat and run," Sam said, remembering the delivery she'd promised by eight o'clock, "but the shop has been crazy this week. I swear the third week of June must be the one everyone picks to get married. I've got six deliveries today and several more tomorrow. I better get going."

"Maybe we can have dinner tonight?" he suggested.

"I'd love it. And speaking of weddings, I've got news about our own. I talked to Zoë about it yesterday and I'll fill you in."

His mood had brightened considerably, Sam was happy to see. She left him waiting in line at the cashier's desk, with a promise to touch base by phone later in the afternoon.

On the way back to Sweet's Sweets, Sam cranked up the van's air conditioning as high as she could stand it for seven in the morning. With luck she could get four of her six cake deliveries done before the sun became blistering hot. The remaining two were specifically not to be delivered before three p.m. She scanned the intense blue sky for any sign of a rain cloud. Nothing.

Chapter 21

The wedding deliveries went well—aside from the first one, where yesterday's customer to whom she'd had to apologize was practically tapping her toe. A complimentary large box of breakfast scones seemed to soften the woman's temper and Sam managed enough obsequious moves to get her to say that she would patronize Sweet's Sweets again.

Luckily, the other three deliveries were right on time and those customers raved over the results. By the time she'd dropped off the last one, she was feeling the normal letdown after a night of hard work, magical influences or not. She phoned the shop to be sure there were no emergencies and that the rest of the weekend's orders were on schedule. Then she stopped by her house, dropped her pack and jacket on the kitchen table, and set her alarm for noon.

When it went off she felt refreshed, although tempted

to take the afternoon off and lounge around in her pajamas eating potato chips and watching daytime TV. Since that was not an option she washed her face, brushed her teeth and ran her fingers through her hair. Donning a fresh jacket and reminding herself that she better run a load of laundry very soon, she headed out the door.

Two small puffy clouds sat on top of Taos Mountain, giving Sam hope that maybe their bigger brothers would soon show up. The news still carried stories of forest fires all around the state. Even if rain weren't predicted anytime soon, cooler temperatures would be most welcome.

Back at the shop, everything seemed to be running pretty smoothly. Becky was diligently rechecking every order before it went into the fridge, and Jen commented that several people who'd picked up their cakes were very pleased. Sam looked around. Things hadn't run this smoothly in weeks and she felt like a surprise was going to jump out at her any minute.

Beau phoned just as she was leaving to make the final two wedding deliveries of the day and they made plans to meet at their favorite little Chinese place at seven.

"My, you sure do look nice," he said in his most gentlemanly Southern tone when she walked into Yu Garden.

She smiled, not admitting that she was wearing her last clean blouse. The dirty laundry still had not made it as far as the washing machine. While they perused the menu she filled him in on the wedding plans she'd discussed with Zoë. She left out the choicer moments of yesterday's phone call with her mother. Beau would soon enough learn more about his future mother-in-law.

"I cruised by that so-called church you attended the other night," Beau said after they toasted each other with glasses of Tsingtao. "You're right, it sure looks like a warehouse to me."

"Anyone there?"

"Not at first. I had some paperwork to fill out so I sat down the block for a few minutes. A car pulled up—unfortunately, not the Toyota—and some young guy offloaded a couple of guitars and amplifiers."

"They must be having another service tonight," she said. "There was guitar music last time."

"So, you want to go to church after dinner?" he asked with a glint in his eye.

"Absolutely not. I did my duty by snatching a plastic cup from the place. I probably have some kind of holy mark on my forehead, branding me as a thief." She rubbed her sandal clad toes against his pants leg under the table.

His smile lit up. "I highly doubt that, ma'am. If you're going to hell for anything, it'll be for the lewd thoughts you're having about me right now."

"You got that right." She laughed heartily for the first time in days. "I plan to have my way with you. And then I plan to get a good night's sleep. Another early morning, and then I have a day off."

It was almost tempting to call on the wooden box for another shot of energy so she could stay longer at Beau's and then work like a demon through the next day and night.

"Anyway, before you so deliciously distracted me with carnal thoughts," he said, "I meant to tell you the rest about Redfearn and his church."

She paused and lowered her beer glass.

"Marshall Gray showed up while the young guy was unloading the guitar equipment."

"Really. I thought he left town."

"He was back today. They spoke for a few minutes. Of course all I got from down the road was hand movements and body language. But it looked like angry words . . . not the kind of thing you'd see in church, if you know what I mean. Gray stomped around while the young guy looked baffled, and then Gray got into his car and roared away. Maybe I should have grabbed him for a speeding ticket." He looked genuinely regretful at that last part.

Sam mulled over the new information while they finished their mu shu pork and paid the tab. She still hadn't come to any conclusions by the time she'd followed Beau's SUV out to the ranch.

"I'll be glad when you've moved in," he said, nuzzling her neck in the kitchen.

He poured them each a brandy and they carried the drinks upstairs. For the next hour Sam didn't think of nursing homes or men with shady police records. Beau's bedroom with the rustic log walls and Indian art sheltered them in their own little cocoon, and she reveled in their lovemaking.

Afterward, although she was tired, she found herself too keyed up to fall asleep. Beau snored softly with his arm draped over her, but her eyes were wide open. She gently picked up his wrist and slid out of the king-size bed. Wrapped in her cotton robe she padded barefoot downstairs in search of a glass of milk.

Iris's bedroom door stood closed, as it had since the day she died. Sam knew that Beau hadn't yet been able to go through her things. Maybe she should take the initiative and offer to help sort the clothing and personal items. He would surely be able to move on more quickly without that task hanging over him. She opened the door and switched on the overhead light.

A cardboard carton sat on the bed, which he'd left neatly made when Iris was admitted to the rehab center last December. Sam stepped into the room and raised the flap on the box. A lightweight plastic pitcher and drinking cup with a straw lay on top; these were the things Iris had in her room. She lifted out the first few items. Below the hospital-issue stuff were some personal things—her address book, a pair of reading glasses, warm socks, and a few get-well cards from her friends. As Sam picked up the cards a business card drifted to the bedspread. She reached for it.

Joe Smith, Attorney at Law. As on the card Renata had given her, there was no address, just a phone number.

She stared at it for a full minute. A dagger of ice sliced her spine. How and when had this come into Iris's possession? Other than Beau, Kelly and herself, Iris had had few visitors. She jammed the card into the pocket of her robe and flipped through the stack of greeting cards. A pamphlet, longer and narrower than the cards, stuck out of the pile.

It was just like the one Sam had found in Lila Coffey's home. The Fellowship of Good Works Church, Ridley Redfearn, pastor. She grabbed it up, letting the other cards fall to the floor.

"Beau! Beau!" She raced up the stairs and into the master bedroom.

He rolled over, a sleepy, sexy smile on his face.

"Look what I found!" She sat on the edge of the bed beside him and held out the brochure.

He came to attention immediately. "Where did you get this?"

She quickly explained. "The preacher who went by to see Iris was Ridley Redfearn. The guy who got his degree from some online diploma shop."

Beau's face went white. "The director told me—"

"Iris was incapacitated by that first stroke. Even if she wanted him out of there she probably couldn't get her wishes across."

"Exactly. And if she couldn't order him out, what kinds of things did he say to her? What might he have done to her?"

"Oh, Beau. You think . . . oh, god, could he have somehow been involved in her death?"

He gulped. "Here we've been thinking that the men who married these old women—the husbands—were harming them. But what if it wasn't them at all? What if this Redfearn guy is behind the whole thing?"

He got out of bed and pulled on his jeans. "I've got to talk to that director again."

"Hon, hold on a second." She reached a hand out to him. "It's after ten o'clock. The place probably has minimal night staff on duty right now. Wait until morning. It won't change anything."

He paced the floor. "It might save some poor woman's life."

"Call over there," Sam suggested. "Tell whoever's on duty not to let Redfearn in until you've had a chance to speak to the director in the morning."

He pulled the telephone directory from a drawer in the

nightstand and paged through it with shaking hands.

"Let me," Sam said, taking the book. She thumbed the pages until she found the listing for Life Therapy. "Calm down. Here's the number."

She read it out and he dialed. Once he'd confirmed that Bob Woods wasn't in, he conveyed the message about Redfearn. When he hung up he turned to Sam. "I guess that's all we can do tonight."

"I'm still not sleepy," she said.

"Me either."

"Maybe some hot chocolate?" She rose, ready to go to the kitchen.

It was well after midnight when they finally fell asleep and Sam's early alarm was not a welcome sound in the pre-dawn. She tried to leave quietly but once Beau stirred he came wide awake.

"What time will you go down there?" she asked.

"The night nurse said Mr. Woods wouldn't come in until nine. I'll be waiting for him."

"Come by the shop and get me. I want to see what he says." She sensed his hesitation. "Please?"

She raced through the morning prep routine at Sweet's Sweets, seeing to it that Julio and Becky were on track with their tasks. By the time she heard Beau's voice out front, she'd decorated two wedding cakes and rolled out the fondant coating for the next on her list. She shed her work jacket and grabbed up her pack.

"You look better at this hour than you did last night," she told Beau as they got in the car. "Sorry I shook you up with that brochure."

"It just caught me so unaware," he admitted. "I couldn't believe Mama had anything to do with that sleazy preacher.

I wish I had gone through her things months ago."

"We'll see what they can tell us."

Life Therapy was gearing up for a busy day, Sam thought, as they entered the front door. Beau's uniform got the desk clerk's attention and she paged Robert Woods immediately.

The manager's voice held a little uncertainty. "What can I do for you this early, Sheriff?"

"I'm interested in a man who claims to be clergy, who visited my mother at some point during her stay here," Beau said. "Ridley Redfearn."

"I'm familiar with the name," Woods said. "Spiritual counseling is often a part of a patient's healing process. Several ministers make regular visits here, and of course any patient may request the counselor of their choosing."

"My mother was not a religious woman, and she would have never invited a man like Redfearn to visit. Yet his pamphlet was among her things."

Woods shrugged. "I don't know what to tell you. He may have simply left the materials with her."

Sam twitched in her chair. If Iris didn't want the man around she would have certainly not kept his information. Of course, she'd had limited speech after the stroke and maybe she hadn't been fully able to say what she wanted. And she'd been wheelchair bound even before the stroke, so getting out of bed and tossing something in the trash wasn't an easy task either. Still . . . Iris had been capable of getting her ideas across, especially with Kelly. She would have to ask her daughter about that later.

She nudged Beau and whispered in his ear.

"Another patient was here until just a couple of weeks ago," he said to Woods. "Lila Coffey. Was Mr. Redfearn her pastor as well?"

"This line of questioning falls under patient confidentiality," Woods said, stiffening a little in his chair.

"I'm not asking about anything they might have said to each other. Just whether he visited her."

"I believe so. But that's all I can say. I'm sure you understand."

Sam wanted more but realized they weren't going to get it. Beau was probably lucky to get answers about his own mother. After a couple more questions that went largely unanswered, they stood up.

Out in the vestibule they encountered a flurry of activity. A new patient had just arrived by ambulance, a woman in a wheelchair with her neck in a sturdy brace and her left leg in a heavy splint. Two male orderlies in blue scrubs hovered around the chair, propping the double doors open and wheeling the chair into position. A perky girl in a brightly flowered pink top spoke to the patient, assuring her that they would soon be getting settled in her new room.

Sam and Beau stepped aside to make space for the entourage to pass. As the wheelchair approached her, Sam got her first real look at the patient's bruised face with a long row of stitches across the forehead. Before the injuries it had been a beautiful face, and although the red hair was limp and stringy, there was no question about her identity.

It was Renata Butler.

Chapter 22

Sam stepped into the path of the chair. "Renata, what happened to you?" she blurted out.

Renata rolled her eyes upward, unable to tilt her head. Sam squatted down beside the chair.

"Ma'am—" One of the orderlies started to interrupt but caught sight of Beau in uniform. He stepped back.

Renata looked confused for a moment, then her mouth stretched into a tentative smile. "Madam Samantha? Is that you?" Her Russian accent seemed more pronounced today.

Sam touched Renata's hand. "Yes, it's me. What happened?" she whispered.

The bandaged woman patted Sam's hand with her free one. "It was car accident. A silly thing, really."

It didn't look very silly to Sam.

"We need to get her settled into her room before her

pain meds wear off," the perky girl in pink said. "You can come back to visit later if you'd like."

Sam pressed Renata's hand gently and said she would come back. As she stood up she saw James Butler in jeans and a t-shirt approaching the front door. She stepped aside to allow Renata's chair to pass by, then she and Beau closed in so Butler couldn't follow it without stopping first.

"James." Sam let the single syllable hang in the air.

He gave her a quizzical look.

"Samantha Sweet. I made the cake for your reception."

He put on his show smile. "Oh, yes, how have you been?"

"I guess the more pressing question is how have you and Renata been? She's awfully banged up. An auto accident?"

He clearly resented her tone and started to push past but Beau stepped in closer.

"Let's chat a minute," he said to Butler. "They need your wife alone in there for a little while anyway."

He took Butler's elbow but the dark-haired man yanked free. He didn't make any rash moves, though, merely walked along beside Sam with Beau close behind.

Out in the parking lot the heat pressed in. Beau put on his straw Stetson but James Butler had no such advantage. Sam wished she could edge to a shady spot but she saw the benefit to getting quick answers from Butler if he were uncomfortable in his surroundings.

"Tell me about the accident," Beau said with no smile on his face.

"I don't know much about it," Butler said. "Renata went out alone, a quick errand, she said. She apparently missed a stop sign and someone plowed into her. At the hospital they said she was lucky to be alive."

And how lucky are you feeling, Mr. Butler? Sam thought.

"Is your wife normally a safe driver?" Beau asked.

"She only started driving a few years ago. She came from Moscow and never owned a car before coming to America. Her car was bought for her by her first husband. It's a big, sturdy Mercedes. Probably the reason she survived the crash."

"And what about the condition of the car?"

"We're waiting for the insurance company to look at it. Decide if they will considered it totaled or not. I imagine they will. I hear it's pretty messed up." Butler shifted his feet on the hot asphalt. "Now if you don't mind, I'd like to be with my wife."

Beau nodded, watching him closely.

"Samantha, it was good to see you again." He walked back into the building.

"Pretty cool customer," Beau said.

"Unlike me," Sam complained. "I've got to get out of the sun."

"I'll track down the wrecked Mercedes and have it thoroughly checked. I don't trust that guy an inch." He started the cruiser and powered the windows down.

"Thanks. I told you I was suspicious of him. And now that Renata's in that home, I'm more scared for her safety than ever."

"Well, we can't read 'serial killer' into it just yet. Sometimes accidents really are just that."

But the fact that James Butler had attended school with Ted O'Malley and his own sister had convinced Renata that she and James were meant for each other . . . Sam couldn't let go of the bad feeling in her gut.

* * *

"Sam, I'm so glad you're back," Jen said the second she walked in the door. "We've got a problem."

Another one. How surprising.

Sam put away the sarcasm long enough to find out that the big disaster involved a bride who'd suddenly discovered that she had miscounted the wedding guests. They would need cake for fifty more people than planned. Since the cake was already done and due to be delivered this afternoon, Jen hadn't known what to tell the distraught young woman.

"I'll give her a call," Sam said, switching mental gears rapidly as she walked into the kitchen and picked up the phone.

Once she got past the girl's hysterics she suggested that they provide a sheet cake that could be cut and set out on plates by the banquet hall staff. None of the guests would ever be the wiser. Now she just had to get the sheet baked, iced and decorated so everything could be delivered by two o'clock. An impossible challenge always made her day.

Julio, bless his heart, had pulled the large sheet pan and started assembling ingredients before Sam even finished the call.

"Vanilla or chocolate?" he asked.

"This girl's vanilla all the way," Sam joked.

He dumped butter and sugar into the mixer and started the big motor running. An hour later the cake was in the fridge so it could cool quickly enough that the buttercream wouldn't melt when it touched.

Meanwhile, Sam reviewed the orders to be sure no other disasters would smack her late in the day. As much as she wanted Sunday off, it looked like she would need to come in, at least long enough to place a supply order and get things organized for another crazy week. As she remembered that July Fourth was coming up and made a note to order a bunch of flag themed decorations, her mind kept darting back to Renata Butler's accident and all the questions surrounding it.

She skipped lunch when the others ordered sandwiches from the deli down the block and by one-thirty she was on her way to deliver several cakes, starting with the bride who had panicked this morning.

The rented banquet hall was bustling with activity and she recruited a couple of helpers to get the tiered cake to a special table near the dais, while the sheet cake went to the kitchen. She might have stayed to admire the elaborate flower arrangements and draped tables but the van was idling outside and other brides awaited.

After the fourth delivery she realized she was famished and pulled through the drive-up at McDonald's for some chicken nuggets that she could nibble while driving. The deli sandwich at noon would have been a healthier choice, a reminder that she better be taking care of herself if she planned to make it through this crazy season.

As she pulled away a persistently beeping horn caught her attention. A woman in a yellow Volkswagen beetle was trying to flag her down so she pulled to the far edge of the parking lot.

"I saw the van," the woman panted. "I need a birthday cake."

Sam counted to three. Did this lady actually think the van just drove around with a selection inside and she could just grab a cake? She left the air running while she jotted on a napkin. The party was actually the following afternoon and Sam made notes about the child and the party theme, reminding herself to keep her suggestions simple. She described one of their standard Barbie doll cakes for the six-year-old and quoted the price.

"My shop is closed on Sundays," Sam explained. "But if you don't mind paying in advance, I can have the cake delivered in the morning."

She accepted the lady's cash on the spot and wrote down the address. Now if she could just avoid losing that McDonald's napkin. She sat in the van and watched the VW drive away. People never ceased to amaze her. Might as well get this one on the schedule. She phoned the bakery and recited the details to Becky, who assured her she was getting it all down on an order form.

"If Julio can bake the cake this afternoon, I'll decorate it in the morning," Sam said. "Unless you have some spare time this afternoon."

The groan at the other end of the line answered that question.

"It's fine. I have to come in tomorrow anyway. As long as we have the ingredients I can whip it out pretty quickly."

She no sooner ended the call than the phone rang in her hand. Beau. With a quick glance at the dashboard clock she let it go. Even though she was itching to know what he'd found out, she would be late for her final two deliveries if she took the time to talk now.

By the time she'd handed off the last of the wedding cakes she felt frazzled and as damp as an old mop. She pulled into the shade of a huge tree near the courthouse and dialed Beau's number.

"Hey there," he said. "I guess I caught you at a busy time."

"Very busy. But I'm eager to know—did you find out anything about Renata's accident?"

"Quite a bit. It's not good. I pulled the accident report. Luckily, the other driver didn't hesitate to talk to me without waiting to have an attorney. You never know, these days. Anyhow, the man was driving along on Paseo, at the speed limit, early morning and there was light traffic. Says the Mercedes pulled right out from a side street without even slowing down. He braked, in his words, for all he was worth but he hit her anyway. His airbag smacked him in the face, but otherwise he wasn't hurt.

"Renata Butler wasn't so lucky. Multiple fractures of her left leg, trauma to her neck, a gash to her temple. She was hospitalized for two days before being moved to Life Therapy. She may be there for weeks."

Sam's attention had grabbed onto one fact. "Why didn't Renata slow down before pulling out onto such a major street?"

"Well, inexperience wasn't the reason. I've just been on the phone with the mechanic that I asked to re-examine the car. Her brake line was tampered with. There wasn't a drop of fluid in there."

"How did she get that far from home without noticing?"

"There would have been enough pressure in the line to stop the car at slow speed, maybe a time or two. That probably got her out of her driveway but by the time she reached Paseo there was nothing left. Stomping on that pedal would have been completely useless."

Sam let the information settle.

"Beau, I'm worried for her. Clearly, someone tried to kill her and make it look like an accident. Now that she's lying there helpless in a bed, they'll come back after her." The words rushed out faster and faster. "Post someone by her door, Beau. Someone has to keep her safe."

"Darlin' you know how understaffed I am for the next couple weeks. Guys are on vacation. Two of my deputies were out sick this week and somebody always calls in sick Sunday morning."

Hungover.

"It's almost a sure thing." He paused but she didn't argue with him. He sighed. "I'll call over to the rehab place and ask that they keep an eye open for trouble, but I can't put one of my own men out there for at least a few more days."

Sam opened her mouth. Closed it again. He would do whatever he could.

"I gotta go," he said. "Somebody's tapping on my door."

Sam closed her phone and tried to come up with a good answer. But no brilliant ideas presented themselves.

Chapter 23

She realized she was tired but she forced her attention to the road and drove toward Sweet's Sweets. Kelly was just walking out the back door of Puppy Chic when Sam pulled up.

"Leaving early?" Sam teased.

Kelly pushed her damp curls off her forehead. "It was a little slow today. Like the calm after the storm," she said. "How about you?"

"Crazy. Every bride thinks hers is the only Saturday wedding in town."

Kelly followed her up the steps to the bakery's delivery entrance. "Are you coming home tonight or going out to Beau's?"

"Home, I think. He's swamped at the moment. Lot of overtime for him, since some of his guys are out on vacation. I need to catch up on my sleep."

Kelly gave her a knowing glance.

"For your information, Miss, I just couldn't fall asleep last night. I got to looking through some of Iris's things. Beau hasn't done anything toward clearing out her room yet. I guess he's just not ready."

"It's been hard, losing her," Kelly said with a catch in her voice.

"If you want to lend a hand here until closing time," Sam said, "I'll spring for dinner. Your choice, anything you'd like."

Her daughter gave it about three milliseconds of consideration. "Italian? I hear that new place is fabulous."

"Call for a reservation. If we can't get in by eight, it'll have to be another night. But yeah, I've been wanting to try it too."

Sam did a quick visual survey of the kitchen while Kelly pulled her phone from her pocket. Becky had a mass of sugar wildflowers in front of her—asters, lilies and sunflowers. Sam remembered taking the order from a middle-aged couple who definitely looked like the earth-child types. Their cake would be simple but beautiful. Julio was taking the half-sphere of cake that would form the skirt for the last-minute Barbie cake from the oven.

"Mom? We can grab a five-thirty reservation or there's nothing until after nine."

Sam glanced at the clock. She would have less than an hour to shower, change clothes and be there but she could make it. "Earlier sounds better."

"Kel, can you gather these decorating tips that I left out earlier? Toss them into that tub of soapy water in the sink, then store the pastry bags and extra icing in the fridge?"

She stepped to the front to see how sales had gone for the day. Jen was alone and the displays were nearly empty.

"Let everyone take whatever they might use at home over the weekend," Sam told her. "There's not really enough here to make a donation to the homeless shelter. A slice of cheesecake, two turnovers and three cookies might only cause a riot there."

A woman walked in just then and took the two turnovers. Sam threw in the cheesecake for free and told Jen that the employees could divvy up the cookies however they saw fit.

"I'll donate mine to Becky's little boys," Jen said. "My waistline is already suffering from this job."

Sam considered her own width compared to her slender helper, remembering the sting of Nina Rae's comment about Sam losing weight before her wedding. As a teen she'd been called curvy, later it was voluptuous, and in middle age she knew she was just plain chubby, even though working with sugar and chocolate all day had somewhat dimmed her own taste buds for desserts. She vowed to order a small portion of whatever she chose tonight at the new Italian place.

She left Jen in charge of the final locking up and by the time she and Kelly arrived at Venezia she got a hint of its popularity. The restaurant consisted of one narrow room, lined with tables full of chattering people, the air filled with the voice of Andrea Boccelli. Their last-minute reservation netted them the tiniest table near the kitchen but the smells coming through that door literally made her mouth water.

Once their glasses of the house red wine were delivered, Sam chose a spinach ravioli and Kelly opted for a baked ziti dish. They clinked glasses and didn't do a very good job of ignoring the plate of foccacia bread the waiter deposited in front of them.

"So, Mom, you said you were going through some of Iris's things last night?" Kelly said through a mouthful.

"There was a box of stuff the rehab center sent home with Beau, just the few things she had with her." Sam pulled her hand away from the bread plate. "A couple of things disturbed me."

"Like what?"

Sam told Kelly about the lawyer's business card and the religious pamphlet. "Beau says Iris would have never given that preacher the time of day."

"That's an understatement," Kelly said. "Boy, she told me some things . . ."

"Really?" Sam knew Kelly had developed a great fondness for the old woman and had spent a lot of time with her, visiting and reading books to her.

"She was down on religion big-time after Mr. Cardwell died. What was it she said? 'When my Matthew died, those people came swooping in and wanted to run the show.'"

"Really? What did she mean?"

Kelly sipped from her wine. "I guess his mother—that would be Beau's grandmother—donated a lot of money. At one time she even left the church some land. Iris gave me the impression that her mother-in-law's generosity left some of those church people with the idea that they could show up anytime they wanted, with their hands out."

"And by the time Matt died the family didn't have anything to give. Beau told me how tough things were for them financially, how they lost their ranch. I had no idea what was behind it. I'm not sure he even knows."

"Well, don't quote me. I got those details in bits and pieces. I'm just saying . . . Iris wouldn't have welcomed anybody who said he was a clergyman into her room. If he left a pamphlet, that thing would have been in the trash."

Their dinners arrived and Sam's first bite of the rich, smoky marinara sauce caused her to moan. "Oh my, that is *so* good."

Kelly's baked dish was so steaming hot that she had to stir it to let the heat escape.

"Anyway," she said as she watched tendrils of steam rise, "I wonder why Iris *did* keep that pamphlet. There has to be a reason."

"Did she ever say anything to you about it, that or the business card, specifically?"

Kelly took a tentative bite and thought about it. "You know, she might have. I'd forgotten all about this. Twice when I visited her she talked about some bad men who were not to be trusted. One time I thought she said they were coming after her."

Sam stared.

"But you know, Mom, how garbled her speech was. And I think that place . . . I think they gave her sleeping medications at night. You know, to keep her from getting up and trying to wander around or something. Some of the things she told me seemed like pure fantasy, like she'd dreamed them. The part about the strange men seemed so farfetched that I chalked it up to that. And the part about not trusting, well, she got to where she was untrusting of nearly everyone. I could see this suspicious look in her eyes, even when *I* came through the door. At least until she recognized me. I mentioned it to a nurse once. She said paranoia and fears were very common when elderly people were put into a new environment."

Sam chewed slowly, trying to absorb this new information. Back then she'd been so busy with the

Christmas holidays and then the new year and trying to plan for her own wedding. She hadn't gotten by to see Iris nearly enough, and then she was gone so suddenly. What if Iris *had* been begging for help? She needed to talk to Beau about this.

* * *

That proved more difficult than Sam anticipated. She and Kelly gave up their table at Venezia, as a crowd of people formed near the door. From the passenger seat of Kelly's little red car, Sam dialed Beau's cell phone, only to have it go to voicemail. No answer at his house either, but that wasn't surprising. He'd hinted that he would probably be working late. The desk officer answered the sheriff's department line and told Sam that, yes, Beau was in but he was on another call and three others were on hold. Could a deputy help her?

"I'll just catch up with him later." She redialed and left a message on his cell to call her whenever he had some free time, but she really didn't expect to hear from him before morning.

When they got home, Kelly said she was going to change into something looser and watch her favorite reality show. Sam agreed about comfortable clothing but once she'd changed she couldn't settle on the couch and become interested in the television. She busied herself cleaning out the refrigerator—something she hadn't done in weeks—making space to store their Italian leftovers.

By nine, she still hadn't heard from Beau but her eyelids were drooping. She said goodnight to Kelly and hit the bed hard.

When she rolled over and glanced at the clock it was only 1:37. Odd dreams—probably sparked by the rich food and unsettling conversation—punctuated her attempts at sleep and she finally decided to go to the bakery at her regular time, even though it was her only day off.

The streets were deserted at this hour on a Sunday morning, and the cool air felt good on her face as she drove with her van's windows down. She parked in the alley and went into the kitchen. Her only "must do" tasks for the day were to decorate the Barbie doll cake for that woman who had flagged her down yesterday, and to check her supplies and place an order online. She would deliver the birthday cake early and be free. With luck, she might get sleepy enough to go home and get a few more hours rest. One thing she'd learned about her work schedule—she had to grab sleep when and where she could.

She found the dome shaped cake that would form the doll's skirt. Julio had placed it in the fridge after it came out of the pan. Plenty of pink and lavender frosting was already made up in tubs and Sam set that out too, gathering her tools and the plastic doll's head and torso, which, when assembled and decorated would look like a slender princess wearing a ball gown. While the icing reached room temperature she booted up the computer and then made the rounds of the kitchen, checking her inventory of everything from flour and sugar to toppers for wedding cakes and tiny flags for Independence Day cupcakes. She jotted notes on a scratchpad. Better check the coffee and beverage supplies while she was at it, she decided.

The sales room was in night mode at this hour, with only a hint of the lightening gray sky outside. She switched on the overhead track lights and started toward the beverage bar when something caught her eye. A square of white paper lay wedged under the front door. Someone must have dropped a napkin and Jen missed it. Sam walked over to pick it up.

Not a napkin. The folded sheet looked like standard copy paper. She opened it and stared in disbelief.

STOP MEDDLING YOU BITCH!! was hand printed in bold black marker.

Sam's heart raced. Who—? She stared at the block letters.

Her thoughts zipped every which way. Had she made a customer angry? Had someone targeted her business? She reread the note four times. Meddling, bitch. No, this wasn't about business. This was personal. And it probably had to do with the questions she'd been asking at the nursing homes. Instinctively, she held the note by one corner, although something told her that her prints were already all over it.

She carried the note, like a disgusting dead thing, to her desk and dropped it there. Beau should see this. But it was way too early to call a man who'd put in a very late night. She paced the floor, too full of adrenaline to settle back to her work. Finally, she realized the futility of it. Nothing could be accomplished until she could talk to Beau. And she wasn't going to be such a baby that she had to go crying to him at five in the morning.

She slipped the note into a plastic bag and set it aside. Then she speed-walked through the shop to the front door to be sure it was securely locked, although clearly the note had been stuffed underneath. She locked the back door and shook her arms and hands to work out the tremble.

"Okay, nothing has changed from an hour ago. I just need to get to work."

But her hands shook as she tried to pipe flounces on the doll's skirt and she gave it up after a few minutes. Typing on the computer was marginally easier and at least she could go back and erase her mistakes. She finished the supply order and looked at the clock. Nearly six, but that was still too early to disturb Beau.

She stretched her limbs and discovered that her hands were steadier now, so she began work on the cake. When her cell phone rang she literally came off the floor and icing squirted across the work table.

"Damn!" She dropped the pastry bag and wiped her hands on her jacket as she walked toward the desk.

The readout showed her home number and a dozen scary thoughts went through her head. But it was only Kelly, telling her that she'd gotten an invitation to drive up to Eagle Nest Lake with some friends and not to worry if she was late getting home. They would probably stay and picnic by the water.

The normalcy of Kelly's voice reminded Sam that things really were fine and she shouldn't be so jumpy. She wiped up the string of pink icing and stretched her fingers again, then finished the cake without further incident. Deciding that Beau would surely be up by now, she punched in his cell number while she carried the dirty utensils to the sink.

"Hey, darlin'," he said. "Did you and Kelly have a nice dinner last night?"

She'd practically forgotten about that. "It was great. Look, where are you right now?"

"Just leaving home for the office. But I don't have to

stay all day, only long enough to get some assignments handed out. Why?"

"Let's just say that someone left me a little present and I better show it to you."

"Sam—"

"It'll make more sense when you see it. I've got a cake to deliver and then I'll come by your office."

Showing up at her customer's house before eight a.m. might be risky—they could be asleep or leaving for church or something. Sam called the number the lady had provided and verified that someone would be home to accept the cake. Then she rechecked the shop's doors, turned out lights and put the cake in the van.

Twenty-five minutes later the cake was safely in the hands of the customer, with one little girl excitedly dancing around in anticipation of her birthday party later in the day. Sam turned the van around and drove the back roads to Beau's office.

"So, what's this little gift you said you got?" he asked after they'd retreated to the privacy of his office.

She pulled the plastic bag from her pack and handed it over. "I touched it before I thought about there possibly being prints on it."

He plucked it out by one small corner and shook it open. His jaw tightened when he read the words. "Where was this?"

"Jammed under the front door of my shop."

He looked up at her.

"I'm sure it's for me, not my employees. The part about 'meddling.' Somebody knows we've been asking questions."

The note still dangled from his fingers. "Who, I wonder. Or maybe I should say, which one?"

"I have no idea. None of the suspects have ever confronted me, especially with that kind of language."

He dropped the note to the desktop and sat down, tapping his index finger against the laminated surface. Sam pulled one of the spare chairs closer and flopped onto it.

"On another subject—or maybe it's a related one, Kelly told me some interesting things your mother had said to her, that Iris was afraid of someone. Did you know about that?"

He went dead still. "Tell me."

She repeated what Kelly had told her, as word-for-word as she could remember, including the parts about how garbled Iris's speech had become and why Kelly wasn't even sure she'd heard what she thought she'd heard.

"She would have come directly to you, hon, if she'd believed there was a real threat to your mother. You know that."

He nodded slowly. "What I think we better do now is to revisit that place and ask some tougher questions."

Chapter 24

Traffic was light and the few drivers who saw a department cruiser come up behind them quickly changed lanes and cleared the path. They arrived at Life Therapy within fifteen minutes and Beau took a parking slot near the door.

Robert Woods came out of his office after they pressed the issue with the receptionist.

"Another visit," he said, ushering them into his office. "To what do I owe the pleasure?"

Sam noticed the vaguest hesitation before he actually said the word pleasure.

"I'd like for you to pull my mother's file," Beau said.

Woods remained in his chair. "Might I ask why?"

"I don't want to turn this into an official investigation, but I will if I need to," Beau said. "I have some questions and I'd like to see what the records indicate."

Sam could practically see the word *lawsuit* zip through Woods's mind.

The man finally rose from his chair and walked to a set of file cabinets. He pulled a slim folder and sat back down.

"Your mother died of a massive stroke, her second, I believe," the director said after a quick glance into the file.

"That may be. But my questions relate to something else. I'd like to see that file, please. Unless you plan to demand a warrant. I can get one."

"What, specifically, do you need to know?"

"I'd like to refer to the nurses' notes, to see whether anyone noted that my mother was being harassed by a man who came to visit her. Whether anyone bothered to pay attention to the fact that she was afraid for her life."

"What are you saying, Sheriff? That we have killers roaming the halls?" Woods's hand shook. "That's preposterous!"

Beau held out his hand.

Woods thumbed through the sheets of paper that were clipped to the manila folder at the top. "I see nothing here."

"I'd like to look." Or there *will* be a court order, his look said.

Woods slapped the cover closed and pushed the file across the desk. Beau opened it and scanned the pages. Beside him, it appeared to Sam as if the sheets referred to medications and treatments.

"You have to understand that many of these older women have paranoia issues," Woods said. "It's not at all unusual for them to have groundless fears, and while we would never ignore a genuine concern . . . you understand that we don't make notes of every little thing they say to us either."

"So you often simply ignore their fears?" Sam asked.

"Not at all. I never said that." He splayed his manicured hands on the desk top. "We want their time here to be as comfortable and quieting as possible. It's important to their cure, to the body's natural healing ability."

Beau flipped to the final page of the folder, read down it quickly, and closed it. "I think I understand," he said as he laid it down. He stood up and the others followed suit.

"If there is anything else, at all . . ." Woods said.

"I'll be in touch," said Beau.

He didn't say another word until they were out in the parking lot and he'd unlocked the doors to the cruiser.

"Looks like Kelly was right about Mama being sedated. I recognize the names of some of those medications."

"Do you think they over—"

"I'm not saying anything, really. And I'm not looking to start a lawsuit or place blame. Mama's gone and we can't be sure exactly what happened."

"Do you think her fears could be tied in with these recent cases, Beau? Sadie Gray or Lila Coffey?"

He cranked the ignition. "I have no idea. But I know someone I can ask."

He backed out of the parking space and turned east out of the lot. Sam tried to get her mind around the new information, to figure out his train of thought.

"One of Mama's nurses was a gal named Sally Roundtree. I saw her name in the file just now, and I happen to know that she no longer works at Life Therapy."

Sam sent him a questioning look.

"She's a nurse at my doctor's office now, just started there a couple months ago, and she remembered me from when Mama was out here."

"And she might remember more of what Iris said back then."

"And she will most certainly be more willing to talk about it than that little condescending corporate flunky."

Away from the nursing home Beau pulled off the road and grabbed a telephone directory from under the car seat. A couple of minutes later they had Sally Roundtree's address.

He pulled up in front of a tiny bungalow with neatly landscaped yard and bright flowerbeds. A woman in her forties, with soft Tewa features and long black hair done in a braid down her back, was standing in the midst of them. A stack of wilted weeds lay at the edge of the lawn.

"Miss Roundtree? Beau Cardwell. Remember me?" He crossed in front of the cruiser and stood outside her gate.

"Well, Sheriff, sure I do. You were in the office a few weeks ago. Is there a problem?"

"I'm just fine, thanks. This is actually about the time when my mother was a patient at Life Therapy, about six months ago," he said. "Could we ask you a couple of questions?" He quickly introduced Sam.

"Absolutely! But let's get inside. This sun's getting to me." She motioned them through the gate as she stepped away from the flowerbed, leaving the weeds where they were. "I swear I'm losing my natural ability to deal with the heat. My mother could work in the fields all day long, winter or summer. Not me. I've been in air conditioned offices too long."

Sam and Beau followed her up a flagstone walkway to the front door and she led them inside.

"Let's have us a lemonade," Sally said, leading the way

to a kitchen wisely placed on the north side of the house.

While she rinsed her hands at the kitchen sink Sam admired her oven, which looked fairly new, and the collection of cookbooks on a shelf above it.

"You like to bake bread?" Sam asked, noticing a common theme among the books.

"When I get the chance I try to. Work takes up a lot of time, and I still can't duplicate my mother's Indian bread. She sells it up at the Pueblo, you know. Everybody wants Mary Roundtree's bread. I use her recipe, I try all these others . . . I just don't have that knack, I guess."

She poured three glasses of lemonade and carried them to the table.

"So, Sheriff, hearing about Indian bread isn't why you looked me up."

"No, actually. And call me Beau." He complimented her on the lemonade before he continued. "You were one of my mother's favorite nurses at Life Therapy."

"And Iris was one of my favorite patients. Well, everyone's really. Such a spunky lady, a real fighter. She was making real progress with her speech therapy and getting better movement too. If only that second stroke hadn't happened. I was so sorry to lose her."

Beau nodded. "Thank you. We all were."

Sam sensed that he wanted her to introduce the other subject. "Sally, Iris told my daughter some things, and we've become a little concerned recently."

"Your daughter was Kelly, wasn't she? She was always there, always so good to Iris."

"She's a great young woman. Anyway, she just recently told me that Iris was convinced that some men were spying on her at the care home and that Iris felt she might be in danger. Did she ever say anything like that to you?"

Sally's face went bland, her Indian inscrutability showing.

"You certainly won't be in any trouble for telling us," Sam hastened to add. "Neither will the home. We just have reason to believe that two men who might have visited Iris are now involved in something . . ."

"Other women, in other care homes, have died, Sally," Beau said. "A lawyer named Joe Smith visited both of them, and we found his card among my mother's things too. And there was a preacher named Ridley Redfearn. Mama would have never given a preacher the time of day, but she kept a brochure from this one."

"Oh, dear." Sally's expression had crumpled. "I know what you're saying. I remember the brochure you're talking about. Iris told me she didn't want that man around. The preacher, I mean. Well, you have to understand that her speech was impaired, but she communicated with me pretty well. She had me toss the brochure in the trash right after he left it on her nightstand. But later that afternoon, I was in her room and she indicated that she wanted it back."

Sam leaned forward.

" 'Put it away. In case.' That's what she said. You know, as much as she *could* say it."

"In case of what?" Sam asked.

Sally shrugged. "I don't know. I'm sure she didn't mean in case she died. She would not have had that man do her funeral service."

Beau spoke up: "No way. She wanted what we did, the small memorial with friends and family."

"Did you ever see Redfearn around the home again?"

"Oh, lots of times. He visited several of the patients."

"Do you remember specific ones?" Beau asked, pulling a pen from his pocket.

"Not really. He was just, you know, *around*."

"What about the business card from the lawyer, Joe Smith. Do you remember him?"

Sally shook her head. "Not really. I think I do remember there being a business card. It might have been his. That was another thing Iris asked me to put away, in case."

They asked a few more questions, but Sally didn't seem to be able to describe Smith or even remember specifically who he was. Feeling at a dead end, they thanked her for the lemonade and left.

"She didn't exactly confirm that either the preacher or the lawyer threatened Iris's life," Sam said as they drove back toward Beau's office. "But obviously, your mother didn't want them around. And I do believe that she felt threatened in some way."

"Mama had good instincts about people. Before she got sick she would ask me about my cases. She'd say 'I got a feeling about that guy,' and I was amazed at how often her feelings about somebody turned out to be right."

Sam rode in silence, wondering once again about the note she'd found at the bakery this morning. Somebody knew she was asking questions and that person was afraid enough of the answers to threaten her.

Chapter 25

Beau parked in his reserved spot at the department and asked Sam if she wanted to come in. But she knew how busy he was.

"Hey, since this is actually supposed to be a day off for both of us, how about I get away from here as early as I can and we'll do something fun for a change. A movie or a picnic?"

Anything would be better than constantly worrying about bogeymen lurking around corners and leaving notes under doors.

"Call me when you're free," she said. "I'll be home later and we can make a plan."

For all her desire to stop thinking about nursing homes and the problems of the older ladies whose lives had crossed her path recently, she still wanted to check on Renata Butler.

If she didn't try harder to stress the warning about watching her back, Sam knew she would be letting her new friend down. A quick visit surely couldn't hurt.

The parking lot at Life Therapy was more crowded now and Sam parked her van as far from the administrative office windows as she could. Encountering Robert Woods after the tense visit earlier probably wouldn't serve her present mission. She learned Renata Butler's room number with a quiet inquiry at the desk and ducked down the hall.

Renata's bruises had reached the yellow-green stage now, but she lay in the bed with her eyes closed. Her legs were propped on a stack of pillows and the stiff collar still encircled her neck.

"Renata?" Sam whispered. "Are you awake?"

She stepped closer to the bed and watched Renata's eyelids flutter open.

"It's me, Samantha Sweet," Sam said. "How are you feeling today?"

The patient's mouth moved but it took awhile for her to get any words out. "Samantha? Why are you here?" It came out as *whyr here*.

"I wanted to see how you're doing."

"Medicine. Sleepy."

"I won't stay long. But I'm worried about you. Has James been here with you?"

Renata's dark eyes moved back and forth. "Jimmy, are you here?" Again her words were slurred and run together.

"He's not in the room now, Renata. Was he here earlier?"

She nodded and started to raise her head from the pillow. "Ooh. Dizzy."

"Don't try to move."

"Do you remember the accident, what happened with the brakes not working?"

A cautious nod.

"Had anyone worked on your car before you drove it that day?"

Renata's eyebrows drew together and she winced at the stitched gash on her forehead. "Don't rememmer any work." She glanced sideways and noticed the plastic cup on the nightstand.

"Water, please."

Sam picked up the cup and aimed the straw so Renata could sip. After a couple of long draws she took a deep breath and became more alert.

"Sorry, Sam. I guess it's . . . the medication." She paused for a breath. "I'm supposed to get much rest so I can start exercises soon."

"Honey, I brought—"

Sam turned to see James Butler stop abruptly in the doorway.

"Hello, James. I just stopped in to see how Renata is doing."

"I didn't realize you were such a caring friend," he said, sidestepping around her and standing at the foot of the bed. He had a blanket draped over his arm.

"I brought you this extra blanket, sweetheart," he said to his wife. "Last night you kept talking in your sleep and saying your toes were cold."

Renata smiled at him. "I don't remember."

"Well, you're still a little loopy from the medicines. But that's why I'm here. To take care of you." He said this last bit somewhat pointedly, letting Sam know she wasn't needed.

She met his stare, wondering if he was the one who'd

slipped the threatening note under her door. A smile masked the fact that her teeth were clenched. She'd wanted to tell Renata about her suspicions, to warn her to be very careful. But what could she say, really? Nothing, with James standing right there.

He circled the bed, tucking Renata's blankets around her, patting her hand, laying his wrist against her forehead. He clearly wasn't going anywhere as long as Sam was in the room.

There didn't seem much more to say or anything Sam could do, so she wished Renata well and left. At the end of the hall a nurse stood at a desk, preparing little white paper cups with medications for each room.

"Excuse me," Sam said. "Is Renata Butler supposed to be on strong sedatives?"

The nurse shot her a look. "Are you a relative, ma'am?"

Sam's hesitation gave her the answer and it was pointless to try to bluff her way through with a lie.

"I'm sorry, I can't share any information about a patient's care except with relatives whose names we have in our charts."

Well, what did I think? Sam fumed. *They weren't just going to confide in me because I asked.*

Sitting in her van while the air conditioning blew the pent-up hot air out the open windows, Sam went back over her list of suspects. James Butler seemed the most likely to have sent the threatening note. He'd just seen her when Renata was admitted, the afternoon before the note was left. Ridley Redfearn's name had come up in questions to both the nursing home director and the nurse, Sally Roundtree. But those queries were made after the note arrived.

And where were Marshall Gray and Ted O'Malley all

this time? It was beginning to look like both of them had cleaned out their wives' fortunes and hit the road. Plus, why would either of them threaten Sam now? Both had neatly ducked around all her inquiries and probably just thought she was the chubby baker who stuck her nose in where it didn't belong. Not an actual threat.

And maybe she was just that—the outsider who got involved where she didn't belong. A blanket of discouragement settled on her.

"This is stupid," she said to the bright blue sky. She powered her windows up and drove toward home.

"I am not going to get involved. Not anymore." She practically chanted to herself as she pulled into her driveway and let herself in the back door. "It's not my business, not my problem."

"Mom? Did you say something?" Kelly was standing in front of the open refrigerator.

"Choose something or close that door."

"Geez, sorry."

Sam hung her pack on the hook near the back door. "Sorry, Kel. I just—"

"I know, you've told me a million times about wasting energy."

"It's not that." Sam shuffled across the room, turned around, went to the sink for a glass of water.

"Did you find out something bad about what happened to Iris?"

"No. Well, yes and no." She took a long drink from the glass. "I'm not sure."

Kelly arched her eyebrows and turned back to the fridge, opening the door a few inches and reaching inside, coming out with an apple and closing the door immediately.

"Sorry, Kel, I don't mean to be secretive. We asked a lot of questions but didn't really get any good answers. Beau is discouraged because there's nothing he can change about it. And I'm seeing killers everywhere, but I can't really explain why." She set the glass down on the countertop. "So . . . I don't know what to tell you."

Kelly reached an arm out and gave Sam's shoulders a squeeze. "It's okay, Mom. Everything eventually sorts itself out, doesn't it?"

She went into the living room and the TV came on. Sam remembered her waning supply of clean clothes so she went into her room and sorted the heaping basket into two loads and threw the light colors into the washer. She felt at loose ends but couldn't summon up the energy to tackle in-depth house cleaning. After tidying the kitchen and putting away a few straggler items, she found herself staring at the phone and wondering what time Beau would call about that movie.

Too high school. She dialed him.

"I was about to call, darlin'. This day is just getting impossible for me."

As he'd predicted, two deputies phoned in sick and he'd been called out to restore order to a concert in the park that had gotten a little wild. Sam assured him it was okay.

Running through her list of ways to occupy herself, work always seemed to top it. Hadn't she just been feeling overwhelmed at the bakery because there were too many orders, too little time? So, what better way to spend a Sunday afternoon than making up extra flowers and trims, getting a bit ahead of the game for the coming week?

Kelly gave an agreeable, if distracted, nod when Sam asked if she would mind transferring the clothes from washer to dryer and starting the next load. Sam grabbed herself some leftover chicken salad for lunch and headed out.

Her mood still felt gray. Disappointment over not having the day off with Beau, that vague unease over the way she'd left things with Renata, the nagging doubts over Sadie Gray and Lila Coffey's deaths. And then there were the terse conversations she'd had recently with her mother. And maybe, just maybe, she was hormonal as hell.

She let the thoughts ramble around in her head, hoping they would all vanish once she got to her shop and started creating. No matter how much work it became, Sam knew she would always love that artistic rush she got when she began working with her hands. Dough and sugar and chocolate and fondant were her media, but the satisfaction was the same as if they'd been clay or paint. She sighed and turned her mind to those happy things.

The feeling stayed with her while she pulled into the alley, got out of the van, and walked up the steps. But the moment she reached the back door something felt wrong. The door wasn't shut tight. She pushed against it and the metal was hot. When it swung inward, a billow of smoke hit her in the face.

Chapter 26

Sam reeled away from it, backward, tumbling down the concrete steps.

She scrabbled to her feet, started to run up the stairs, realized the futility of it. Smoke obscured the interior completely. She choked on it and backed down, her heart racing. Grasping for her phone she punched in 911.

"Fire!" It was all she could think.

The dispatcher was talking but Sam could only hear the rushing blood in her head and the crackle of flames from the building.

"Sweet's Sweets, my bakery. It's on La Placita. Get the fire trucks here!"

The female voice said something about staying on the line. Sam couldn't make out the words. Panic rose and she stared up and down the alley, hoping a water hose would magically appear. She forced herself to slow down and think.

"Tell them to come to the alley behind the building. I think that's the worst part." Truthfully, she had no idea.

When sirens began to sound down the street she realized she ought to move the van out of their way. She gave up on holding the phone to her ear and just yanked the door open and started the vehicle. At the far end of the alley she made a quick turn and pulled around to the parking lot in front of the row of businesses.

Ivan's bookshop. Riki's pet grooming. The little gift shop farther down. They could all be lost if the fire spread. Not to mention her life savings and all her work. A lump filled her throat and she couldn't breathe. She whipped the van into a spot away from the building, leaped out and ran for her shop.

Two fire trucks roared past the parking lot and slowed for the alley turnoff.

From the front of the building, Sam couldn't see any smoke yet. She raced to the front windows and stared in. The cakes in the window display sat there as if nothing were happening. Her antique display cases were empty, as expected. The bistro tables and chairs were in their normal spots. So far the fire seemed contained in the kitchen, but it would take nothing at all for it to pass through the curtained doorway and destroy this room as well.

She could hear shouts behind the building. She ran toward them.

Men in black helmets and glow-yellow coats and pants were unrolling hoses. A tall guy of about fifty was shouting orders. He spotted her at the corner.

"Ma'am, stay back!"

"It's my business," she yelled.

"You have to stay back!"

She clung to the corner of the building, daring anyone to make her move away, refusing to lose sight of her back door. Water began pumping and the air smelled of smoke and dampness. A small crowd began to gather. The shouts and sirens and voices blurred into a solid chunk of noise.

A pair of arms went around Sam, coming from behind. She swung out, daring whoever it was to make her move.

"Sam, stop!" It was Beau. "Darlin' hold on. It's just me."

"Oh, Beau, my place is on fire! What—"

"I heard the call," he said. "I was out on Salazar Road or I would have gotten here faster. What happened?"

She told what she'd done, never taking her eyes off the men with the hoses. "I don't know what happened. Everything was fine this morning. I never had the oven on. I can't imagine how this—"

All at once she did imagine. Was this the second warning? The note under the door hadn't stopped her questions.

Beau caught her expression. His face went still.

Sam's mind reeled. What next? How far would they go?

Beau turned her to face him squarely. "We don't know yet, darlin'. We can't assume anything at this point. These buildings are old. Faulty wiring . . . other things."

Sam clenched her teeth. The one bit of faulty wiring in the whole building happened to be in her section of it?

"We have to let them get the fire out," Beau was saying. "We have to let them investigate."

He squeezed her arms. "You do have insurance, right? Even though you're renting, you do have insurance."

"Of course I do. It's just—" Just everything. She had orders due tomorrow, weddings next weekend whose brides weren't going to give a flip that the bakery burned down. Their special day would be ruined without a cake. And nothing inside that shop would be usable. No one would accept a smoke-flavored cake. She felt tears rise and start to spill.

Could this week get any worse?

Possibly, yes.

Through the blur of tears she spotted a reporter from the newspaper. She planted her face against Beau's uniform shirt.

Chapter 27

The rest of the day passed in a blur. The fire engines left but the entire block was cordoned off with barricades and yellow tape, and vehicles kept coming and going as one inspector after another pushed his way through to the scene.

At one point, the building's owner, Victor Tafoya, showed up and gave Sam such a blame-filled glare that she had to turn away. The old man was no friend. He'd been giving her grief from day one. At least the structure was still standing and it appeared from a distance that none of the other businesses had been affected. Julio and Jen stood by her side, the three of them facing down the old grouch.

Erica Davis-Jones, the owner of Puppy Chic, stopped by and gave Sam a long and reassuring hug. Thankfully, no dogs stayed overnight at the grooming shop so Riki's liability was nil. Ivan Petrenko from the bookstore looked more worried. Smoke could ruin his entire stock. Toward dusk one of the inspectors let Ivan into his shop and he came away looking more relaxed.

Beau stayed as long as he could but once the flames were out and the danger past, he really had to start taking radio calls again. He assured her that he would work with the fire department and that he would insist on a full investigation.

She'd called Kelly as soon as she could manage to control her voice, reassuring her daughter that whatever they might say on the news, she was safe and things were not that bad. But she truly didn't know—so far, no one would allow Sam inside and it was that fact that most ate away at her.

Finally, an older guy in one of those yellow jackets came over to her—she assumed, the chief investigator.

"There's good news and bad news," he said.

She gulped. How bad?

"The damage appears to be minimal. That's the good news. But it was definitely arson. An accelerant was poured on the floor. You're darn lucky the vinyl tile was laid over concrete. The tile caused all that smoke. It's a good thing you didn't go inside. That stuff is highly toxic when it burns. Since your appliances are steel, they fared all right."

Sam felt relief flood through her.

"I need to ask you some questions, though," he said. "Tell me about how you discovered the fire."

She went through it all, from the second she parked in the alley to her frantic 911 call.

"Did you see anyone else around? Anyone at all?"

Sam closed her eyes and tried to remember. She was pretty sure the alley had been deserted. She shook her head.

"Any vehicles in the alley that might not belong here?"

"I don't remember any."

"That fire had only started minutes before. Otherwise it would have gone a lot farther. It was inches from touching the curtain that separates your kitchen from the other room. Those hardwood floors and wood display cases would have gone up quickly," he said. "So the person who lit the match had just done it, then they ran."

Sam tried hard to think. "Could they have run out the front while I was back here?"

"Front door was locked."

"He got in through the back," she said. "I remember that being the first thing that didn't look right. The door wasn't fully closed."

"The metal door and frame had pry marks on them," he said. "The fire starter came and went that way, I'm afraid." He stared at the high wooden fence that separated the alley from the building behind, which faced the next street beyond.

"I would have definitely noticed anyone climbing that fence," Sam said.

He nodded. "Yeah. So the guy had to have exited one end of this alley or the other." He wagged his head back and forth. "Well, be sure to let me know if something comes to you."

He handed her a business card and she jammed it into her pocket.

"I can't let you inside until morning. Everything needs to cool down," he said. "Even then I'd recommend that you don't touch anything or start cleaning it up until your insurance adjuster has come out."

Sam braced herself. Clean up. Insurance. The enormity of the task was only starting to hit her.

* * *

Sam lay awake in bed a long time that night. Two showers hadn't quite taken the smoky smell out of her skin and hair. It was as if her nostrils were inundated with it. Not to mention that her mind refused to leave overdrive.

Kelly had offered to make her some dinner but by the time she got home Sam couldn't think of food. They talked—Sam reliving the whole experience for Kelly. Then she called Beau to let him know what the arson investigator had told her.

"We'll catch him, darlin'. I promise you that. I've started investigating already."

His words reassured her, but nothing could put the business back to rights for a long time. A tear leaked down each side of her face.

* * *

She woke at four-thirty in the morning, without need of an alarm clock. For a split second she almost got up and started to dress, ready to start making cakes. Then she remembered.

Her funk from the previous night threatened to envelope her again. Waiting for dawn, with a cup of coffee at her kitchen table, she couldn't stop thinking.

At six there was finally enough daylight to see her way around so she drove there, pen and pad on the seat beside her. How could she possibly condense the enormity of it to a written list?

She pushed the heat-warped metal door open and

stepped into a surreal black-and-gray world. Her dream, reduced to char. The stench made her throat close. Tears spilled.

She gave in to the hopeless feeling for a moment. Then it began to shift, replaced by anger.

"This isn't me!" she shouted to the hollow room. "They aren't scaring me away!"

She pulled out the pen and began to write.

Power to the building had been restored, although her shop wouldn't get back on line until repairs were made and an inspector signed it off. By eight o'clock, when business offices would begin their new week, she was ready to start making phone calls—insurance adjuster, cleaning crew, food suppliers.

She was still deciding which of her baking utensils were salvageable when her cell phone rang. She recognized Zoë's number.

"Sam, what's this about the bakery? I can't believe it!"

"What have you heard?"

"Check the morning paper. Arson? Really?"

Sam didn't want to know what kind of slant the newspaper had put on the story. If they went the typical way, it probably sounded like she'd torched her own business for the insurance money. She gave Zoë the condensed version and assured her friend she was all right.

"Well, if you need my kitchen—you know, to get your orders done—you just let me know. And Darryl says if there are repairs to the shop, you better call him."

Sam's eyes began to sting again.

Zoë's contractor husband had done so much to help Sam get the place ready in the beginning. Of course he would be the one. She blinked and checked that item off her list. The insurance adjuster showed up just as Zoë's call ended. She walked him through the charred kitchen and smoky sales area. While he made notes on a clipboard she jotted down other things she'd thought of. Then her cell phone buzzed again.

"Fingerprints from that note you received match James Butler," Beau said. "I brought him in for questioning. Still tracking down some others, and I'll let you know."

Sam tamped down the desire to rush right over and confront Butler herself. Her secondary temptation was to dash off to Renata Butler's bedside and warn the woman just what kind of snake she was married to. But, frankly she'd lost a lot of her zeal for that mission. Torn between begging Renata to come to her senses and saving her shop, Sam knew that her customers and her own business had to come first.

An hour later, the insurance man had written out some figures for restoration costs and although Sam was under no illusions about how quickly she might see the check she was pleased to see that his estimate seemed fair. She found a company that specialized in fire damage cleanup and begged them to get there as soon as possible.

Sam's energy began to lag by mid-afternoon. She left Jen to oversee cleanup at the shop and to answer the telephone—miraculously, the line still worked. When panicky customers called to find out what would happen to their orders, Jen was to take down all the information and pass it along to Julio, who would be working out of Zoë's kitchen for the next few days. Sam and Becky could do a certain amount of decorating in Sam's home kitchen—after all, she'd run the business from there for several years before Sweet's Sweets came into being. But at the moment she needed a rest.

When she got home she showered off yet another layer of smoky grime and thought longingly of her bed. But when her eyes fell on the wooden box on her dresser, she knew what she needed to do.

Chapter 28

Her phone rang just as she set the box back on the dresser. The wood's glow gradually faded as Sam released it, but her hands retained the warmth and she could feel that vibrant energy singing through her arms, into her torso and legs. Bertha Martinez's voice had said in the dream, *Look to the box for answers*. Sam had a good feeling that was about to happen. She picked up the phone.

"Things are hopping here," Beau said. "I've got two of our suspects in separate interrogation rooms and a material witness on the way. Their stories aren't matching and Butler is getting a little nervous."

"I'm coming over there," Sam said.

"I don't—"

"Beau. This is my livelihood we're talking about."

"I just meant that I don't know if what we're getting

from them is relevant to that. So far, all of my questions have been about Redfearn's connection to my mother and the other nursing home cases. I haven't gotten tough on Butler yet."

"See you in ten minutes," she said. "Don't let them go."

She bent a few traffic rules on the way, but frankly she didn't care. She parked her red pickup next to Beau's cruiser in clear violation of the Department Employees Only sign. If someone squawked, Beau would have to smooth it over.

One of the deputies answered her tap at the back door and she asked where they were holding James Butler. Beau met her halfway down the hall and filled in a few details. Butler and Ridley Redfearn were in the two interrogation rooms, separated by a narrow room that could look in on either suspect through two-way mirrors. She watched him as he spoke and knew that Bertha's advice had been sound. She touched his forearm.

"You'll have to trust me on this," she said. "If you can put me in the viewing room, I can tell you if these guys are being truthful."

His forehead wrinkled.

"Remember that time a few months ago? The candidate whose wife died . . ."

Beau nodded. "It's not exactly according to procedure, but I believe you."

"Go in there and ask James Butler something that we know the answer to—like his wife's name or something," she suggested. "I need to watch him for a minute. Then start asking the questions about the case."

When Butler answered the question about his wife's name, Sam clearly saw an aura of orange-red. His response came to her as truthful, his manner confident.

"Has your wife recently changed her will?"

The aura became darker, more red, a muddied tone when Butler said that she had. Although the answer was probably truthful, something about the question made him angry. Outwardly he concealed it well. Sam glanced at Beau.

"Do you know anything about how your wife's car accident happened?" Beau asked.

"I understand that the brakes on her car failed," James Butler said.

"Do you know why?"

"No! The car was serviced less than a month ago. We thought it was in great shape." That answer appeared to be truthful.

Beau walked to the opposite end of the room and back. "Do you know a man named Ridley Redfearn?"

Butler seemed puzzled at the change in subject. "A little. Not very well."

Truth.

Sam felt a doubt creep in. How could that be? Renata said Redfearn had performed their marriage ceremony. Was her aura-reading ability failing?

Beau offered Butler some water and used that as an excuse for leaving the room. When he stepped into the viewing room with Sam she told him what she'd seen and interpreted. "Renata Butler is in danger. There's a lot of anger in this man, even though I don't think he personally tampered with her brakes. She's helpless, Beau, in that care home. Can you post someone outside her room?"

"We've got Butler here. He can't do anything to her."

"But he's got others helping him. I can feel it. And what about that statement about Ridley Redfearn?"

"Well, think about it," he said. "Renata may belong to

Redfearn's congregation but James could barely know him. Just because he performed their ceremony doesn't mean they are chummy."

When Beau left to get Butler's cup of water, Sam fumed. She felt like she was getting mixed signals.

Beau re-entered the interview room and handed James his water.

"Tell me what you know about Ted O'Malley," Beau said.

"Teddy? We go back to high school."

Sam felt her pulse quicken. That appeared to be the truth.

"And recently?" Beau asked.

"Haven't seen him in a long time. Gosh, years ago." The clear red faded to a dark, murky pink.

"How about Marshall Gray?"

"Never heard of him." Deeper pink.

"Lila Coffey?"

Butler swallowed hard. "I don't think I know her either."

"Sadie Gray?"

James shook his head. "Nope."

"Joe Smith?"

A tiny flicker of a smile went across Butler's face.

Beau pulled his cell phone out and pretended to check the readout. "Excuse me a minute," he said, leaving the room.

"He definitely knows Ted O'Malley," Sam said when Beau joined her. "The part about high school is true, and he has seen him a lot more recently than he admits. He's being very deceptive about all the other names. He knows them, but I can't tell to what degree. They could be acquaintances, or they might have been really tight."

"I've got Redfearn in the other room. We'll let Butler chill awhile. C'mon." He activated the mirror to Interrogation Room B and she saw Ridley Redfearn checking his hair in the mirror. Having him stare directly at her was disconcerting and she stepped to one side.

"Mr. Redfearn," Beau said as he walked in. "Or is it doctor? I don't know exactly what title your degree confers."

Redfearn shifted his weight and Sam saw him hide the real answer. "You can just call me Ridley, Sheriff. I don't stand on formalities."

Beau led with some soft questions to gain Redfearn's trust, then sent the other man a pointed stare and asked why he'd visited so many elderly women in nursing homes.

"Sheriff, I'm sure you are aware that the nursing home is often the final stop on this earth for many of our elderly. Especially for those poor women who've been left alone. Offering spiritual comfort is just one small way in which I can make their last days easier."

While the words were probably true, Sam got a creepy feeling from the man. She caught herself rubbing the slimy feeling from her arms.

Beau ran the same list of names past the preacher. He admitted that he'd performed marriage ceremonies for the three couples—the Butlers, the Grays and Coffey-O'Malley—but said that other than Renata none of them were regular attendees at his church. That much seemed to be truthful. But when Beau asked how well he knew each of the men and Redfearn claimed that they were merely acquaintances, Sam knew he was lying through his teeth.

"Do you know where Marshall Gray is right now?" Beau asked.

The preacher pretended to have no idea. When asked the same thing about Ted O'Malley, Redfearn shifted visibly in his seat.

"Is O'Malley back here in Taos, then?" Beau stood over the man's chair and the difference in their physical sizes seemed magnified.

Sam saw a smoke-filled room, a blue pickup truck speeding away. She rubbed her eyes and the room came into focus again. She found herself breathing heavily. Her hands covered her mouth as the implication became clear.

She stepped out of the viewing room and tapped once on the door to the interrogation room. Through a narrow window, she saw Beau look up at her. She pointed and he joined her on the other side of the mirror.

"He knows something about the fire at my shop," she said. "I saw smoke. And there was a blue truck. It was right after you asked him about Ted O'Malley."

Beau charged back into the room and came down hard on Redfearn. Under direct questions about the fire, the sandy-haired man stayed cool and smooth.

"I have no idea what you're talking about," he began.

"Where's Ted O'Malley right now?" Beau demanded. "If you don't tell me, James Butler will."

The preacher's bland expression twitched a little at the mention of Butler. Clearly, he'd had no idea that the other man was being questioned at the same time. When Beau started to leave the room, Redfearn spoke up.

"If he tells you that I know anything about Ted O'Malley's wife dying, he's lying."

"And why would he tell me that?" Beau said. "I haven't said anything about that. Yet."

Redfearn went silent and Sam got the feeling he was

about to ask for a lawyer. Joe Smith, maybe? She remembered how James Butler had almost smiled at the mention of that name.

Beau walked out, letting the door close hard. He walked past the viewing room where Sam waited but he didn't enter Butler's room. She stepped out to the hallway and saw him turning into the squad room. When he came back he told her he'd just requested information on any vehicles registered to Ted O'Malley.

"The minute we know what he's driving we'll have an APB out on it," he said. He jerked open the door to Butler's room and Sam stepped back into the viewing room beside it.

"So, Ted O'Malley's back in Taos," Beau stated conversationally.

James Butler shrugged. "Maybe."

Beau stared at him hard.

"I guess. Some real estate thing." But he wouldn't admit where O'Malley might be staying. A real estate deal could only mean that Lila's house had sold in record time and Ted was here to collect the money.

"That's about all the questions I have for today," Beau said. "But don't leave town. Not that you would, with your wife's recent accident and all. You're free to go."

Beau walked Butler out of the room and Sam heard them pass her door. She stepped out and watched. When they passed the door to the squad room James Butler started visibly and said something to Beau. With a hand on the suspect's arm, Beau steered him toward the lobby.

When Beau reappeared, alone, Sam sent him a quizzical look. He nodded that she should go back into the viewing room. In less than a minute he brought in Candy Butler aka Madame Zora.

"What was my brother doing here?" demanded Candy Butler the moment Beau closed the door on the interrogation room. Her gray hair hung in limp strands down her back and her loose orange blouse clashed dramatically with the olive green tones in her flowing skirt. "And why am *I* being questioned?"

Sam suppressed a chuckle. Apparently the psychic hadn't seen any of this coming.

Chapter 29

The case broke quickly once Candy Butler realized that Beau knew who all the major players were. Sam watched as the woman crumbled, unable to even keep up the pretense of being an innocent bystander.

"It was all about the money," she said after less than thirty minutes of questions. "It always was."

"Explain," Beau said.

"My brother and Ted O'Malley have been friends since high school. Both of them always had a way of charming girls. Ted charmed Debbie Patrick so well that they had to get married right after graduation. But he never really settled down. He'd take jobs out of town so he could fool around. He figured out if he put on this fake European jet-setter act that he could charm older and wealthier women out of their money. Jimmy just found that fascinating. He never could quite pull off the accent to pretend he was French or English, but he was good at talking his way into a girl's pants."

"Where does Marshall Gray come into it?"

"He might be a little older than Jimmy and Ted but he's exactly their type. I don't remember where they originally met. There used to be talk. How they could find rich women and scam some money off them." She shrugged. "You know how it is. There's never enough. They started out taking a few grand . . . Pretty soon they wanted to have it all. For that, they had to get themselves written into the woman's will."

"Ridley Redfearn married them . . ."

"Yeah. And then somebody, usually Marshall, would pretend to be a lawyer. He would advise the women and then draw up papers changing their wills so that the new husband inherited everything."

No big revelation to Sam. They'd pretty much figured out that part of it.

"What about Joe Smith? Is there such a person?"

"Not in this game," Candy admitted. "Marshall just wanted a generic name."

"You said it was all about money. What was your role?" he asked.

"Yeah. Huh. I got five thousand apiece for the setups." She snorted. "Pah. They end up with a hundred thousand or so, I get five. Whenever I bitched about it they'd throw me a little extra. I was about to tell Ridley I was done with the game. Although . . . even five grand is better pay than a lousy twenty or so for a reading."

Candy sat up a little straighter. "I've always had a bit of ESP, some pretty good psychic abilities. I just used it to steer the women toward whichever of the guys had her in his sights. I could usually manage to convince them."

Sam felt a jolt go through her. Renata was lying helpless in that home and her new husband had just been released. He knew Candy was in here. And he probably knew that as an unhappy member of the team she was the weak link. If he had any hope of grabbing Renata's money he had to move fast. Sam ran out the door and pounded on the one where Beau and Candy were.

"I have to go," she said. "I need to check on Renata. Now."

Before Beau could protest she'd taken off down the hall. Would James Butler kill his wife, even knowing he was under suspicion? Or would he just head for the bank and try to clean out her accounts? An innocent life was more important. Sam interrupted Deputy Rico who was filling out a form in the squad room and convinced him to go with her out to Life Therapy.

He glanced toward the hall, clearly wanting Beau's approval first.

"Please!" she begged. "Butler could be killing her right now."

With lights and sirens screaming they roared through town and Rico whipped the cruiser into the lot. They raced inside, ignoring the stares and the demands of the director, Robert Woods. Sam led the way to Renata's room.

James Butler stood over the bed, talking in hushed tones to his wife who appeared to be unconscious. As Sam watched, Butler pushed a pillow over Renata's face. He backed away and pretended to be doing something else the moment Rico shouted at him. Sam rushed to check on

Renata, calling for a nurse, while Rico whipped handcuffs off his belt and advised Butler of his rights.

As the husband was hauled away, Sam listened to Renata's breathing. It seemed steady. She'd probably been fed extra sedatives, but she was alive.

Chapter 30

A week later, Sam watched with tears in her eyes as a line formed outside Sweet's Sweets. It was seven in the morning, her first day back in business.

"I can't believe how much we all did to get the shop open again," she said, looking around at Jen, Becky, and Julio. "Thank you. And be sure to thank each and every person who walks through that door today."

She stepped forward and unlocked the door. There was free coffee and cookies, but that wasn't the real reason for the crowd. Muffins and cakes and pies and cupcakes got boxed up and went out the door all day. It was mid-afternoon before Beau got the chance to stop by and Jen told him to go straight back to the kitchen.

"The place looks amazing, darlin'," he said. "You'd never know how smoky it was a few days ago."

She pressed her lips together, nodding. "I could have never done this by myself."

"This, and helping me solve a whole series of killings."

Sam glanced toward the two employees who were working at their own projects, but there was really no need for secrecy. The story had made the papers, big time. Once Candy Butler's statement was signed and sealed, she didn't have much choice but to agree to be the principal witness when the case went to court. The prosecutor's office had agreed that trying all four men as a group would reinforce the fact that this was a coordinated plot, not just some boys-will-be-boys scam as a single defendant might try to claim.

Candy Butler had called it a game as she revealed details. The men agreed in advance that each would be responsible for killing his own wife. That way, all were equally guilty and all shared the spoils. Did they think of their sick game as 'Killing for Dollars' or some such, Sam wondered.

Ted O'Malley's blue pickup truck tied him to the arson. Sam's vision provided the clue, but the fool still had a can with traces of the same accelerant used at the bakery. He would stand trial separately for that. In O'Malley's truck Beau's men had also found the tool used to puncture Renata's brake line, apparently when Ted got tired of waiting for James Butler to do it himself. That explained why James could truthfully say he didn't know anything about the tampering on the Mercedes. Marshall Grey, in addition to causing Sadie's death, would have some answering to do for the fact that he'd impersonated an officer of the court.

"It's anybody's guess how severe the sentences might be," Beau said. "But the prosecutor plans to come down hard."

Still feeling for Debbie O'Malley, whose rotten spouse

couldn't resist even her small cash hoard, Sam asked Beau how soon he thought the stolen funds might be recovered. "Could we see that Debbie gets her money back?"

"It's done," he said. "I raided Ted's wallet and sent her the two thousand dollars I found there. We're still tracking down what he did with the bulk of Lila's money."

Her heart filled with love for this man who cared more about justice than about whether he might get in trouble for doing a good deed.

Sam thought of Iris. Beau saw the shadow cross her face. "At least we know that Mama wasn't one of their victims. If she had been, you'd have had a hard time keeping me from smashing a few of those guys to smithereens. Not that Lila and Sadie weren't just as important."

"I know what you're saying." Sam squeezed his hand. It was a bittersweet resolution to the cases.

Jen stuck her head through the new curtain in the doorway. "Sam? Someone to see you."

She started to pick up her order pad but Jen shook her head. "It's not that."

Puzzled, Sam walked to the newly cleaned and refreshed sales room. A huge bouquet of red roses filled the doorway. Then it dawned on her that the flowers were surrounded by people.

Zoë rushed forward to hug her, and Sam spotted Darryl, Ivan the bookseller, Riki from Puppy Chic, her longtime friend Rupert Penrick, Kelly, and a number of her regular customers—all the friends who'd helped so much. Beau stood close by as each person offered hugs, congratulations and good wishes for the shop.

"You had something to do with this," she said, twisting to stare up at him.

He spread his arms wide. "Not me. I can't take any credit. You've got a big bunch of friends and admirers, is all I can say." His smile lit up his face.

"I can't even—" Sam's voice cracked.

The crowd divided and someone began to step forward. Slowly, learning how to operate her crutches, Renata Butler came toward her.

"Samantha, you have saved my life. Your shop has made very many people happy. We want you to have—how do you say?—greatest of success. This really is 'bakery of magical delight'." She got a little round of applause and Sam watched through blurry eyes as Darryl helped her to a chair.

Sam turned to see where her employees had gone, wanting to publicly thank them.

At that moment Jen pulled the doorway curtain back and Julio and Becky emerged carrying a cake Sam had not seen before. Made in the shape of a baker's jacket, it had Sam's name in purple script over a tiny replica pocket, with the store logo on the other side. Candles stood where the buttons would go, sending a glow onto their faces.

"Make a wish, Sam, and then we're all having cake!" Becky announced.

Sam could think of only one wish. She closed her eyes and blew out the candles.

Connie Shelton is the author of the bestselling Charlie Parker mysteries and now the Samantha Sweet mystery series. She has taught writing—both fiction and nonfiction—and is the creator of the Novel In A Weekend™ writing course. She lives in northern New Mexico.

Sign up for Connie's free email mystery newsletter at
www.connieshelton.com
and be eligible for monthly prizes, notices about
free books, and all the latest mystery news.

Contact by email: connie@connieshelton.com
Follow Connie on Facebook and Twitter

30477958R00157

Made in the USA
Charleston, SC
17 June 2014